The Truth About Comfort Cove

TARA TAYLOR QUINN

HARLEQUIN®

entertain, enrich, inspire™

Recycling programs
for this product may
not exist in your area.

ISBN-13: 978-0-373-71829-0

THE TRUTH ABOUT COMFORT COVE

Copyright © 2013 by Tara Taylor Quinn

ABOUT THE AUTHOR

With fifty-eight original novels, published in more than twenty languages, Tara Taylor Quinn is a *USA TODAY* bestselling author. She is a winner of the 2008 National Reader's Choice Award, four-time finalist for the RWA Rita® Award, a finalist for the Reviewer's Choice Award, the Bookseller's Best Award, the Holt Medallion and appears regularly on Amazon bestseller lists. Tara Taylor Quinn is a Past President of the Romance Writers of America and served for eight years on its Board of Directors. She is in demand as a public speaker and has appeared on television and radio shows across the country, including CBS Sunday Morning. Tara is a spokesperson for the National Domestic Violence Hotline, and she and her husband, Tim, sponsor an annual in-line skating race in Phoenix to benefit the fight against domestic violence.

When she's not at home in Arizona with Tim and their canine owners, Jerry Lee and Taylor Marie, or fulfilling speaking engagements, Tara spends her time traveling and in-line skating.

Books by Tara Taylor Quinn

HARLEQUIN SUPERROMANCE

MIRA BOOKS

*Shelter Valley Stories
**Chapman Files
†It Happened in Comfort Cove

Other titles by this author available in ebook format.

SINGLE TITLE

For my precious Claire Claire.
I love your stories and will always
listen to every single word.

CHAPTER ONE

A BOTTLE CLINKED.

She knew the sound.

Waking from a fitful sleep that Saturday morning in early November, Lucy jumped up from her mother's couch, pushing her short blond hair away from her face, before her eyes were fully focused.

"Mama…"

Lucy moved toward the sound, her gun still on the coffee table where she'd set it when she'd finally dared to try and sleep.

Standing in front of the closet by the front door, Sandy Hayes wore an all-too-familiar guilty look as she turned to her daughter.

"I wasn't going to drink it, Luce, I swear. I just…you know how I get…and with the…thing…this morning…" Sandy continued to ramble as Lucy took the opened bottle from one of her mother's hands, and the top from the other.

"I… The panicky feeling was there and I just had to see that I had relief if I needed it," Sandy said, talking to Lucy's back as she followed her daughter into the old but clean kitchen.

Lucy's own bungalow across the street was a bit newer than her mother's but equally clean.

"You promised me no more hidden stash, Mama." Lucy opened the cupboard over the sink and slid the bottle onto the lower shelf. "No more games," she said. "And no drinking until after we go down to the station this morning."

Not only was Lucy tired from a night spent on her mother's

rock-hard, faux-leather couch, she was angry. And a tad disappointed. "I get that you aren't going to stay sober for yourself," she said. Crankiness made her add, "Or for me. But this is for Allie, Mama. This man took Allie."

Dressed in last night's dark slacks and a wrinkle-free pinstriped blouse—her daily detective attire—she faced her mother down. "This is important, Mama. Maybe more important than anything we've ever done. The prosecutor says that if you ID this guy, his case is open and shut. And once he knows he's going to prison for life, maybe he'll talk to us. Maybe he'll make a deal."

Sandy stared straight at Lucy, who knew what was coming next. Yep, there they were. The big pools of tears that spoke of a pain so deep her mother couldn't find a way out of its grip.

"You said they have his DNA."

"And the prosecutor is afraid that the defense might be able to lay some doubt regarding the sample they took from you twenty-eight years ago. Apparently there's some question about the collection process they used. You know this, Mama. I told you all about it."

"You also said you thought you'd be able to get the guy to confess and I wouldn't ever have to appear."

"He lawyered up before I got to him the second time. There was nothing I could do about that."

"I can't face him in court, Luce. Not after what he did to me."

"You promised you'd come through for me, Mama." Lucy stopped short of stamping her foot—not that the gesture would have had much impact coming from five foot two inches in stocking feet.

"I promised I'd stay sober and I am, Luce, I promise."

"I know you are. Because I've been awake most of the night making certain that you would be sober this morning. I need you to keep it together until we get this done."

"I will."

"You'd better."

"You're angry with me."

"Yeah, I guess I am. It'll pass. How about you go get in the shower, put on those jeans with the embellished back pockets that you like and your new fleecy sweater, and I'll take you out to breakfast and for a drive down by the river as soon as we're finished this morning."

"Can we stop in at the Belterra?"

A casino on the Ohio River. Another place an addict could find escape for a while.

"Yes, but only for a little while. I have to work today."

Sandy turned toward the bedroom, and then stopped. "When are you going to shower?"

So Sandy would have a chance to hit the bottle?

"I showered and changed last night before I came over," she said drily. "I'll wash my face and do my makeup alongside you. My suit jacket will cover up any wrinkles the night brought."

Sandy's shoulders slumped and contrition hit Lucy hard.

"I wouldn't put you through this if I didn't have to, Mama."

"I just wish… I've spent almost thirty years trying to forget everything about that man, Luce. I'm scared." She shuddered and her eyes glazed. "I don't want to see his face again. The nightmares will come back and… His hands…oh, God, Luce."

Sandy started to cry, buckling in on herself, and Lucy stepped forward, using her body to hold her mother upright as she wrapped her arms around Sandy's upper arms and back. "Shhh. I'm right here, Mama. And I'm always just across the street. If the dreams start again, I'll sit with you. Remember all the good times we had, sitting up watching movies and eating ice cream and popcorn in bed when I was little?"

Sandy lifted her head, wiping her eyes as she tried to smile. "Yes, of course I do. You are the best thing that ever happened to me, Luce. I just wish I'd given you a better life."

"You gave me a fine life. You were always there for me,

too, Mama." Not always sober, but always there. "I had what I needed." Food, nice clean clothes, help with homework and projects. A parent sitting in the front row during the Christmas play. And on the sidelines the year she'd taken up cheerleading. In the bleachers the year she'd gone out for volleyball. And at her police academy graduation, too.

"We have to do this for Allie, Mama. Try not to think about what this jerk did to you. Think of him as the man who can tell us where Allie is."

Sandy's chin stiffened, her eyes hardening. "Yes. He will pay for taking Allie from us."

Lucy was hoping he was eventually going to lead them to her older sister. Allison Elizabeth Hayes. A girl she'd never known. A baby who'd been abducted before Lucy was born.

"You have to hold it together this morning, Mama. If you exhibit signs of instability that the defense will be able to use to discredit your testimony, the prosecutor might choose not to use you. Then we'd be left taking our chances with the possibly contaminated sample of DNA. This guy could walk."

Nodding, Sandy backed up a couple of steps. "I'll try."

Lucy straightened to her full five-feet-two. "'I'll try' isn't good enough this time, Mama. I have to know I can depend on you."

"I won't let you down."

Lucy didn't relent, her gaze boring into her mother as if she could inject Sandy with the strength she didn't have. Lucy had lost count of the number of times she'd heard her mother's promises only to end up on the other side of another broken vow.

"Do you hate me, Luce?"

"No, Mama." Pulling the slightly taller woman back into her arms, Lucy held her tightly, held her in the cradle of her heart, just as Sandy had done for Lucy in years past—both sober and drunk. "I love you."

"I love you, too, Luce. More than anything." Sandy clung

to her, burying her face in Lucy's neck. "You know that you are the most important thing to me on earth. The only important thing."

Because Allie was gone. "I know."

She did know.

Just as she knew she'd never be enough. They needed Allie.

"RAMSEY, IS THAT YOU?"

Leaning back in the well-used rolling desk chair, Ramsey Miller looked around the vacant office of the Comfort Cove detective squad early Saturday morning. There were six full-time detectives, among the more than fifty officers who made up the Comfort Cove Police Department. Others would be filing in soon, but for now he had the partitioned detectives' office to himself. "Yeah, Dad, it's me."

"How are you, son? It's great to hear from you! You getting enough rest?"

"Yeah."

"And enough to eat, too? You know your mother's going to ask."

"How is Mom?"

"She has her good days and her bad days, but overall we're doing just fine."

He wanted to ask if she knew his father. If the dementia had robbed his mother of her memories of Earl yet. But he didn't. Just like he hadn't during last month's call. Or the calls before that. If his mother had worsened to that extent, his father would only lie to him about it.

And to himself, too.

Earl Miller was never going to admit that his wife was leaving him, slowly but surely, one day at a time. He wasn't going to give up on her.

Or see that she didn't have enough love left in her heart to keep her with him. He had love enough for both of them.

At least, that was Ramsey's take on the situation.

"What are you guy's doing today?" he asked now, avoiding the pile of paperwork on his desk—two cold-case records that had been his evening fun the night before.

"Mom's doing the dishes right now and then we'll be heading over to Louisville for their leaf festival. You know how she loves the colors."

"And you like the fudge," Ramsey said, figuring his dad must have been right—his mother had to still be hanging in there if she was cognizant enough to do the dishes before seven in the morning.

"Yep. I get to sample all the flavors. Only thing that would make it better was if you were here to go with us, son."

"I know, Dad. I'll try to get some time off soon."

How long had it been since he'd been back to his Southern Kentucky home? One year? Two?

"We'd love to have you here for Thanksgiving, Ramsey. Your mother's cooking."

"Mom doesn't need me around giving her more work to do." Reminding her of the daughter she'd lost because of him.

"She needs you, son."

Every time he'd been home in the thirteen years since his sister's death—a tragedy due to Ramsey's negligence—his mother had had an emotional relapse.

"I'll see what I can do." He eyed the papers in front of him again. Two more missing-children cold cases that had fallen to him. Little girls, less than two years of age. Both from the Boston area. Both disappearing in August 2000.

Nothing else about them was similar. Not race or parentage, not neighborhood, doctors, schools, hospitals. Their lives had been opposites: one rich, one poor, one had a nanny, one didn't. Their parents had never met or worked in a place where they could have known the same person.

One had been taken at a mall. The other from a park by her home. Neither had been unsupervised for more than a minute.

Both had disappeared without a trace.

Ramsey was certain the abductions were connected to each other somehow, but, thank God, they were not connected to Peter Walters—a pedophile and murderer who was currently incarcerated, apprehended by Ramsey and who Ramsey was going to see in hell. The Boston girls' DNA had been tested and they were not connected to items removed from Walters's home.

"…that little place down by the corner." Ramsey blinked. He'd missed the entire gist of what his father had been saying. "They say they're going to put up apartments, but I don't see why. Can you imagine who in this town would fill up an apartment building?"

Ramsey couldn't. "Maybe they're hoping more young people will move to Vienna if they build housing for them," he said.

"There's no jobs for them," Earl said. "And without jobs how are they gonna pay their rent?"

The little town Ramsey had grown up in had been thriving once, back when the tobacco industry had still supported much of rural Kentucky. Today it was mostly inhabited by people like his folks who just wouldn't leave.

"Who's the developer?" Ramsey asked, hoping that his father hadn't already told him.

"Same guy who built the big-box store outside of town."

"So maybe he's providing housing for all the people who got jobs when the store came to town."

"Maybe. It wouldn't be a bad thing," Earl continued. "Kind of exciting, watching the thing go up from scratch. They dig down first, then pour the foundation and…"

Earl went on to give Ramsey a blow-by-blow of the beginning of an apartment construction project, and Ramsey listened. Because Earl was his father. And he deserved to be listened to.

"Sounds like you're getting to know these guys," he said when his father finally paused.

"I offered to help out," Earl said. "You know, odd jobs, if they need anything. I know just about everything about everything around here...."

His father sure didn't need any extra cash. The farmer had done well for himself and his family. Well enough to be able to retire in comfort when no one wanted to buy tobacco anymore.

"Maybe it's time you get to know someplace new," Ramsey said, knowing he was wasting his breath.

"This is our home, son, mine and your mom's. It's familiar to her."

"Is it still, Dad? Does she know where she is?"

"Of course she knows. She gets a little lost sometimes. Especially when something reminds her of Diane...."

"Everything there reminds her of Diane."

His slightly older sister had been the life of Vienna when she'd been in high school. She'd loved their little town. Had planned to get married and have enough babies to fill up the school.

Until she'd fallen in love with Ramsey's friend from nearby Greer, Tom Cook. And Ramsey had broken a promise to his mother. And Diane had ended up dead.

"Our life is here," Earl said. Just as he had every other time they'd had this conversation.

"I know. It's been good talking to you, Dad."

"You hear anything from Marsha?"

"Not since the divorce. Alimony was paid in full a couple of years ago so we have no connection at all anymore."

"Jimmy Downs says he saw her over in Greer a couple of months back. Says she's married to some banker there and has a couple of kids. Twins."

Jimmy Downs, owner of the gas station in town—one of America's last full-service stations—talked too much.

"I'm not surprised she moved back home," Ramsey said. He was a cop. He knew exactly where she lived. He knew she'd remarried, too. And didn't care. "She wasn't happy in Massachusetts. Too cold for her."

Comfort Cove's frigid winters hadn't bothered his ex nearly as much as the chilly atmosphere inside their home had. His fault, according to her.

"Think about Thanksgiving, will you?"

"Yeah."

But they both knew he wouldn't be home. Not for Thanksgiving. Or Christmas.

"Don't let the next time you visit be for a funeral, Ramsey."

"I have to go, Dad."

"Take care, son. I love you."

"Yeah, me, too."

Ramsey dropped the phone on his desk, thinking about funerals. And Vienna. His father might be a simple man living a simple life, but he knew how to put the hook in his son.

Ramsey didn't blame Earl.

He just wished things were different.

CHAPTER TWO

"YOU READY, MS. HAYES?" Detective Amber Locken stood next to Sandy at the one-way glass.

Watching from the back of the small room, about two feet behind her mother, Lucy bit her lip. Sandy was sober. And she was on the brink of a breakdown.

"I'm ready." The tremor in her mother's voice tore at Lucy. Sandy had been traumatized enough—too much for any woman to endure and find a way back to normal.

"Okay, as soon as I give the signal, the curtain is going to open and you'll see five men standing on numbered spaces. I need you to tell me if you recognize any of them. Then I'm going to ask you which one or ones you recognize. You'll give me the number of the space the man is standing on. And then I'll ask you where you know him from. I need you to tell me, as precisely as you can, where you remember seeing him and what he was doing at the time, got it?" Amber Locken, the Aurora, Indiana, detective in charge of the Sloan Wakerby case, spoke gently.

With her hands clutched together, Lucy sank back against the far wall. She was an observer, not a participant. She couldn't save Sandy this time. She needed to. She wanted to. But she couldn't.

She'd be here, though, ready to pick up the pieces.

Get through this, Mama. I'm right here.

Sandy's trembling was visible from several feet away as Locken tapped on the window and the curtain slowly slid away, exposing five men, all around six feet tall, sixty years of age, white and muscled.

Sandy bowed her head.

Lucy knew that Sloan Wakerby was number four. When he'd first been brought in, she and a visiting missing-child cold-case detective, Ramsey Miller, had done their best to break the man. And just because a good lawyer could maybe prove that the fluid recovered by the hospital after Sandy's rape was not up to court standards, could maybe get it thrown out of court, did not, in any way, prove that the man was not guilty of raping her mother and abducting her sister.

Lucy wanted him dead.

As soon as the piece of shit told them what he'd done with baby Allie. She prayed to God he sold the baby as opposed to... Black-market babies brought a hefty price—she knew that all too well since breaking the Buckley case eight years before.

Sandy's head was bowed, her eyes pointed at her feet.

"Ms. Hayes? We need you to look through the window," Detective Locken said.

The good thing about black-market babies was that, once they made it to their homes, they were generally loved and adored and spoiled by the desperate couples who were willing to pay huge sums of money for children they couldn't have on their own. Allie could be happy and healthy and just unaware that she had a family out there. A family whose lives had been irrevocably torn apart by her absence.

"Ms. Hayes? Are you okay?" Amber sent Lucy another long glance.

"Look up, Mama." Lucy had agreed not to speak. If she influenced the ID in any way...

But if there was *no* ID...

Lucy watched, as her mother slowly raised her head.

"Ms. Hayes. Do you recognize anyone there?"

Sandy's head jerked forward. And back. Her dyed blond

ringlets moved up her neck and back down to the top of her lumbar.

"I need you to speak, Ms. Hayes. Do you understand? We're recording this session."

"Yes!" Sandy's voice was loud. Too loud. "Yes," Lucy's mother said more calmly. "I do understand that you are recording this. My daughter told me what to expect. And no, she did not tell me what to say."

"It wouldn't matter if she did, Ms. Hayes. Lucy had no way of knowing who would be in this particular lineup or on what space. You indicated, by a nod, that you recognized someone through the window, Ms. Hayes. Can you verify that?"

"Yes. I… Yes."

Sandy's voice lost any strength it had had.

Get through this quickly, Locken. You don't have much longer....

"What number do you recognize?"

Lucy held her breath. What if her mother's memory played tricks on her? Sandy had tried so hard to forget. To survive.

"Number four. I know him."

Lucy's muscles gave way, weakening so much she had to sit down.

"Who is he?"

"The man who… He…"

"It's okay, Ms. Hayes. We're here with you now. Tell us where you know this man from."

"He…raped…me…."

Lucy was directly behind her mother, holding Sandy's weight with her own. Locken would need more. The prosecutor would need more.

But the ID had been made.

Sandy needed Lucy now.

RAMSEY HAD LAST NIGHT'S files on the nightstand and his laptop computer open and booted up on his chest when the phone rang Saturday night.

"Lucy?" He pushed the call button the second he saw the long-distance number. "I expected your call hours ago."

As a favor to Lucy, a fellow missing-child cold-case detective, he'd flown from Massachusetts to Indiana to sit in on the interview when Wakerby had first been apprehended.

"She ID'd him, but collapsed. I had to bring her straight home."

"That bad, huh?" Where was Lucy now? At home alone? Like he was?

"Worse."

"Did seeing him spark any new memories?"

"Not that she's saying."

He wished he was there. And then wondered what in the hell he was doing. This was about the job. His life was about the job. Period.

"I couldn't get her to rest. Or to talk," Lucy said. "She cried most of the afternoon and evening. And clung to me. I finally sedated her, Ramsey. I feel bad for doing it, but she was making herself sick."

"Her doctor gave you the pills for that reason, Lucy. No need to feel ashamed for using them."

"Maybe not."

But it was clear she did. And there wasn't a damned thing that was going to change that.

Ramsey knew all about the guilt that parents managed to instill in their offspring.

"Give me another rundown of the case again." He offered the one thing he had to give—the one thing she'd accept—professional expertise. "Start at the beginning."

They'd been through it all before. Ramsey had read the police report shortly after he'd "met" Lucy by phone when evidence he'd found in Peter Walters's basement had had a possible link to her sister's case.

But they were cold-case detectives. They didn't stop when

they reached a dead end. Their job was to keep looking for the missing child. Until they found a link, a clue, an answer.

"My mother was nineteen. A single mom living alone in Aurora with a six-month-old baby girl."

"Where was the father?"

"Gone. Out of state. She didn't know where. He'd split right after she had the baby. She got checks in the mail, though, randomly, with no return address. Various postmarks. She can't remember where from."

"Seeing Wakerby today didn't spark any of the memories she'd lost?"

Lucy's sigh was heavy. And deep. "No. Not consciously, at any rate."

He could picture her in the precinct room at the station, at her desk along the far wall—he'd only been to Aurora once and had never seen her home—in slacks and a blouse and blazer. As far as Ramsey could tell she wore the same kind of plainclothes "uniform" every day. Just like he did.

"The memory lapse is understandable." Something in her voice pulled the words out of him. "She suffered a horrendous trauma that night. Her mind is protecting her from what she can't handle."

"I know. It's just…so frustrating. I look at her and I know the answers are in there. And sometimes I think it's not just the trauma blocking the memories. It's the alcohol. If I could just keep her sober for enough days in a row to clear her head—"

"She still might not remember." Cold hard facts. Victims, especially emotionally sensitive ones, couldn't survive without deleting particularly damaging images from their psyche. "And she's been sober for a couple of months, at least," he reminded her.

Lucy had told him that her mother had been in rehab. When, or how many times, he had no idea. But she'd completed the inpatient program at least once fairly recently.

"Okay, so, she leaves her job as a department-store cashier

near a mall in Cincinnati on a Saturday afternoon in August, picks up Allie from the mall day care, drives to the bank to deposit her paycheck at the after-hours depository, drives back toward Aurora, stopping at a grocery store in Lawrenceburg.

"She remembers getting Allie out of the car seat. She remembers standing in the baby-food aisle at the store. She remembers that the cashier was pregnant and she remembers that it was almost dusk when she pushed her cart, with Allie in the seat, out of the store. And then…nothing…" Lucy's voice broke slightly.

"The police report said that she was taken from the parking lot." Ramsey jumped in with what he knew to keep her on track. "They think she made it to her car, because it was found with the door open."

"Right. It was a '74 Ford Pinto. Lemon colored. With a dent in the left back fender, and the driver's side front wheel well was rusted out. It had close to a hundred thousand miles on it and a half a tank of gas. Her mother, who'd gotten pregnant with her in high school and never married, had given it to her just before she found out my mom was pregnant and kicked her out of the house."

"Her mom lived in Aurora, too, right?"

"Yeah. But she was in prison by the time Allie was born. She was drunk, ran her car off the road and into a yard, hit a six-year-old girl and then left the scene of the accident. The little girl later died. My grandmother got six to ten."

"Was she back in the picture when she got out? Did you ever know her?"

"On and off. Prison roughed her up a bit. And she hung with some unsavory folks. Mama didn't want her around me. Last I heard she was living in Florida with some guy. We don't even get Christmas cards from her anymore."

Ramsey had been spoiled by all four of his grandparents growing up. And watched all four of them die, too. One at a time. As cancer and old age and too many years of hard work took their toll.

"So the night of the rape…your mother was found, unconscious, on the bank of the Ohio River between Aurora and Rising Sun."

"Right. She couldn't remember how she got there. But she kept describing a face. And hands. She remembered him touching her, but details of the attack were lost. She remembers him slapping her but has no idea how her arm got broken."

"And she has enough of a memory of the actual rape to convict him of it in case the judge throws out the DNA evidence."

"Yes." Her voice broke again and silence hung on the line. Ramsey pushed aside his laptop, sat up and pulled on a pair of shorts.

"But she has no memory of Allie at all. The baby was in the grocery cart, and then nothing." Lucy's exhaustion pulled at him.

"I remember reading that Allie's car seat was in the Pinto when they found the car abandoned in the grocery-store parking lot."

"Yes. But by the time Mama was found, the car had already been moved to a back lot at the police station. The store manager had called it in half an hour after Mama left the store because of it being unattended with the door wide-open."

"Police were on alert for her then, almost as soon as she'd been taken."

"Yeah."

"And when they found her, there was no sign of your sister."

"Right. Nothing. Not a diaper, or a shoe. Nothing. It was like she'd never been there."

"But then, they don't think the rape took place where they found your mom."

"Right."

"We need Wakerby to tell us where he initially took your mother. We need to know where he raped her."

"I know. If we had a crime scene…"

"We need to know what vehicle he put her in when he took her from the parking lot. Even the type of vehicle would be good."

If the rape had happened recently, they'd have surveillance tape to refer to.

"I need my mother to remember something besides a slap and a face. I need to know what the walls looked like, if there were walls. And if not, I need to know that. What did the ground feel like beneath her? Was she in a bed? On a floor? In a car? I need to know if there was more than one person and whether or not she heard Allie crying—"

"All we need is a place to start," Ramsey interrupted softly. Calmly. He couldn't work the case officially. But there was nothing to stop him from using his professional skills to help if he could. "One piece of information inevitably leads to another."

"I know."

"So…how are you?"

"Fine."

He stared out his bedroom window toward the fenced and very dark backyard that held nothing but a gas grill and lawn that was more dead than alive. "Rough day?"

"Yeah."

"I'm glad you called."

"Me, too." Her tone told him what she would not. She needed a friend tonight.

He couldn't afford the temptation. And felt like a heel.

His life in a nutshell.

CHAPTER THREE

MONDAY'S MAIL BROUGHT an invitation from Emma Sanderson and Chris Talbot. The pair were having a wedding and reception on a friend's boat in Comfort Cove, Massachusetts, on Saturday of Thanksgiving weekend.

The invitation bore a handwritten note from Emma, telling Lucy she'd really like her to be there.

And while Lucy had only met the other woman a couple of times, sitting in on a case of Ramsey's, this was one wedding she would not miss.

Filling in the RSVP while sitting in her car, Lucy sealed her acceptance and tucked the envelope in the front pocket of her purse to be dropped into the outgoing mailbox at the station.

The wedding wasn't until the Saturday, so she'd be home to have the traditional holiday dinner with her mother on Thursday—hopefully Sandy would be coherent enough to do the cooking herself. Her mother's cooking skills were much better than Lucy's.

And then she'd escape the rest of the painful weekend—Sandy hadn't had a sober holiday yet—leaving her mother in the care of Marie Kolhouse, Sandy's caregiver and best friend, whose salary was provided by Sandy's emotional disability social security.

Marie was a godsend. She got Sandy to her doctors' appointments when Lucy couldn't. She helped keep the house clean. Made sure Sandy had groceries.

Had Ramsey received an invitation to the wedding? She

couldn't imagine that Emma and Chris would ask Lucy and not Ramsey, the lead detective on the case.

Would Ramsey accept the invitation?

Picturing the cute black dress she'd purchased on a whim a couple of years before to wear to the chief of police's annual Christmas party, Lucy put her car in Drive, skidded too quickly down her driveway and sped away. The reception was on a boat. She wouldn't be wearing high heels.

And what Ramsey Miller thought of anything she might have on her body was not food for thought.

Another trip to the penitentiary was.

MRS. GLADYS BUCKLEY DIDN'T resemble any convict Lucy had ever seen. Even after six years of incarceration—and two years on house arrest before that while she awaited trial—Gladys had the bearing of a rich and privileged woman.

"New hair color," Lucy said as she sat down across the standard oblong table in the small, caged interview room at the minimum-security state penitentiary where Gladys would be living out the rest of her days with no chance for parole, thanks, in part, to Lucy.

Lucy had found out about Gladys through Sandy and called the police—not that Gladys knew this.

"There's a girl on my street, licensed from one of the expensive salons with superior training," the older woman replied. "She does it for me."

Gladys spoke like she still lived in her mansion on the hill, when her street, these days, was a cell block on the second floor of the prison.

"I'll bet you pay her well." Gladys could use commissary funds, monies given to prisoners for services rendered incarcerated, which went a long way when you were "decorating" a six-by-twelve foot abode.

Dressed in expensive-looking brown slacks, a white blouse and an orange-and-brown flowered jacket, she looked more like a model from the pages of a fashion magazine for older women than a prison inmate as she nodded. "Of course. Good work deserves ample reward."

And money bought loyalty. A moral code from Gladys's world that had served her well for more than two decades. Until Lucy, wearing a wire with a direct link to the Aurora Police Department, had posed as an unwed mother and blown Gladys's black-market baby business, and her world, to hell.

"I have some questions for you," Lucy said now, looking the older woman straight in the eye. When she'd first met Gladys, when she'd first spent time in Gladys's home, she'd liked the woman. A lot.

"I'll answer what I can," the sixty-three-year-old said as gracious as always, her manicured hands calmly folded on top of the table. She'd been offered a plea deal, minimum-security housing with every freedom she could be allotted while still being a guest of the state, in exchange for full cooperation.

"How did you meet Claire Sanderson?" Lucy spoke slowly, choosing her words carefully as she slid the photo across the table. She wasn't there under any official capacity. Gladys's case was closed. Unless Lucy turned up any unaccounted-for children who Gladys had sold.

Gladys looked at the photo and slid it back with one finger. "I don't know her."

They'd been through this before. The month before. With Ramsey Miller, who was officially working the Sanderson cold case.

Lucy and Ramsey were long-distance friends. With no lives outside work. He sat in with her on the Wakerby case. She sat in with him on the Sanderson case. And the Walters case. All cold-case child abductions. They'd proven that Lucy's sister, Allie, was not one of Walters's victims. And the previous month, they'd celebrated with Emma Sanderson when DNA from her missing little sister, Claire, had turned up negative for a Walters match.

"Look again, Gladys. Please." Lucy met the woman's gaze, taking imaginary deep breaths while she reined in her frustration. "She's two years old in that picture." Taking another photo from the folder she'd brought in with her, Lucy put it in front of the woman. "This is an age-progressed photo. Possibly what Claire looked like at four."

Emma and her mother, Rose Sanderson, had paid for a private age progression to adulthood a few years before. They'd posted it on the internet and taken it with them to speaking engagements. And received nothing but false leads.

The more time that had elapsed between one's disappearance and an age progression, the more chance there was for no likeness at all. Age progression was a science based on average calculations and no one was completely average.

Still, at two, or four, those changes would have been fewer, the progressed photo more accurate.

"I don't know her."

"Evidence says you do."

"It's wrong."

Detective 101. Evidence didn't lie.

"Her DNA was on a hair ribbon found in your home."

"I had a drawer full of ribbons. Most of them from my nieces when they were younger."

"Did you have a niece that looked like Claire?"

"No. They were dark haired. They grew up in Florida and still live there. Kasey and Kylie. They're my younger brother's girls. You can verify the truth. Ask the girls to give you DNA samples and check them against the ribbons you found and I'm sure you'll find that they match. And before you ask, the girls are in their late thirties—thirty-seven and thirty-nine—so they don't fit your girl here."

Gladys shook her head softly, her lips pursed in confusion. "I turned over all of my records," she said. "I handled hundreds of babies. Not a single toddler. I'd remember a two-year-old. You can come visit me once a month for the next twenty years if you'd like, hon. I don't mind the socializing. But I don't know this child you keep insisting I know."

Lucy didn't trust the woman. But Ramsey's words from two nights before held the truth that drove Lucy back to see her again and again. *One piece of information inevitably leads to another.* Emma Sanderson's invitation had spurred on this visit.

Lucy had promised Emma she wouldn't stop looking for Claire.

And while Lucy was certain that Gladys Buckley had associated with Sandy Hayes but had never seen Allie Hayes, she was equally certain that Gladys had some connection to Ramsey's missing Claire Sanderson....

Claire Sanderson. A two-year-old blonde sprite who'd disappeared from her home twenty-five years before and never been seen or heard from again. Emma Sanderson was four when Claire went missing. And her life had been irrevocably changed. Much like Lucy, Emma had grown up with a mother so stricken with grief that the daughter left behind had never had the chance to be a kid.

Or to be innocently happy.

Lucy had recognized a kindred spirit the moment she'd met Emma the previous month.

Folding her hands on the table, Lucy leaned forward. "I don't doubt that you have nieces who live in Florida and that their hair ribbons were among those taken from your home. What I need to know is how a hair ribbon worn by Claire Sanderson happened to be among them."

"I have no idea," Gladys said. "And no reason not to tell you if I did know."

Unless there was some as-yet undetected crime that Gladys had committed. Her plea agreement stood only for the charges already made.

And Lucy had done what she could for the moment. At least as far as the Claire Sanderson case was concerned. So she should go. But she had a more personal matter…. One that, ethically, she couldn't discuss. One she hadn't discussed with Gladys Buckley in all the years she'd been aware of the woman's association with her mother.

"I was going through names and numbers in your business address book yesterday," she said. "I came across a name with no corresponding records attached. And no notes designating that the contact had failed to produce…anything."

There'd been coding for every aspect of the baby business. Including those for referrals or leads that did not result in a baby to sell.

"There were a lot of names in that book. I can't possibly remember them all."

"The name was Sandy." No last name. Years before, while examining her mother's papers, Lucy had found a peculiar scrap of paper with Gladys's number written on it. That had been the beginning of the end for Gladys's operation. Later, when Lucy had access to Gladys's private information, she'd come across a record of her mother having called the older woman.

Not that Gladys had any idea who Lucy was, apart from being the cop who'd helped bust her.

Gladys didn't know how Lucy had stumbled upon her operation in the first place. For her mother's sake it had to stay that way. But she'd had a hellish weekend with Sandy, who hadn't been sober since Saturday morning's ID, and she was sitting right across from a woman who might be able to help her.

The focused look on Gladys's face told Lucy she'd hit a mark. "That was a sad one," Gladys said.

One piece of information was all they needed. Ramsey said so. And it didn't look like they were going to get the information from Sandy—or Sloan Wakerby—anytime soon.

Last month, Lucy had scored the DNA match of a lifetime and found the guy who'd ruined her mother's life. She'd always assumed that would be the hardest part. Finding the guy. After that all the pieces would fall into place.

Her mother's memory would be jogged.

The guy would talk in a bid for leniency.

Neither one of those things had happened. And here she was, a month later, and no closer to finding her sister than she'd ever been. She was getting desperate.

She'd exhausted every lead she had from her mother's life in Aurora—which were precious few.

Based on key evidence, the police had determined all those years ago that the abduction/rape had been a random stranger attack. There'd been no sign of anyone following her mother. Or of the attack having been planned. Quite the opposite. The busy parking lot, the open door, the body dumped by the river, were all signs of a spur-of-the-moment act.

A classic fit for one of the FBI's most dangerous classifications of rapist profiles.

And a dead end when tracking reasons and motivations.

Amber Locken was doing the follow-up on Sloan Wakerby's past. His associations. Any sightings of him with a baby almost thirty years before. So far, she'd turned up a big fat nothing.

Lucy didn't know where else to turn, but Gladys. And she was here, anyway—here because she'd promised Emma Sanderson she wouldn't quit looking for her sister until Claire was found. Or evidence of her death was found.

Her mother hadn't been in contact with Gladys until after the rape. After Allie's disappearance. There was no way Gladys could lead her to the man who'd raped her mother and taken her baby sister.

"Tell me about Sandy," she said, after taking a moment to second-guess herself. This line of questioning wasn't within protocol. It probably wasn't smart.

But then it wasn't the first stupid thing she'd done in her mother's case. On her own time, her own dime, she'd identified Sloan Wakerby as a person of interest, but until she had his DNA she couldn't arrest him. And without arresting him she couldn't get his DNA. She'd tampered with his car—breaking both taillights—and given the police a reason to arrest him. Then she'd called and reported him. Sometimes, when there was no other way, you did what was necessary.

Gladys's watery gray eyes were shadowed as she looked at Lucy. "Did something happen to the poor girl?"

"Tell me about Sandy," Lucy repeated.

"I don't know a lot. She was raped. Her baby was taken at the time of the attack. It was in all the papers, names withheld, of course. But I watched for the baby to come through. I only dealt with newborns, but that wouldn't prevent someone from contacting me if they had a baby to dispose of quickly."

Lucy's palms started to sweat. "Did someone contact you?"

"Yes."

Lucy's mother lied and "forgot" by habit. But she'd believed Sandy when she'd told her this woman hadn't found Allie.

"Who? When?" Her interrogation skills were slipping.

"Sandy did. After the attack. I'd all but forgotten about it, but then I got this phone call. The girl had been asking around downtown Cincinnati, in places a nice young woman shouldn't have been, for ways to get rid of a baby. Someone sent her to me."

"She wanted to hand over a baby?" Lucy asked, because she would've asked that if she didn't already know.

Gladys shook her head. "She was trying to find out where people took babies they didn't want. She wondered if whoever had taken her daughter had brought her there."

Sitting back, Lucy waited for her stomach to settle.

Gladys was telling it to her straight. And Sandy had, too. Their stories matched explicitly.

"I only heard from that young woman once. Never even met her. But I never forgot her, either. I always kept her name and number just in case I ever heard anything. I'd have found a way to get her reunited with that girl. That's one mama who needed her baby home."

Sandy had kept Gladys Buckley's number, as well. And Lucy found it when she'd been going through her mother's things, getting rid of stuff, when it looked like they were going to lose their home her junior year of high school.

Sandy's social security had come through in the nick of time and they'd stayed put. But Lucy had held on to the phone number.

And when she finally got her mother to tell her what Gladys Buckley did for a living, shortly after Lucy had graduated from the academy, she went straight to her mentor—Amber Locken—and volunteered to be an unwed mother in their sting.

She didn't find Allie. But she got Gladys Buckley put behind bars.

"Why are you asking questions about Sandy?" Gladys asked softly. "Did they find her little girl?"

"I'm not at liberty to say." Lucy gave the answer by rote.

She slid one more photo in front of the woman.

"Do you recognize this man?" Sloan Wakerby's picture was current, but Sandy had recognized him.

Gladys studied the picture. And again she shook her head. "I've never seen him before in my life. And that's not the type of face you'd forget."

"You're sure about that?"

"Absolutely sure. I know what you all think of me, selling babies for money, but the way I look at it, I was offering a service to people who needed it. The babies who came through my home were mostly drug babies, or the results of teenage pregnancies. They were unwanted. And I put them in the arms of parents who wanted them enough to pay a large sum."

"You don't think you ever sold any babies who'd been kidnapped by scum out to make a buck?"

"Not to my knowledge."

Lucy had a mouthful to give the older woman—they'd discovered at least a dozen of the children that Gladys had sold had been reported missing—but she saved her breath.

"You ever hear of a guy named Sloan Wakerby?" she asked instead.

"Sloan? I've never known a Sloan in my life."

If Gladys was lying she was damned good at it. But then, the woman had made a career out of lying in a big way.

But she'd kept records—listings that had allowed them to match more than a dozen missing children to their biological parents. And there'd been no Sloan or Wakerby listed in those records.

Lucy was done here.

"Thank you for talking to me."

She gathered up her things, shook the woman's hand and motioned to be let out.

She'd already had two strikeouts on this visit, and she had an entire evening ahead of her, filled with investigative avenues to pursue.

But first, she got into her Ford Escape, drove down to the river, headed southwest on the road along the shore and called the only person she wanted to talk to right then.

The one who'd care about both strikeouts.

The only one who'd understand.

She called Ramsey Miller.

He didn't pick up.

CHAPTER FOUR

"HEY, MILLER, YOU GOT a minute?"

With his arm halfway in the sleeve of his brown suit jacket Wednesday evening, Ramsey looked over at Bill Mendholson, a detective five years his senior and Ramsey's mentor. Bill had been out most of the day.

Ramsey had made a connection between the two Boston missing-child cold cases. He'd gone through both evidence boxes, including trash found in the area, and read all the reports written by everyone who'd done any work on the cases, or who'd been on the scene and made a statement, and the only similarity he could find was that chocolate-bar wrappers—not the common kind found in drugstores and supermarkets—had been found in the vicinity of both disappearances. Might not mean anything. Probably didn't. But as long as those girls' disappearances were unsolved, he wasn't going to stop checking out every single possibility. No matter how remote.

He'd been researching chocolate, chocolate manufacturers, the effects of chocolate, perps who offered chocolate, for most of the day. He'd been immersed in chocolate. Chocolatiers in Boston. Chocolate distributors in the Boston area in August of 2000. Establishments that sold chocolate bars. He'd exhausted every possibility he could think of for connections between the two abductions that took place in the same city in the same time period twelve years before, and he knew he had to take a break.

So he was on his way out to check a name and address that

had finally come in on a person of interest in the Claire Sanderson case. An address he was off to investigate.

"Yeah, Bill, what's up?" Five o'clock was quitting time for both of them and only an hour away, but with all of the papers spread on Bill's desk, it didn't look as if he'd be heading home any time soon, either. Mary must be working late.

Ramsey would be spending most of the night with the Sanderson files. Another cold-case toddler abduction. This one from right here in Comfort Cove, twenty-five years before. And also cleared—thank God—due to recently obtained DNA evidence, from any connection to imprisoned child molester Peter Walters.

But Claire wouldn't let him go. He had to find her. Lucy Hayes's voice mail on Monday had delivered yet another dead end. She'd come up empty after talking with Gladys Buckley. Again.

"Dead body on East Main, male, nineteen to twenty-five, called in at five this morning. No ID. No wallet, tattoos, keys or cash on him. He was in the gutter, dirty, like he was homeless, torn clothes that didn't fit, long hair, unshaven. Empty bottle about a foot away. Strange thing is, he didn't smell, no body odor or alcohol. No needle marks. His teeth were white, straight. Buzz has him—I'm waiting on a tox screen, but I'm certain it's going to come out clean."

Jacket on, and a bulging folder under his arm, Ramsey leaned his shoulder against the pillar on the right side of Mendholson's partitioned space and said, "You're thinking the homeless thing was a setup."

"Yeah. It was too perfectly staged."

"Did you check out his fingernails?"

"Yeah. Pearly pink and manicured. No discoloration. No grime. No broken edges. No match for prints, either. And there's nothing on missing persons."

"Cause of death?"

"Still waiting on the official determination, but he'd been stabbed."

"I'm assuming he bled out where you found him?" Because if not, Bill would have said so.

"Yeah."

"So it wasn't a dump."

"Nope."

"Who called it in?"

"A shopkeeper. Older guy who owns a bakery around the corner. He was out walking around the block to get away from the hot ovens for a minute—"

"You wouldn't be talking about Chet Barber, would you?"

"Yeah. You know him?"

"Yeah, I do. When I first moved to town I rented a place two doors down from Chet's place. He used to give me day-old bread in exchange for me keeping an eye on his place. He's a good guy. The neighborhood watchdog and do-gooder."

"I thought I remembered that you'd lived down there. Any thoughts on what I'm looking at?"

"Besides the obvious, a mediocre murder cover-up? A piss-poor attempt at losing a body?"

"With the ocean ten miles away, why dump a body on a city street?"

"Could be someone from the docks who wanted to point suspicion away from him. You know anytime something turns up in the water, the first place we look is the fishing docks."

Gomez and Anderson, two middle-aged detectives, walked past. "Night," they called.

"Night," Ramsey and Mendholson said in unison. Ramsey straightened. "If your vic was in homeless garb as a cover-up why was he on the street, dressed that way, *before* he was dead?"

"Not sure."

"Any indication that he was from around here?"

"If he is, he doesn't spend much time on the water. His skin's spa soft and white as a baby's butt."

"You got a picture?"

Bill handed it over.

"I'll head down there and see if I can get someone to talk to me."

"Thanks, man." Bill was already studying notes in front of him, his glasses perched on his nose.

"No problem." Pulling his keys from his pocket, Ramsey held his file against his body with his elbow and made his way toward the elevator. Wednesday night and he'd already worked an almost forty-hour week.

"Hey, Miller, I was just coming to see you. I've got the mock-up you wanted on that Jack Colton guy," Kim Pershing said, getting off the elevator he'd been waiting for.

Though Kim had been a cop for ten years, she'd just made detective over the summer. She'd been a great cop. And was going to make an even better detective.

"Thanks," Ramsey said, taking the folder she held out and tucking it under his arm with the other one, backing up to let the elevator go without him. Kim's timing couldn't have been better. He was on his way to pursue a lead on Jack Colton—the guy who just happened to have been driving a delivery truck in Claire Sanderson's neighborhood the day she went missing.

"Anything noteworthy?"

With a sympathetic smile, Kim shook her head, her shoulder-length dark curls bouncing around her shoulders. "No rap sheet, which you already knew. His DMV record is clean. He's lived between here and Boston his entire life with the exception of a semester at the University of Cincinnati on a baseball scholarship. He didn't make the team, dropped out of school, moved back to Massachusetts and has been here ever since."

University of Cincinnati. Handy that the well-known institution of higher learning was less than an hour's drive from

Lucy Hayes. Something she could check out for him. An excuse to give her a ring.

"What about family?" Focus, man. The case was all that mattered.

Kim gave him another soft smile as she shook her head. "His folks moved to Florida ten years ago. Dad's dead, heart attack. Mother's in assisted living with early onset dementia."

"Siblings?"

"Nope." She looked like she was going to say more so he waited. And then she didn't. She was looking at him, as though waiting for him to do something.

He held up the folder. "Thanks," he said, pushing the report against his side as he stepped back.

"You want to have a drink or something?" Kim hadn't moved. Her smile had changed, become more personal. She was looking fine in her dark slacks and white blouse and appeared far more fragile than he knew her to be.

"Can I take a rain check? I'm on my way out to do a canvass for Bill."

"You ever get tired carrying around all that weight, Miller?"

Pushing the elevator button he glanced back at her over his shoulder. "What weight?"

"The million or so rain checks you've asked for and never cashed in."

Lucky for Ramsey the elevator door opened and sucked him in, forestalling his need to reply.

RAMSEY SHOWED PICTURES of Bill's vic to half a dozen people before he got a hit. A wino he knew—an ageless and mostly toothless guy who'd hung out on Ramsey's doorstep with him back when he'd been a beat cop nursing a broken marriage, a guy he knew only as Pops—admitted to Ramsey that he'd taken twenty dollars from the guy in exchange for his clothes.

"Guy give me 'is suit, doo," Pops said in the voice Ramsey knew well. He'd never been able to tell if Pops slurred because he was drunk, or because he was ancient and toothless. Over the years he'd talked to Pops at all times of the day and night and the old man always sounded the same.

The mostly homeless loner always smelled the same, too. Rank. In spite of Ramsey's repeated attempts to help the man.

Two of his first real street lessons he'd learned from Pops. People are what they are because of the choices they make and sometimes they're going to be homeless no matter what kind of help they get—because they continue to make those choices.

"This guy was wearing a suit?" Ramsey asked now, glad he'd pulled his coat out of the backseat of his sedan before he'd hiked his way to the not-so-nice end of Main Street. Darkness had lowered the temperature considerably.

"Yep." Pops's intonation went down instead of up. "Give id do me, doo," the old man said in a language Ramsey understood from years of communicating with the guy.

"You still have it?"

"'Pends."

Reaching into the pocket of the brown slacks that matched his brown tie, Ramsey pulled out a twenty. "On what?" he asked, slipping the bill far enough into Pops's ripped shirt pocket that it didn't immediately fall back out.

"On if you wanna look innat bin." Pops pointed to a half-smashed cardboard box, about the size of a large microwave oven, that was crammed under a couple of broken cement steps outside an old Laundromat.

A couple of minutes later, with the suit safely tucked in a shopping bag that he'd used his badge to procure from the convenience store on the corner, Ramsey was heading up the walk of an apartment complex that he'd passed countless times back when he'd lived in the area, but never had reason before to visit.

The address he'd acquired earlier that day—a woman who might know delivery driver Jack Colton.

He knocked. With his hands tucked into the deep pockets of his tan, calf-length overcoat, he pulled the edges of the outer garment together while he waited. And then knocked again.

A shuffling noise sounded from the other side of the door. The porch light came on. And then a dead bolt turned. The door opened a crack and a wrinkled, pert-nosed face peered through the small opening.

"Yes? Can I help you?"

"Are you Amelia Hardy?"

"Yes. How can I help you?"

The elderly woman's forehead barely measured as high as Ramsey's chest. She was plump and stooped. And sounded like sunshine.

He smiled. Kept his voice easy as he introduced himself, stated his precinct and showed her his detective badge. "I'm looking for someone who lived in this building about twenty-five years ago," he said. Reaching into the pocket of his sport coat, he pulled out a photo of a younger Jack Colton. "This man. Do you remember ever seeing him before?"

"Hmm." Amelia frowned and bent over his hand until her nose was almost touching his palm. "I'm not sure," she said. "Can I take it inside to get a better look? I have my magnifiers there."

"Of course," Ramsey said, his hands folded in front of him as he waited.

And waited.

Five minutes later he was pretty sure Amelia had forgotten him.

And then there she was, back at the door. "I'm sorry, young man," she said, smiling at him as she handed him a cup filled with what smelled like chocolate. Ironic after the day he'd spent researching choclatiers.

Or fitting.

The photo he'd given her was nowhere to be seen.

"I made a phone call to make sure you are really a cop

and then put on water for some of my homemade cocoa mix. Would you like to come in?"

He had hours of work ahead of him, things to do before he was due back on shift in the morning.

"I'd like that," he said without hesitation, and with a short movement forward, he stepped back in time.

CHAPTER FIVE

LUCY WAITED A DAY and a half before making another trip to the lockup without obtaining permission to be there. Amber Locken might not have agreed to let her at her perp if she'd asked. Amber had made no secret about the fact that she thought Lucy was too emotionally connected to the case to have any official involvement. Their captain had agreed.

Amber and the captain didn't know Lucy well enough.

She let herself into the jail just after the dinner hour on Wednesday, swiped her detective badge, made it through the next set of doors, swiped her badge again and then requested a visit with prisoner 281.

Two-eighty-one was housed on the long-term-stay, dangerous-crime block. He was a man who had not yet been sentenced to prison. But he would be.

Sloan Wakerby agreed to her request to see him. And why not? He didn't have anything to lose.

Used to interrogating suspects—dangerous ones—Lucy nonetheless second-guessed the advisability of what she was doing when the guard left her alone in the room with Sloan Wakerby. But the armed officer was just on the other side of the glass, watching every move that was made. She was perfectly safe.

She wanted Wakerby alone. The guy didn't respect women. He'd had a smirk on his face every single time she'd asked him a question the one other time she'd had a go at him. An official go. Ramsey Miller had been present that time. He'd flown in specifically for the interview.

She'd asked Ramsey to come. But that was before Lucy had had a full handle on Wakerby.

Her new theory was that if there were no men around, Wakerby might get cocky enough to give her something.

She wasn't choosy. Any little thing she could work with would do.

"You ever hear of a woman named Gladys Buckley?"

"If you think you're pinning something else on me, you'd better give it up, lady."

"Gladys wasn't raped."

"I don't give a…"

Lucy tuned out the rest of the man's colorful reply regarding his lack of caring.

"She's an older woman," she said instead.

"I don't have to talk to you without my lawyer present."

"That's right, you don't. I'm here to talk. You just listen."

Wakerby's stare was harsher than the string of words he'd just hurled her way.

"You were made," she said as she set down her portfolio and took the cold hard metal seat across the scarred conference table from the slime who'd ruined her mother's life.

Wakerby grinned—an expression that only engaged half of his mouth—and shrugged.

"You're going to prison for the rest of your life. At the very least."

"Because of that bitch who ID'd me? Her testimony won't hold up in court."

"Oh, no? Why not?"

His full smile showed a row of broken and rotting teeth. Remembering what her mother had told her this man had done to her, Lucy almost threw up.

"Talk to my lawyer," Wakerby said.

"I'm talking to you." She would find her sister. Period. "I heard your victim describe what you did to her." Her voice was calm. Nonjudgmental. "I've been at this awhile. Heard a lot of testimony. But what you did—original…and smart. The perfect crime. If technology hadn't caught up with you, you'd have gotten away with it forever. You'd have paid a ticket for that broken light on your car when you were brought in and you would have walked free. What you did to that woman was wrong, but I have to tell you, I'm impressed by your ability to pull it off."

There were days Lucy didn't like how the job made her act. This was one of those days.

Sitting low in his chair with his ankle across his knee, Wakerby watched her, the slimy smile on his face making her angry enough to cry.

"Yeah, you were the man," she continued. "You did what other men only dream of doing. Had yourself a beautiful young woman, did exactly what you wanted with her and then threw her to the curb."

Wakerby's smile grew.

"Except now there's a snag," she continued. "A DNA snag."

He was still smiling. But the smile had stopped growing. Lucy registered the hit. The interrogation score.

"You're with Judge Landly," she continued. "He's a good judge. Intelligent and fair. He listens to both sides and pays attention to mitigators.

"You know what those are?" Lucy asked, her voice soft. Curious.

"I know what they are, *bitch*." Wakerby wasn't smiling now.

Lucy used every ounce of her strength to sit there, to keep her demeanor soft, feminine and calm. "Yeah, extenuating circumstances that will reduce your sentence. And that's what you need to be thinking about right now. You need to figure out how you're going to spin this to make you look less like the fiend the jury is going to find you. You know, why you couldn't help doing what you did."

She paused. Now was the time, while it was just the two of

them, for Wakerby to start justifying what he'd done. If she was doing her job as well as she normally did.

Judging by the twitch in his chin, she was pretty sure she was doing fine.

Wakerby's smile had faded to a grin. He still watched her, saying nothing.

Once she'd unearthed the identity of a man—Sloan Wakerby—who'd fixed a broken awning at a bar down by the river twenty-five years before, Lucy had only needed perseverance to find him.

She was going to get this piece of shit.

"Here's another little hint about Judge Landly," Lucy added. "If you're honest in his courtroom, you've earned yourself a mitigator."

The man across from her didn't budge.

"You know what the penalty is for child abduction and murder in this state, Mr. Wakerby? Child abduction and rape carry significant penalties. The *minimum* sentence for murder is forty-five years."

Wakerby's grin grew tight.

"Ok, Mr. Wakerby. I guess we're done here, then." Picking up her folder, Lucy stood. She motioned for the guard and moved to the door. Just before the uniformed man let her out, she turned back.

"You'll be hearing from your lawyer soon, Mr. Wakerby. You aren't just up for rape. Your victim had a baby with her who hasn't been seen since you kidnapped them from the grocery store that day. We're going for murder." The D.A. hadn't made a decision yet on the murder charge. But Lucy was pretty sure he was going to. "Have a good day."

Amber Locken might have her ass for the visit. But she'd wiped the smile off Sloan Wakerby's face.

AMELIA HARDY WAS ALMOST ninety, with steel-gray hair pinned in a tight bun on the back of her head. She'd been in the same apartment, about seven miles from the ocean and twelve from the Comfort Cove tourist district, for more than seventy years, she told him. Using the same furniture, Ramsey suspected. The small living room was clean, uncluttered and yet very full. Books lined the built-in shelves and figurines stood in front of them.

The claw-footed cherry coffee table and matching end tables bore white doilies and live plants, clear-glass coasters and magazines.

"Please, have a seat," Amelia said in her slightly unsteady birdsong voice. Glancing between the claw-footed embroidered sofa and the claw-footed matching peach wingback chair, Ramsey chose the chair. Amelia put his hot chocolate on a coaster on the end table beside him.

"You have a nice place here," he told her, noticing the drywall tape coming through the wall in one corner of the small room.

"Thank you."

"Does your landlord help you with the upkeep?"

"No. I own the place."

"The whole building?"

"No. Just this unit. The building was sold and turned into condominiums about ten years ago. Funny, you know." She sat on the sofa and faced him, her feet, encased in black leather slip-on shoes, resting on an upholstered step stool, her calf-length silk dress pulled down over her knees. "*Condominium* sounds like such a fancy word. But this place is still the apartment I rented when I graduated from teacher's college when I was twenty-one."

"You taught here in Comfort Cove?"

"No, at a private school for girls in Boston. For the first few years I roomed on campus during the week and drove here for the weekends. I grew up in Boston, but I always loved the ocean and knew this was where I wanted to live."

The place smelled like…lilacs, maybe. Reminding him of

his mother's bedroom when he was a kid. Or maybe her bathroom. After she'd showered, he'd go in there and the floor would be lightly dusted with a white powder that smelled just like Amelia's living room.

Amelia had few photos. A young woman and a young man, standing on the beach. Next to a tree. In front of a car.

"Did you ever marry?" he asked her, sipping cocoa when he should have been finding out what she knew about Jack Colton and then getting the bag bearing the dead man's suit back to the precinct for processing.

"No, sir. My Hank was called up to go to war six months before our wedding. He never made it back." Her smile bore the sadness of many ages as she glanced toward her photos.

"So he never made it here? To this apartment?"

"No, Hank never made it here, but you guessed that I got this place while he was away, didn't you? In preparation for him to come back. In preparation for our marriage."

"I suspected." Because the room spoke of standing still. And the only clue to the reason was those photos.

"This was to be our first home," she said then, sitting back with a faraway look. "I spent hours furnishing the place. Sewing curtains and quilting a spread for the bed. I'd saved every memento from every date we ever had and put the knick-knacks up on the shelves. Every time I added something new, I took photos and sent them to him. I'd make the hour drive from Boston every Friday night and spend the evening here writing to Hank. He'd write back to me that he laid in bed at night and pictured me here—us here. He'd tell me of the things we'd do as soon as he got home...."

Ramsey would bet his life that Amelia still had every single one of those letters. And that she read them regularly, too.

He sat listening as, over the next half hour, Amelia talked about the three years her fiancé was away. About the wedding plans that she made, in anticipation of him coming home, and then had to put off. Again and again.

He was waiting for the story to turn tragic, for the phone call, or the knock on the door, that would signify the end of Amelia's hopes for the future. But before she got there, she sat forward, clasped her hands together and smiled at him.

"You wanted to know about that young man, Jack," she said, sounding as happy and content as if she'd been offering him the cup of cocoa. Standing, she moved to an old secretary, a three-foot-wide china cabinet with drawers and a pull-down desk shelf. Ramsey's grandmother had had one that she'd passed down to his sister, Diane. It still stood in Diane's bedroom in their parents' home, filled with Diane's things. As far as he knew, his mother still dusted the antique every week, when she cleaned the rest of Diane's room.

"I do remember him." Amelia's voice sounded distant, and Ramsey realized the woman was looking at the picture he'd handed her earlier. She'd obviously set it down on the secretary. The magnifying spectacles were perched on the end of her nose.

The old woman walked toward him, handing him back his photograph as she held the glasses and sat on the end of the couch, her knees almost touching his.

"That's Jack," she said, and then continued. "Mostly he was a boy of few words, but I'd say I knew him fairly well. You see, I, too, am a pretty good judge of character," she said. "It wasn't that long ago that he was here."

"How long ago?" Ramsey's demeanor didn't change. His focus was acute.

"I'm not sure. He was still living here when I retired, I know, because I'd be walking down to the bakery just after six when he left for work in the mornings. One of the pleasures of my retirement was that I could be at the bakery as soon as the last loaves of bread came out of the oven. There's nothing like freshly made bread. Don't you agree, Detective?"

Ramsey had a flash of his mother, standing in the kitchen, hands covered in flour, and Diane beside her, flour on her cheek and on her chin, as she tried to get the hang of kneading bread.

He nodded at Amelia. And quickly asked, "When did you retire?"

"Nineteen eighty-six. I was sixty-seven and getting a little nervous about the hour's drive to Boston during the winters. After those first few years, I commuted back and forth every single day." She frowned, and then her expression cleared. "After I retired, I taught kindergarten at St. Francis down on High Street, and I remember your young man helping me carry my trash down one morning when I had my hands full. You remember St. Francis, don't you? It burned down a few years ago...."

Fifteen years ago, before Ramsey had moved to Comfort Cove. Even before he'd met Tom Cook and introduced the citified Greer boy to his older sister.

"Was this young man still living here when St. Francis burned down?" he asked.

Frowning again, Amelia shook her head. "No, you know, I don't think he was. I'm sure he wasn't. Because we were all gathered out on the stoop that night. We could see the flames from here. And the nice young woman who married that teacher from the high school in town was talking to me. She moved into Jack's apartment not long after he left. Cheryl, her name was. I can't remember her last name. Doesn't matter, though, since she's married now. I don't remember her husband's name, either. Dirk, I think."

"Do you remember Jack's last name?" Ramsey asked. Had Colton been living under an assumed name?

"No," Amelia frowned, shaking her head. And then her brow cleared. "It started with a *C,* though. Jack C. I know that because of his mailbox. Our mailboxes are all lined up together in the laundry room. He was the only person who put just their last initial instead of their whole last name on the box. He'd written his first name too large and couldn't fit the whole last name on the little tab. Funny the things that stick with you, huh?"

And not funny at all the things that you couldn't get rid of. Claire Sanderson's case was one that was haunting Ramsey. He'd been on it for months and couldn't get a break.

Or get rid of it, either, physically or mentally.

It stuck with him day and night. And it wasn't funny at all.

CHAPTER SIX

JACK COLTON HAD BEEN a delivery truck driver twenty-five years earlier. A house on his regular weekly route was two doors down from the home where two-year-old Claire Sanderson had been abducted. Jack's truck had been seen on Claire's street the morning she went missing—a piece of information Ramsey had only just uncovered, when he'd reopened the cold case over the summer, to find out if Claire Sanderson was one of Walters's victims.

"What else do you remember about Jack?" he asked now, his voice as kind as it got.

"Nice young man," Amelia said. "Polite. Hard worker. He drove a truck. He was always so punctual, and when I asked him about it he said because time meant money. He delivered meat, which couldn't just be left at someone's door. The customer had to be present to take delivery. He had a set route with regular customers and he got paid per stop. The more timely he was, the more customers he'd be given. He had his schedule down almost to the minute."

Jack hadn't told Ramsey about being compensated per job, or about the schedule he'd kept, when the now forty-eight-year-old semitruck driver came in for an interview over the summer. But what Amelia said made sense.

"Did you ever see the truck?"

Shaking her head, Amelia said, "He never brought it home. It was against policy. He caught the bus down at the corner and rode it to the warehouse where he picked up his truck."

Colton had been delivering meat to a home two doors down

from Claire's every Wednesday morning, at the very same time, which was partially what had helped him pinpoint more accurately the window of time in which Claire disappeared. Amelia's insight into the driver's schedule fit squarely with what Ramsey already knew.

Colton's presence near the scene had never come up in the initial investigation and Ramsey was the first and only officer to question Colton on the matter. So far, there was no reason to suspect the guy, except that he'd been in the area. A normal occurrence for him and not a crime.

"Do you know if Jack ever lost a stop for being off schedule?" Ramsey asked.

"I have no idea. If he did, he never said so." She glanced toward the photo on the table closest to her. "My Hank was a hard worker, too. He was in college, in Boston, when he was called up. That's how we met. In college. And in the evening and on weekends, he stocked shelves at his daddy's hardware store. Jack kind of reminded me of Hank the way he was so good at fixing things."

"Your Hank had you." Ramsey took the lead she'd offered. "Did Jack have a girl in his life?"

Was the man as upstanding as he'd seemed? Or had Jack and Frank Whittier—the live-in fiancé of Claire's mother, Rose Sanderson, and the only suspect in the case—somehow been partners in the most hideous of crimes? There was a lot of money to be made at selling children on the black market and Frank Whittier had been taking on the responsibility of a new wife and two children, in addition to his own son. Three more mouths to feed. Two more college tuitions. By all accounts little Claire had been a handful. And a charmer. Rose had been completely devoted to her. Frank could have been resentful of all the attention the woman gave to the toddler. Or jealous of the fact that he hadn't fathered the little girl.

It wouldn't be the first time Ramsey had seen something like that.

A couple of months ago, Jack had cleared Frank's name in the case, releasing the sixty-two-year-old from twenty-five years of suspicion. Frank was back in school, taking the continuing-education classes that would allow him to get his high-school teaching certification again. Before his initial arrest, he'd been the principal of a well-known boy's school, and a winning basketball coach at a public school, as well.

When Ramsey had finally located Jack Colton, based on private writings that Cal Whittier, Frank's son, had turned over to him, Jack had testified that he'd seen Claire Sanderson alone in her front yard, watching as then seven-year-old Cal walked down the driveway, on his way to school. He said that Claire had gone back to the house. Because she'd only been two, he'd swung back by after making his delivery to make certain that she'd made it inside, and he'd seen Frank Whittier, alone, open the back door of his car—exposing its emptiness—to drop his briefcase on the backseat. The man had then gotten in the front of his car and driven off to work.

His testimony and timeline followed Frank's own testimony from twenty-five years before regarding his actions that morning. He'd come out of the house at 7:20 a.m., five minutes later than usual, dropped his briefcase on the backseat of his car, climbed in the front and driven away. He'd never seen Claire outside of the house.

He hadn't seen her inside the house just before he left, either, but that wasn't unusual as she'd have been back in the bedroom with her four-year-old sister, Emma, waiting for their mother to brush their hair and put it in ponytails.

The only unusual thing in their routine that morning had been the babysitter's call saying she was sick, which meant that Rose was on the phone trying to make other arrangements for Claire and Emma, and for Cal, for when he got home from school. She'd been on the phone when Frank left.

"Jack didn't just have one girl, like my Hank did," Amelia was saying. "He had a few of them."

New information. New leads?

"He had them here?"

"Yes. They were sweet girls."

"And it didn't bother you that Jack wasn't faithful to them? That he had more than one of them?"

"Oh, my, Detective, I'm sorry if I misled you. He didn't have them at the same time! There was one girl he dated for a bit, but it didn't last long. I remember seeing her a time or two. She had red hair, I think. And then there was the girl who moved in with him. I never met her. I was filling in for a dorm mother at school and was only home on Sundays the semester she was here. She broke up with him. I know about her because I heard him crying one night and I asked him about it. I knew, you see, that Jack wasn't close to his family. He was the only child of an older couple who never quite made room for him in their lives. He learned how to fend for himself quite young. But a man that young shouldn't have to fend for himself all the time. Growing up is hard. Being an adult is hard. If I could give him some advice, then that's what I had to do. He was embarrassed that I knew he'd been crying, but I told him that all men cry now and then. It was nothing to be ashamed about. Don't you agree, Detective Miller?"

Hell, no, he didn't agree. Not all men cry. Ramsey needed information. He nodded.

"So then, after this girl broke his heart, did he live alone?"

"For a while. And then another girl moved in. Melanie was her name. I liked her. But I don't think it worked out, either. I asked him once if he was going to marry Melanie and he told me that he wasn't in love with her like a guy should be in love with a girl he was going to marry. I'm not sure what ended up happening, though. Jack moved out and I lost track of him."

"He never came back to see you?"

"I'm not even sure he was in state. He'd said he wanted to travel. And to make more money."

Ramsey, with all his senses tuned in and alert, relaxed farther back in his chair. "These girls he was friends with, did any of them have kids?"

Say, two-year-old blonde girls?

"No. I'm absolutely certain about that. Hank and I planned to have a house full of children, and anytime there was a little one living here, I made certain I was first on the list for babysitting duty."

"So you'd have noticed if there were ever little children here, even just for visits?"

"Absolutely. Except that semester I was gone."

"Were you here on October 13, 1987, in the morning?"

It was a long shot. There was no way anyone could be expected to remember a specific day more than two decades before.

Unless it stood out in their minds for some reason.

Like maybe Frank showing up in a vehicle—his delivery truck—with a precocious toddler in tow?

Amelia didn't immediately shake her head as he'd expected she would.

With her magnifying spectacles in hand, the older woman stood. She went over to the bookshelf—a couple of shelves filled with black leather bindings. Putting on her glasses, she pulled out one black binder, and then another. Thumbed through that one until she found what she'd obviously been looking for.

"Yes, I was here." She shocked him with her answer.

Amelia was old. And obviously spent a lot of time alone. Wouldn't be at all unusual for the woman to get confused.

Or to want to please him just to keep him there.

Ramsey watched her closely and said, "You sound sure about that."

Making her way slowly toward Ramsey she gave him the book. "I have a calendar for every year of my life here," she said. "Originally I kept them as part of an agreement between Hank and me, a plan we had to keep close to each other. The three years he was overseas, I cataloged my days so that I could share them with him. After…well, I was so used to keeping the books that I continued to do so. I thought about quitting a number of times, but I like having them there. I never married, never had children. There's no one to help me remember the things an old lady might forget. I've got my books to remind me."

Ramsey looked at the entry for October 13, 1987. Amelia had been home that day waiting on a delivery of fabric she was using to make dresses for the church disaster-relief closet. The fabric had arrived at two and she'd had the first dress done by six.

And she'd watched the news.

"You wrote about the little girl who was kidnapped."

"Claire Sanderson, yes," Amelia said. "She was from right here in Comfort Cove and close to home, you know? I felt her disappearance personally, like it happened to me. Followed the case for years. Her mama and sister lived here and I could just imagine how it would feel, always waiting.…

"I used to think I might run into them someday, but then I heard they were speaking locally and I didn't go. I just hurt too much for them. I couldn't go see them hurt."

Ramsey had met the woman the month before. And Amelia was right, it was worse when you watched them hurt. Much worse.

"If Jack, or any of his girlfriends, had brought a child to visit that day, you might have missed them, then, if you were sewing." Stick with the case. The investigation. The search for facts.

"Nope." Amelia let him keep the book as she took her seat on the couch. "My sewing room—what used to be the spare bedroom when this was Hank's and my home—is directly beneath the unit where Jack lived. If he'd had a child up there, I'd have known."

Unless the child had been unconscious.

"Does that room have a window?" Ramsey asked.

"Yes, sir, looking directly out at the street. That's why I chose that room to sew in. So I can see what's going on."

"You keep pretty good track, then, of who comes and goes around here?"

"Not like I used to, but yes, a girl living alone has to always be aware of her surroundings to keep herself safe."

True. Wrong that it should be that way, but true.

"Did you ever notice any other visitors to Jack's place?"

"No. Nothing that stood out. The boy worked so many hours it would have been hard for him to do much entertaining. Besides, Jack was a quiet boy. He liked to read. Watch TV. And work. He was always concerned about saving his money. Didn't waste it on eating at restaurants. That boy would paint a room in exchange for some of my stew. I'd give him soup and two days later the bowl would be outside my door empty and clean. I started leaving him a list of things on sale at the grocery store every week and the next thing I knew, he was insisting I leave my trash just outside my door, and it would always disappear."

So Jack needed money, too. Motive.

"Did you ever know him to drink?"

"Alcoholic beverages? Jack? Never. He didn't use tobacco, either. He lived right above me, Detective, and he never gave me one bit of trouble."

Amelia nodded toward his mostly full cup. "You aren't drinking your cocoa, Detective Miller."

Ramsey wasn't real fond of hot drinks. And after a full day of investigating chocolate in relation to two missing little girls, he didn't relish it, either. But the obviously lonely woman had taken the time to prepare it for him so he picked up the cup.

"Is there anything else you can remember?"

She watched him sip. "Mmm, good," he said, winning him another one of her smiles.

"Jack liked my cocoa, too," she told Ramsey. "He helped

me out in exchange for my homemade cooking, but he made
extra money doing odd jobs around here for the landlord and
was called upon to change my furnace filters a time or two.
And to fix the leak in my kitchen drain. He put new flooring in the bathroom, too, a real nice tile instead of linoleum.
You want to see?"

He had to get going. Ramsey drained the now-cooled cocoa
and stood. "Sure," he said, slipping Jack's picture back into
the inside pocket of his suit coat.

Slowly leading the way down a narrow hall with gleam-
ing hardwood floors covered with peach throw rugs, Amelia turned left at the first door and flipped on a light switch.

"There, see?" She pointed toward the floor.

Ramsey glanced, and did a double take. The flooring was
clean, but the edges were sharp in places where the mortar
had worn away. The tub was claw-footed. In pristine condi-
tion. Probably worth some money.

The bottom of the toilet was missing mortar or caulk, and
the crevice in between the porcelain and the tile was an ugly
brown.

The bathroom floor was as clean as the rest of the house;
the peach and white swirled tiles sparkled. All the room
needed was a little TLC—a little time.

Looking at the floor, he tried to picture Jack Colton there,
down on his haunches, helping an old woman in exchange for
cocoa and the probable pittance his landlord would have paid
him. The image fit.

Ramsey should help her caulk her floor. She'd given him
cocoa. And information.

No. He had work to do.

She was lonely.

He was a loner.

He followed Amelia back out to the living room. "Thank
you very much for your time," he told the older woman, mak-

ing his leave known before she sat back down and had to get up again to lock up after him.

"Come back anytime," she said, her smile still broad as she stood, hunched, in the middle of her living room.

He made it to the door. She wasn't following him. Probably something to do with the limp that had become more pronounced, the gait that had slowed considerably, on the short walk from the bathroom.

"I noticed some drywall tape coming lose in the corner over there." What in the hell was he doing, making her worry about something she obviously couldn't fix? Or afford to hire out? She was a retired teacher. From a small girls' school. With no apparent kin.

"Oh?" Wide-eyed, she turned, and Ramsey was fairly certain that, although she studied the wall, she couldn't see the damage he referred to.

"I could fix it for you." No, he couldn't.

"You could?"

Technically. He knew how. Thanks to his father who made certain that Ramsey knew the basics of home maintenance and repair.

"Yes." He could bring his caulk gun and redo the bathroom, too. The kitchen sink should probably be checked and…

"Then that would be fine," Amelia said. "When will you be back?"

"Sunday, does that work?"

"As long as it's in the afternoon, then yes, it does. I go to church in the morning."

He opened the door, and realized that she was going to have to follow him over there to refasten the dead bolt behind him. He wondered why she didn't have a cane. Or a walker. Or…

It was none of his business. Amelia Hardy had gotten along just fine without him for almost ninety years.

"Detective?"

He turned back. She hadn't moved. "You never did tell me

why you wanted to know so much about Jack. He isn't in any kind of trouble is he?"

He couldn't give information from an ongoing investigation. "No, ma'am, he isn't," Ramsey said.

Standing where she was, Amelia nodded. Ramsey looked at the woman, at the lock, stepped back into real time and closed the door behind him.

He was outside her door, five minutes later, when he heard the dead bolt click into place.

CHAPTER SEVEN

THE NIGHT WAS DARK and there was no moon, making Lucy's bedroom a box of shadows in black. She'd acted rashly. Her visit with Sloan Wakerby that evening would not go unnoticed by her superiors.

The possibility of being reprimanded was not what was keeping her awake.

The sister she'd never met was doing that. She had her mother's rapist. The man was going to pay for what he'd done to Sandy. Maybe she should just let it go.

If Allie had survived the abduction almost thirty years ago, she'd be an adult now. Living her life with no knowledge of Lucy or Sandy. Who was to say the woman would even want to know about them? If she'd been sold to a decent couple, she'd probably had a great life. Was most likely still having a healthy, normal life.

So was Lucy's hell-bent determination to find her sister more for her own sake than for Allie's?

Sandy would have a better chance of rehabilitation, of getting off the booze, staying off, if she knew that Allie was safe and happy.

But then she'd want to see her.

And what if Allie didn't want to see Sandy?

Or worse, what if Allie was dead? What would that knowledge do to Sandy? While there was still hope that Allie was alive Sandy had something to live for. To hold on to.

If they knew Allie was gone, would Sandy give up completely?

The thought reminded her of Emma Sanderson. Not too long ago, the Comfort Cove high-school teacher had said the same thing about her own mother regarding her little sister, Claire.

Lying flat on her back in panties and an extra large T-shirt, with the sheet pulled up to her ribs, Lucy stared wide-eyed into the darkness, her gaze pointing toward the ceiling she knew was up there.

She'd only known Emma Sanderson for a short time, and didn't know her all that well. But the memory of the woman stuck with her. They had one thing in common: they were both the surviving daughter of a single mother, with a sister who'd been abducted. They'd both grown up with grief-stricken mothers. They both had mothers who leaned on them unnaturally, relied on them almost exclusively, needed them to the point of emotional exhaustion.

Or maybe it was just Lucy who was exhausted. She closed her eyes and willed unconsciousness to follow. Since the night she'd broken the taillight on Sloan Wakerby's car, Lucy hadn't slept worth a damn. She was tired.

Still, Emma was getting married. Lucy smiled in the darkness. In the midst of pain and sorrow, there was happiness. In the aftermath of tragedy, joy was still attainable.

Maybe she should quit the investigative profession and become a poet, she thought, staring at the ceiling again. No one lived or died because of a poem.

Emma had talked about writing her own wedding vows. Traditional promises didn't run deep enough for her. Or fit her, either.

And how would Emma's wedding fit Rose Sanderson, the mother who clung to her so voraciously? In some ways the day wouldn't be easy.

Would Ramsey Miller attend the wedding? She'd never seen him outside of his professional capacity. Never even so much as had a drink with him.

Not that she needed to. She liked having a professional soul mate, of sorts. That was all.

He'd be in a suit, of course. In the handful of times she'd actually seen him, he'd never worn anything else. Pants, jacket, matching shirt and tie and shoes. That was Ramsey Miller.

If a woman were to have sex with him, she'd get to peel away all those layers....

Ramsey worked all hours of the day and night, but he was human. All man. Built just right in all the right places. It stood to reason that he had sex regularly with someone.

Not her.

With Lucy he was always in control.

But would he loosen up after a glass of champagne? Did he drink beer?

Or dance?

People danced at weddings. With their arms around their dance partners.

Ramsey's shoulders were broad. His arms would be strong. And warm. His thighs rock solid.

It had been so long since Lucy had been held....

Why had she never put a night-light in her bedroom? They were in every other room in the house—softly illuminating her space so that she could see, the minute she walked into a room, that she was alone.

Would she always live alone? And maybe just have a lover?

Someone who was passionate about what he did? Who cared about outcomes? Someone who hurt for the babies who were lost?

Someone whose hands would caress her skin with the tenderness he kept hidden so deeply inside?

Someone who didn't want to get married any time soon...

Sandy would be front and center if Lucy ever married. The thought was enough to make her stop thinking about weddings.

The fact that her phone was ringing helped, too.

Grabbing the cell phone from her nightstand, she expected to see either her work number or her mother's number on the caller display.

It was neither. And if her caller had been reading her thoughts a few minutes earlier, she was going to just go ahead and die.

Mental telepathy wouldn't be so cruel....

"Hello?"

"Did I wake you?" The deep tenor of Ramsey Miller's voice shook her insides and she welcomed the darkness that had been closing in on her just seconds before.

It was almost midnight. Her shift started at eight in the morning. So did his. "No, I was awake."

He couldn't know she'd been thinking about his fingers on her naked skin....

"I have a favor to ask."

About his thighs pressed against hers...

"What do you need?" Her words came out too soft, too intimate, like he was there, lying in bed with her. Lucy cleared her throat. If Ramsey had a favor, it was strictly business. "What's up?" she said loudly while her toes curled and her naked thighs felt exposed, in spite of the sheet covering them.

What in the hell was the matter with her? She was a professional. Always.

"Jack Colton."

"The delivery truck driver?" Lucy sat up, the sheet pooling over the bottom of her T-shirt, pretty much forgotten. Ramsey had said he was going to do some more checking up on the guy. This was bigger than sex. Bigger than any personal life she'd ever have.

"It bugs me, you know? I can't let this Sanderson case go."

"Then you must be on to something. There've been other cases you've looked at in relation to Walters, found that the DNA didn't match and been able to move on from."

"I have them all in a stack on a corner of my desk."

The news didn't surprise her. She had a stack of cases, too. Ones she'd pulled while looking for connections to Allie. Ones she'd found during the Gladys Buckley investigation. Ones she'd get back to.

"Maybe it's because we worked with Emma Sanderson. Because she was willing to risk her life to find her sister. Or because I think Cal Whittier is an honest man who deserves to have his father exonerated once and for all, or be tried for his crimes. Or maybe I'm just turning into an old coot who can't let go of a bone."

"You aren't old." Lucy chuckled. "And Claire Sanderson's case is different," Lucy said, feeling more like herself. "You go looking for DNA to either tie her to Walters or free her from him, and instead, you find that the box of evidence pertaining to her case is missing. You couldn't just let that go. You had to find out who took it and why. Any good cop would."

"And I did."

"Yes, but in the meantime, you met Cal Whittier, the only suspect's son, and you found a piece of new evidence in the case, evidence the detectives who had the case twenty-five years ago didn't have. You have to follow up, Ramsey. Just like I'm doing with Wakerby."

Maybe she and Ramsey were meant to be married to their work.

"How's that case going?"

She'd let Sloan Wakerby take away her ability to be peacefully alone in the dark. She'd rather think about Ramsey's arms, holding her close on the dance floor.

Or any other floor.

"We can talk about my stuff in a minute. You called about Jack."

"Yeah. He went to UC for a semester." He gave her dates. "Maybe there's still someone there who'd have been around then, someone who knows something."

Something Jack Colton wouldn't want them to know.

"Are you getting a warrant?" They'd need access to records.

"I should have it on my desk in the morning."

"Are you there now?"

"At work? No. I'm home."

Which, based on the work habits he'd confessed to during one of their late-night conversations, probably meant he was in bed with his computer propped up on his chest.

Lucky computer.

"Do you know where Colton lived when he was at UC?" She forced herself to think about things that mattered.

"No idea. I'm hoping a dorm."

She was thinking the same thing. Thank goodness. Back on track. "We'd have more chance of finding someone who knows him, that way. There'd be records of resident assistants. Dorm managers."

"We could get lucky and find that his dorm manager is still working there."

"And if he had a roommate we'd have another possible witness. There could be a suite mate, too. Or even a floor mate who remembers him."

"Things happen for a reason," Ramsey said, almost to himself. "Any good cop knows that."

"And?"

"When I called Caleb Whittier this summer to tell him about the box of missing evidence in Claire Sanderson's case…"

Because some of the missing evidence had pertained to Cal.

"…he told me about the book he'd written, putting events from his life in chronological order. He told me for a reason. He gave me Jack Colton."

"He told you about the book because he was trying to get you off his father's back."

"Knowing about the book gave me the ammunition to bribe him. Either he let me read what he'd written or I'd go hard on his father. He put himself in that position by telling me the book existed in the first place."

"Maybe, unwittingly. But you said that he didn't even realize the information about the delivery truck on the street that day was in the book."

As a traumatized teen, Cal had written about the day Claire Sanderson had been abducted. Cal remembered that morning as the day his father had made him go to school against his wishes. He'd hidden behind Jack's truck in order to find his way undetected to the backyards in the neighborhood to gain access to his own backyard without being seen. He'd planned to stay there until the coast was clear—meaning Claire's mother, Rose, and Cal's father, Frank, had both left for their jobs at their prospective schools—so that he could go back into the house with the spare key he always carried.

It was the first account that had been given of the delivery truck. And Cal's father, who'd spent twenty-five years as the only suspect in the case, had been exonerated by things Jack had said when he'd finally, twenty-five years later, been questioned.

"Just because Cal Whittier said he didn't realize that mention of the truck was in the book, doesn't mean that he was telling the truth."

Ramsey's fatigue sounded loud and clear through their cellular connection.

"You think Cal was handing you Jack?"

"I think it's possible."

"Cal couldn't have known that Colton had anything to say that would clear his father's name."

"Unless he knew exactly that."

"You're saying you think that Cal and Colton have been in contact? That a deal was struck for Colton to clear Frank Whittier?"

"It's possible."

"You checked phone records."

"They could have used prepaid cell phones. Or snail mail. Or...maybe I'm digging up dirt where there is none."

"Jack Colton was driving a delivery truck on the street where an abduction took place at about the same time it happened," she reminded him.

"Just as he did every other Wednesday before and after that. A guy's not a criminal for doing his job."

"Could be someone knew about his route and purposely chose the date and time so there'd be a suspect." She played Ramsey's theory out because that's what good cops did for each other. And because being Ramsey Miller's sounding board was a good part of her life.

"'Someone' being Frank Whittier?"

"Maybe." Emma adored Frank's son Cal, the boy she'd loved as her big brother—and the man he'd become, too. But Emma hadn't said a lot about Frank. "Who'd have figured that no one would mention the delivery truck having been on the street that day?"

"Or the fact that young Cal had cut school. If the boy had been where he was supposed to have been he'd never have seen that little girl in his father's car that morning," Ramsey added, his voice gaining momentum.

"If Cal hadn't seen Claire in Frank's car, Frank would never have been a suspect and Jack, as the only other occupant of the street at the time, would have been the prime suspect. You think Whittier chose that particular day and time to do something with Claire because he knew the delivery truck would be there and could be a diversion?"

"It happens."

"But no one reported seeing the delivery truck that day," Lucy repeated, frowning in the darkness, needing answers while not yet sure they had all the right questions.

"Young Cal and the neighbors were asked if they saw or did anything unusual that day, anything outside of their normal routines. That truck was routine. No one reported the cars that were usually parked on the street, either. Or seeing their neighbors going to work. They only said they didn't see anything different or unusual."

People noticed what they expected to notice. "And unless we're going to believe that the neighbors also had something to do with Claire's disappearance, then we have to believe that they were all engaged in their own lives, their own mornings, and didn't notice anything unusual or someone would have seen that little girl snatched away from her home in broad daylight."

"Exactly. How did that happen?" Ramsey asked what she knew was a rhetorical question. And it wasn't.

"Unless someone who was supposed to be on that block, someone who knew her, took her. What I remember from the police reports is that Claire didn't cry out. Or scream. Her mother would surely have heard that."

"Right. No one heard anything."

"She wouldn't have gone willingly with Jack Colton. She didn't know him. Which is why we're right back to Frank Whittier."

Ramsey's angle was a good one. The most likely one. Probably the right one.

If Frank wanted the delivery guy, Jack Colton, to be a suspect, he'd have mentioned the guy when he'd first been questioned twenty-five years before. To divert attention from himself, if nothing else.

"Maybe there's someone else," she said, anyway, to keep them both sharp enough not to overlook anything. Not to miss what might be right in front of them. The evidence told the truth and they just didn't have enough of that yet. "Someone who also knew Jack's schedule. Someone unrelated to either him or Frank. Because if Frank timed his move in line with Jack's truck on the street, wouldn't he have led the police in that direction by mentioning that he saw the truck there?"

Theories were an important part of police work, she reminded herself. Theories led to questions, to quests for information, that often led to evidence. To the truth. They just didn't want to get so lost in one theory that they missed another. Or lost sight of facts.

"Someone could have silenced the child before she had a chance to scream for her mother," Ramsey said. "Jack could have been working on his own. Other than the fact that he's a great guy who cares about old ladies and saving money and is faithful to his girlfriends, who pays his taxes on time, has no police record and not even points on his driver's license, he could have done this."

She empathized with his frustration. Felt it along with her own mass of tumbling emotions that night.

"You know something?" she said as she sank a little deeper into her pillows.

"What?"

"I'm glad that I had Allie's missing-person's file checked out when you went looking for it to find out if she was one of Walters's victims."

"Why?"

Just like a guy was her first thought. He couldn't intuitively understand an emotional outpouring and return it in kind? "Because you called me to ask about it and I found out that I'm not the only person whose every waking moment is centered on searching for missing children." Because he'd called her and become her best friend in the world. "This quest just never lets me go. Ever. And it's the same with you, isn't it? You've got Claire Sanderson and I've got my sister."

"I saw the evidence in Walters's basement."

He cared so deeply.

And she wanted to feel that intensity in a physical sense.

She rubbed the back of her neck. "I'm glad that we found each other," she admitted, the darkness, her meeting with Wakerby, messing with her.

It wasn't that she needed Ramsey. She was just feeling… glad that he was on the other end of her line.

"There's no off time for us," she rambled on. "Any time of the day or night, we're ready and willing to talk about a case. Before you, I had to wait for a decent hour to run things by a colleague."

In other words, they were both fully engrossed in work to the exclusion of any other aspect of life. They were two-dimensional human beings living in a three-dimensional world.

Could sex be two-dimensional, too?

"I'm accomplishing a lot more on my cases, in less time, because of you," she finished.

"Speaking of which, what's the latest on Wakerby? Have they indicted him?"

"For rape, yes. Not for murder yet."

Beyond that she couldn't think about the man any more that night. She needed daylight.

"I received an invitation to Emma Sanderson's wedding today." Why was she doing this? Clearly Ramsey Miller wanted nothing personal between them.

She wouldn't, either, once the night was done and she was in her right mind again.

In complete control again.

The thought had Lucy sitting straight up in bed.

Somehow Sloan Wakerby had taken away her sense of control. And she hadn't seen it coming.

Damn him.

"Did you get an invitation, too?"

"Maybe. There was an envelope with Emma Sanderson's return address. I didn't open it yet."

After contacting Cal Whittier regarding Claire Sanderson's missing evidence box—and ultimately finding Jack Colton—Ramsey had contacted the second person with evidence in that box, Emma Sanderson.

Emma was four when her little sister was abducted. And her life, like Lucy's, had been abnormal ever since.

Ramsey had reported the missing evidence, interviewed Emma regarding anything she might know about anyone who might have stolen the evidence and then asked Emma to bring in some of Claire's belongings so that the lab could try to extract some of Claire's DNA to either identify her or rule her out as one of Walters's victims. Ramsey was determined to have the man tried for every single child he'd hurt. Lucy figured Ramsey wasn't going to rest until Peter Walters was put to death.

Emma wanted answers about her sister. She wanted closure. She'd agreed to Ramsey's request for Claire's belongings.

And because of a similarity in Lucy's and Emma's situations, Ramsey had asked Lucy to fly in for the meeting with Emma.

Ramsey had been thinking of the case. Of making Emma comfortable so she'd talk. Of using Lucy's interrogation and listening skills to get answers they didn't yet have.

And, in Emma, Lucy had found another kindred spirit. Which meant two in one year. And two in a lifetime.

"I sent my RSVP back this morning." She was going to wear the little black dress.

And she wanted him to see her in it.

"When's the wedding?"

"Thanksgiving weekend." Three weeks away. "On a boat at the fishing docks in Comfort Cove."

"I don't do weddings."

"I'm going."

"You'll be flying in?"

"Yeah. I'd love to have someone there I know." And to dance with him.

"I'll probably be working."

"We could compare notes over a toast."

"You're sure you're flying in?"

"Yeah. I already made my reservation." She'd done that just before going to see Sloan Wakerby that evening.

She'd been thinking about Ramsey then, too.

"What time do you get in?"

"Ten o'clock Saturday morning. The wedding's at four."

"I'll pick you up."

Lucy grinned. A big grin that stayed there. "Then you pretty much have to drive me to the wedding because I won't have a rental car." It didn't occur to her to prevaricate. Not until she'd already spoken.

"It's my fault you got the invitation at all. I can't leave you to go alone."

She guessed that meant they were going together. It shouldn't be a big deal. Tomorrow it wouldn't be.

And with that resolved, she was determined to get back on track. "You know what's bothered me all along about Jack Colton?"

"Other than the fact that he was there that morning?"

"He admitted, when you questioned him this summer, that he saw Claire outside her house."

"Right."

"Her disappearance was big news."

"Right."

"While Comfort Cove is bigger than Aurora, it's not all that big now. I'm guessing, twenty-five years ago, it was quite a bit smaller."

"It was."

"So don't you think Jack would have heard about a child missing from a street he did business on? Don't you think, when he heard when the abduction happened, that he'd have called the police and told them that he'd seen the little girl in her yard that morning? Or when he heard that Frank Whittier was a suspect, he'd have called to tell the police what he told you this summer? That he'd seen Frank get into his car alone?"

"I asked him that question last time I spoke with him. He

didn't call because he figured that as soon as he did, he'd be a suspect. He was a young kid on his own. With no money. He couldn't afford to lose his job. Couldn't afford to be brought in for questioning. Couldn't afford a lawyer. Short answer is, he was afraid."

"So he let Frank Whittier hang?"

"He said that he watched the news enough to know that Frank Whittier wasn't charged and that was good enough for him. He didn't realize the hell Frank's life became because of the ongoing suspicions against him. He did say that he'd been feeling guilty for years about not coming forward, but thought that to do so so late would only raise more suspicions about his possible involvement. And he's right on that score. I am suspicious."

"Basically, he turned a blind eye to save his own ass," Lucy summed up drily.

"You know as well as I do that folks do it all the time. Colton said that he was afraid that if he came forward, the real kidnappers would come after him and it wasn't like he had any information that would actually help the police find Claire Sanderson. He saw her in her front yard and she was fine. And when he drove by again, she was gone. He didn't see anyone in the area and has no idea what happened to her."

"Do you believe him?"

"You got time to make a run to Cincinnati to check him out?"

"You bet." She'd make time.

For Emma. For Claire Sanderson and Allie and all of the other children who'd been ripped away from the families who loved them.

And for Ramsey Miller.

CHAPTER EIGHT

RAMSEY WAS OUT ALL DAY Thursday and Friday, pursuing leads. Late Friday afternoon, he rode the elevator with Bill up to their desks.

"Think Walters will get life without parole when he finally goes to trial?" Ramsey asked Bill.

Bill shrugged. "I hope so. But hindsight tells me not to hold my breath."

It told Ramsey the same thing. Which was another reason he couldn't rest until he found the rest of the pervert's victims. The man had to pay for each and every one of them.

And families needed answers.

Kim Pershing met Bill at his desk. "We got a hit on that homeless guy," she said, looking from Bill to Ramsey.

"The lab lifted fingerprints from his suit, but he wasn't in the database. The suit was custom made, though, and I tracked it down to a place in New Haven, Connecticut. From there, I was down to three men who purchased the same suit in that size in the past year. I was able to reach two of them. The third is an Ivy League human-studies instructor at Yale who took this semester off to finish writing his doctoral dissertation. Joel Randolph. Twenty-eight. Part of his thesis required that he spend a week on the streets, with no connections, no one knowing where he was." Kim pursed her lips.

Ramsey and Bill exchanged glances. "Sounds like your guy," Ramsey said.

"Have you contacted the family?" Bill's question was directed at Kim, who, in expensive jeans and a fitted long-sleeved T-shirt, did not look the detective part at all.

"No, sir. I didn't want to give anything away." Notification was up to Bill. Kim's job, as support person, was to investigate possible identities for their dead body. "Their information is on your desk." The woman nodded toward a manila folder in the middle of Bill's desk, atop various papers and charts strewn across every available inch of space. Bill used to be completely rigid, too. A place for everything and everything in its place. And then he'd fallen in love with Mary. He was as committed to stopping crime as ever; he'd just relaxed a bit when it came to the little things in life.

"You really need to clean that desk up," Ramsey said as he left his colleague and mentor to one of the most unsavory parts of their job. Delivering the final blow to loved ones.

Becoming a bad memory someone was never going to forget.

"You were out of line, Hayes."

"Way out of line."

Standing in the captain's office with the captain and Amber, Lucy looked between her coworker and her superior. "I know," she said. "I apologize."

Amber, who already had her mouth open for a comeback, closed it again, as her expression deflated.

Lucy looked at Lionel Smith. "I have a feel for this guy, Captain," she said. "I know I'm not impartial enough to run the case—Amber drew it and it's hers." With a nod toward the other woman, she continued. "I have every confidence that she'll bring this one home. I just… There's more."

"Your sister."

"Yes."

"We haven't forgotten Allison, Lucy."

"But you'll send him up and leave it at that if you can't get anything more out of him."

"We need evidence, Lucy. You know that."

"If I get the rape charge, and give the D.A. enough to get a conviction, he'll be at our disposal any time we need him," Amber added, her tone mollified.

And if Lucy messed things up, Wakerby could walk.

"I didn't talk to him about the rape." They were three of Aurora's four detectives, discussing their biggest case.

"That's your word against his."

She shook her head. "I had my phone set to record mode the entire time I was in the room with him."

Turning back to Lionel, who stood behind his desk in his black suit and tie, Lucy said, "And if my mother doesn't stand up to trial, and the defense manages to convince the judge that our DNA sample is tainted, he's going to walk and I might never have another chance at him."

Lionel's scrutiny might have been hard to take if Lucy wasn't one hundred percent certain of the case she was pleading. She could get this guy. And now might be her only shot at him. Certainty didn't stop her from sweating beneath her navy jacket and cream-colored silk blouse.

She took a deep breath as Lionel's attention switched to Amber Locken. "Lucy's earned her reputation for interrogation results. Whether it's a good thing or a bad thing, she seems to be able to crawl right up inside the perp and see where to hit so it hurts the most."

Amber nodded.

"She's okay to have her go at Wakerby…"

Lucy's smile was strictly on the inside, but it was a big one.

"…on two conditions." Lionel's firm stare went between the two of them. "First, you keep Amber informed at all times—*before* you visit, and immediately afterward, too. No surprises."

Lucy nodded.

"And second, no mention of the rape, Sandy, any evidence

pertaining to either, any charges that are filed or charges that might be filed. Got it?"

"Got it."

"Amber—" Lionel glanced at the other woman "—as a professional courtesy to one of our own, I'm asking you to keep Lucy informed as you work this case."

"Sure." The thirty-eight-year-old redhead nodded toward Lucy. "I was doing that, anyway."

Amber Locken had been a new detective when Lucy volunteered to be the stoop for the Gladys Buckley sting. She'd been Lucy's guide, her voice of encouragement. Lucy was glad not to have lost that support.

"I grossly overstepped," Lucy said again. "I'm really sorry." She was. Honestly. And she'd do the same thing again if she thought it would help her find her sister. She gave every waking hour to the job. Her life belonged to her mom and Allie.

"Okay, then, I guess we're done here," Lionel said, spreading his hands as he dropped down to the old leather chair behind his desk. That chair and that desk had been sitting in that office in the Aurora Police Department since before Lucy was born.

Lucy waited for Amber to leave. She had something else she wanted to discuss with Lionel. Claire Sanderson was not her case, was not even close to her jurisdiction, but her DNA had been found in Gladys Buckley's evidence—found only because Lucy had made it her personal business to check every missing child she ever heard of through the database she'd had set up after Gladys turned over her records.

"Sir, I visited Gladys Buckley this week…" Lucy started in as soon as the door closed behind Amber.

"You don't have to report to me every time you question a prisoner, Hayes."

"I know that, sir." Lucy sat in the chair in front of Lionel's desk. A place she'd been often during her two years as a detective. "I was doing some research for a friend in Massachusetts."

"Detective Miller?"

"Yes, that's right. And I found a DNA match between a hair ribbon we took from Gladys's place and a two-year-old girl who went missing from Comfort Cove, Massachusetts, twenty-five years ago."

"What did Gladys have to say about that?"

"This wasn't the first time I asked her about the ribbon, sir. Both times she denied ever having a two-year-old in her home. I believe her. And, technically, I'm done with my part in this case. I just wanted to run what I found by you in case you have any ideas."

Lionel had been the principal on the Buckley case.

"I—"

As soon as the captain started to speak, Lucy's cell phone rang. The ringtone told her Marie, her mother's caregiver, was on the line.

"Excuse me, sir, may I take this?" Marie knew she was on duty and wouldn't be calling unless it was important.

Lucy had the phone to her ear before Lionel had a chance to nod.

And was standing and at the door within seconds.

"I'm on my way," she told Marie, and with a hurried, "my mom's in a bad way. I have to go…" toward her boss, she was gone.

THE WEEK'S LACK OF ANSWERS left a bad taste in Ramsey's mouth.

Leaving the office, he thought about going home, putting a steak on the grill, sitting inside while it cooked, nursing a shot of whatever he had in the cupboard above the refrigerator and seeing if there was a ball game on.

The fact that he wasn't even sure what sport was currently in season—had the Super Bowl happened yet?—steered him away from any possibility that a game on television would be enough to distract him from the puzzles that haunted him.

He'd given the Boston girls as much as he had in him that week. He'd spent the night before reading and rereading their files and Boston news articles dating back to 2000. Time for a break, for the distance that would allow him to gain a different perspective.

Time, again, for Claire Sanderson to speak to him. Or rather, for him to clear his mind and listen to her. The toddler who disappeared from Comfort Cove without a trace spoke to him constantly. Every minute of every day. She'd lived in his town. Made no difference to him that he hadn't lived in Comfort Cove when Claire had been abducted. He'd been a ten-year-old boy running wild and free on a Kentucky farm twenty-five years before. But he was in Comfort Cove now. She'd been born here. He lived here. She was his responsibility.

He was on the road out of town, driving along the coast, before he made a conscious choice of where he was headed.

Not that he was kidding himself. He'd been making the trek at least once a week since the previous spring. He'd taken a call on a one-year-old girl, missing from her own backyard. As it did every time he made this drive, the nine-month-old case played itself out in Ramsey's mind as the ocean beckoned off to his right and trees stood proud, and now bare, on his left.

Ramsey had worked around the clock to find the little girl. It had taken three days, and Peter Walters had not stepped a foot outside of custody since Ramsey had personally put the bracelets on him.

Ramsey drove. And turned. And turned again. Walters's place was not easy to find.

Pulling up the long, unpaved drive, he stopped his sedan in the side yard, the building looking nothing like the freshly painted white home he'd first descended upon. Walters's version had had blue curtains in the windows—room-darkening curtains it had turned out—not boards.

A month later Ramsey had returned with a forensic unit from Boston, there specifically to pillage the basement.

Staring at the house, Ramsey could still hear the old man's taunting jeers to Ramsey the day he'd been convicted of kidnapping and battery in the Kelsey Green case. Ramsey had been sitting in court with the prosecuting attorney, and as he'd passed by the defense table on his way out of the courtroom, the defendant had whispered that Ramsey hadn't been able to save the others.

Why?

Why had Walters's moment of truth resulted in a taunt?

Ramsey asked the question again. Did Walters feel even a minute fraction of the conscience Ramsey needed him to have regarding the children he'd hurt? And killed?

Kelsey was the lucky one. Her doctors and family had expected a full recovery, at least physically. And she was young enough, loved enough, to have no subconscious emotional baggage from the agonizing three days she'd spent with the devil.

Days that might have been prevented if Ramsey had been able to get to Walters sooner. If he'd put the clues together more quickly. He'd taken the missing-person call when it had come in, and it had taken him three days....

When he'd put the facts together, he'd gone after Walters, sending Bill after the little girl, whom Walters had left alone in a locked storage shed.

Ramsey had been sitting by himself in a deserted waiting area the night that the doctor had finally finished with Kelsey. Her parents were with her. The rest of the world had been in bed asleep. And there sat Ramsey.

"You still here?" The white coated, middle-aged female doctor had asked him when she'd seen him sitting there on her way past.

"Yes."

"Is there something I can do for you? Do you need to see the family? You have more questions?"

"No."

He just hadn't left.

"She's going to be fine, Detective. And she has you to thank for that."

He'd been working a case, just like any other. No more, no less.

"If you hadn't acted so swiftly..."

It hadn't been quickly enough. No sleep and it still hadn't been enough. There hadn't been an inch of that baby's body that wasn't bruised.

"How many bones were broken?" The question wasn't necessary. The D.A. would have access to all of Kelsey's medical records. But he'd put the answer in his report.

"Fourteen, counting the little bones in her left hand. And three ribs."

He swallowed bile. He'd puked up the food he'd had in his stomach right after turning Walters over to the guys at the jail.

Steeling himself, he stared at the wall across the room from him. "What else?"

"Some internal bleeding, but we've got that under control. Nothing that won't heal. No lasting damage to any of her organs."

"And?"

"That's it. A couple of days in here and she'll be home in her own crib."

He needed to know. Dear God, she was only one year old. And had been found without any clothes on.

But Kelsey deserved respect. And dignity. And while she was too young to demand that for herself, Ramsey would do what he could to preserve it for her. He wouldn't ask.

The doctor turned back toward the hall. "If you need anything, the nurses' station is just around the corner," she said.

"If you'd like me to give you something to help you sleep to-night, have one of them call me."

Sleeping aids were the last thing he'd use. Ever. Alcohol, meth, cocaine—the drugs of choice posed no threat to Ramsey Miller. But something to help him sleep at night? He feared that if he helped himself once, he'd be addicted for life.

"Detective?" the doctor, he'd missed her name, called from the door.

"Yeah?"

"She wasn't raped."

Ramsey watched her until her back was out of range, and only then realized that he had tears on his cheeks.

THERE WERE SUPPORT GROUPS for families who'd lost someone to abduction. Lucy had never attended a support group. Or counseling, either, for that matter. She'd been born into her situation. Living with the ghost of an abducted family member was normal for her.

Sitting in a hospital waiting room needing to hear about a family member was not.

Seven o'clock Friday evening and she was the only person in the small area of the emergency department dedicated to families of those brought in for serious illnesses. Had Sandy had a heart attack as they all suspected? Was it going to be fatal?

Marie had finally gone home, but only after Lucy promised to call her mother's longtime best friend—and paid caregiver—the second she knew anything. And only because Lucy had convinced the older woman that one of them needed to get some sleep so that, together, they could take turns caring for Sandy. Lucy, as next of kin, was the obvious one of the two to sit there. Not only because there was no way she'd leave, but, practically speaking, because she was the only one legally able to make decisions regarding her mother's care.

"Ms. Hayes?" The young male nurse who'd shown her to

the room earlier was back. "The doctor would like to speak with you."

Holding the shoulder strap of her small purse with both hands, Lucy jumped up and followed the nurse's blue-scrub-covered back to a door down the hall.

Inside the small room, she took the seat indicated for her at the oval table. Dr. Paul Sherman introduced himself again, although she'd met him when she'd climbed off the back of the ambulance at the emergency-room door.

She waited for him to say more. Was afraid to ask. To pre-empt the news.

She was scared to death.

"Your mother's resting peacefully." It took Lucy a second to realize those weren't the first words the doctor had said. Just the first she'd registered.

"She's going to be okay?"

"She's going to live." The gray-haired doctor's stern expression wasn't promising. "I take it, from the little bit of medical history we were able to get, that Sandy Hayes is an alcoholic?"

And at forty-five the alcohol had affected her heart to this extent? Sandy had her problems, but she was young. Having Allie at nineteen, being raped at twenty, she'd given birth to Lucy a year later. Sandy had always had age on her side to help combat the toll her life took on her body.

"She drinks, yes."

"In excess."

Lucy had figured that the booze would get her mother's liver first, not her heart. And not for a long, long time. "Yes."

"Your mother is suffering from an alcoholic overdose, Ms. Hayes."

"A what?"

"Her blood alcohol level was close to fifty percent. Most people face death in the forty percentile. As a comparison, the legal limit for motor impairment is point zero eight percent."

"She didn't have a heart attack?"

"No, your mother's heart, believe it or not, is strong and healthy."

Thank God. Relief hit her hard. So much so that she felt the lack of the lunch she'd skipped and the dinner she hadn't yet eaten, in the form of a light-headedness that took her breath for a moment.

Sandy was going to be fine. Her heart was fine.

She'd been scared. So scared.

The doctor was watching her. And Lucy took a firm grip on emotions that had been declaring war on her all week.

"How do BALs rise so high?" She asked the only question that she could grasp at the moment. She was a cop. She knew about legal limits. She'd tested more drunk drivers than she could count. And had never, ever seen anyone with levels higher than two or three times the legal limit.

"By consuming large amounts of alcohol in a very short period of time." Dr. Sherman folded his hands on the table in front of him, his expression softening to one of…she hoped it wasn't pity.

But was fairly certain that it was.

"We're talking the equivalent of twenty-one or more shots of eighty proof in a five- or six-hour span."

For Sandy, consuming an entire fifth in an evening wasn't all that unusual. If she could get hold of one without Lucy or Marie knowing about it.

Which meant that not only had her mother had a stash, but she'd pretty much downed it all at once. Like she'd been drinking a bottle of water.

"It's my fault," she said aloud. Registering the sympathy on the doctor's face, she added, "I made her face something this week that was too much for her. She told me, but I wouldn't listen."

Sloan Wakerby's imprisonment wasn't worth losing Sandy over. If her mother couldn't testify, then she couldn't testify. Lucy wasn't going to push her anymore.

Or was it knowing that the man sat there in jail, with full knowledge of where Allie was without telling them, that was too much for Sandy to handle?

"It was your quick thinking, calling an ambulance for her as soon as you saw the state she was in, that saved her life."

"She was having trouble breathing and showing all the signs of a heart attack."

At forty-five. Sandy might drink a lot, but she was always there for Lucy. Always. Lucy couldn't imagine it any other way.

"We've got her on an IV, fluids and vitamins, and she's fully stable. As a precaution, I'm also keeping her on oxygen for the night. As soon as the alcohol has cleared her system, she can go home. Maybe as early as tomorrow morning."

The constriction that had ahold of her throat was loosening. "I'd like to stay with her tonight, if that could be arranged."

"Not a problem. Would you like me to write an order for a cot? Or there's a reclining chair in the room."

"The chair will be fine. Can I see her now?"

"We're waiting for a room number. As soon as we get one, we'll let you know and you can meet her up there."

She'd be with Sandy soon. All would be well again. "Thank you, Doctor."

Lucy wondered why they were still sitting there. Why wasn't the man going about his next order of business?

Dr. Sherman looked up from what she assumed was her mother's chart. "I see that your mother's been through rehabilitation?"

"Yes, sir," Lucy said quickly. "Several times. She wants to be well, Doctor, and I understand that that's half the battle. You can rest assured that Marie, her caregiver, and I will be incredibly diligent from here on out. We won't leave her alone at all."

Dr. Sherman was shaking his head before she was finished speaking. "Your mother needs to be committed, Ms. Hayes.

I'm sorry, but there's just no easy way to say that. She needs to be in an assisted-living facility with locks on the doors and twenty-four-hour supervision for at least six months. Probably a year or longer."

"You want me to lock her up?" Sandy was grief-stricken, not crazy.

"Those alcohol clinics are expensive and obviously not enough for your mother. My experience tells me that a program isn't going to work for her. She needs something that lasts much longer—that doesn't just dry her out, but that keeps her out of contact with any possibility of alcohol for a much more extended period of time. Assisted living, if I prescribe it, will be covered under your insurance."

Lucy folded her hands on the table, too. "I appreciate your concern, Doctor, but I am not going to have my mother committed."

She didn't have a medical degree, but she knew Sandy. And it didn't matter if they locked her mother up for ten years. If Allie was still missing, Sandy would take a drink the first time she was out. To fill the pain of her daughter's absence.

Or she'd get herself addicted to sleeping pills in assisted living and sleep her whole life away.

No.

Lucy's only hope of keeping her mother alive, of ever having a mother with any semblance of a life, was to find out what had happened to Allison Hayes.

Nothing short of peace of mind was going to save Sandy's life.

CHAPTER NINE

EIGHT O'CLOCK CAME AND WENT. Sandy had been moved into a private room for the night and Lucy had spent the past hour sitting in the chair that was her bed for the night, watching her mother's face, listening to Sandy's easy breaths, paying attention to the blood-pressure monitor that was attached to her mother's finger.

All was well. She could see the proof of that with her own eyes. And was afraid that if she quit watching even for a second, Sandy's hold on life would weaken.

As soon as her mother was conscious, she was going to promise Sandy that she wouldn't have to testify. Or ever be questioned about Sloan Wakerby again.

Lucy had set her phone to vibrate, and she jumped as a sudden pulsing started at her hip. Right next to the gun holster she was still wearing under her jacket, having come straight from work.

Brushing by the gun, she pulled her phone out. Her insides leaped as she saw that Ramsey Miller was calling.

Moving quickly, but watching her mother until she was at the door, Lucy made it out to the hall by the third ring. After the day she'd had, a dose of Miller was just what the doctor would have ordered for her if he'd known to do so.

"Hello?" She moved farther down the hall, motioning to the nurse at the station that she was out of her mother's room as she walked past. She didn't want Sandy to hear her voice and wake up, but she also didn't want her mother unattended.

"It's Ramsey." He didn't usually bother with introductions.

"I know."

"Just wondering if you'd had a chance to get to UC."

Lucy's head hurt. She still hadn't fit dinner in. "I'm sorry, Ramsey. I had plans to have lunch with that friend of mine I told you about who runs a DNA lab in Cincinnati—"

"The one who made the Buckley database for you."

"Right. Anyway, I was going to go to UC after lunch, but I didn't make it to either."

"A new case?"

"No." She walked past patient rooms with lights down low, televisions on softly, and felt like she was on a loudspeaker. "I was called into Smith's office on my way out the door."

She made it to the ward's door, and pushed through, ending up in a deserted elevator vestibule, with a padded bench under a window.

"Smith's office? Why? What's up?"

Making a beeline for the bench, Lucy sat down. "I broke protocol."

"You want to talk about it?"

She *needed* to talk about it. She needed him. But that was against their unspoken protocol.

As soon as she got through this rough patch in her personal life, she'd be just as adamant as Ramsey about keeping herself emotionally unencumbered and singularly focused on the job.

"I went to see Sloan Wakerby on Wednesday."

"You didn't mention it when we talked." The caring tone in his voice tugged on the string unraveling inside her.

"He's messing me up. Maybe I didn't want you to know that."

"Have I done something to lose your trust?"

"Of course not!" It never occurred to her that he'd think so. She didn't want him to think so. So she told him the complete truth. "I didn't want you to think less of me or have less confidence in me."

Because she wanted more between them?

"Newsflash. I figured out you were human pretty much from the beginning, Luce. I don't expect perfection."

So he had expectations?

"He's a perp. I have to maintain my position of control at all times when dealing with a perpetrator or risk contaminating the evidence I need. If I let him get to me and I make a mistake, things could be thrown out of court and he could walk."

"I've seen you in action, Hayes. I'm guessing Sloan has no idea that he has any effect on you at all."

Maybe.

"Did Smith issue a formal reprimand?"

"No. I apologized for making the visit. I shouldn't have gone."

"And you'd do it again in a heartbeat."

"Wouldn't you?"

"Of course."

Relaxing on the bench, her back against the brick wall, Lucy started to feel a little hungry for the first time since Lionel had called for her.

"Tell me how it went down with him."

She needed Ramsey and he was there.

"I didn't ask questions."

"Didn't give him the chance to tell you to go to hell?"

"It started out with him wearing the slimy smile." Ramsey had been with her during the first meeting between her and Sloan. She'd managed to hold it together amazingly well that time.

But that was before she witnessed the effect that seeing the rapist had had on her mother.

At the time of that first meeting, Wakerby's place in her life had been purely cognitive, professional. By the second visit, the reality of what he'd done to her family had taken hold.

"And?" Ramsey's voice brought her back.

"He wasn't wearing it by the time I left."

"You scored."

"I hope so."

"When do you plan to go back?"

"Early next week." Why were hospital walls always white? Like nothing dirty ever went on there. Like white walls could keep filth at bay.

"What are you going to do about Smith?"

"I have his blessing. I just have to keep Amber apprised of my actions."

"You've earned your reputation."

"Yeah, well, now I have to live up to it."

"You doubt your ability to do that?"

Did he ever doubt himself? Of course he did. The question asked and answered itself in seconds.

Still, admission was dangerous.

"Your meeting with Smith was before lunch, you said."

"That's right."

"And it obviously went okay if you got the go-ahead."

"Yeah."

"So what happened to the rest of the day?"

The problem with dealing with cops was that they saw too much, more than other people saw at any rate. At least Ramsey Miller did.

And Ramsey...he knew her. Understood her. Far better than any other peers ever had.

And he had arms made for hugging. Even if he didn't re-alize it.

"Luce? What's going on?"

She could put an end to needing him. An end to whatever was happening between them that neither of them wanted, much less was ready to acknowledge.

She could hang up.

"My mother."

In a few brief words she told him about the call she'd received while still in Lionel's office. And of Sandy's eventual diagnosis and prognosis.

"You're at the hospital?"

"Yes." She hadn't actually said so.

"Are you with your mother now?"

"No." She described her current location. "Mama's been asleep since they brought her up."

"Did you have a chance to speak with her?"

"Not yet. She opened her eyes once and smiled when she saw that I was there. She squeezed my hand, but that's all."

"The alcohol still has ahold of her.'"

"I know." So why was this little-girl fear eating at her from the inside out? She'd been the adult in her and Sandy's relationship since she was about four years old. "Anyway, I'll get to UC on Monday. Marie is prepared to stay with Mama around the clock if necessary."

"Does she get paid overtime?"

"No. But she and my mother have been best friends since grade school. And she's a widow. Mama sat with her many, many nights while her husband was dying of leukemia. I was only four or five at the time. I can barely remember Dwayne, just that he made me laugh. And that we were safe with him."

An odd concept for a five-year-old to have.

Unless you were the five-year-old of a rape victim—and the sister of a baby who'd been abducted and never found.

"Does Marie have kids? Did she ever remarry?"

"No and no. Mama was Mama, even then. Drunk as much as she was sober. Marie took us both on. Mama, and me, too, as much as she could. She still worked full-time back then, and took care of her own mother, but she got money from Dwayne's death, too. I guess he'd taken out a fairly nice life-insurance policy before he got sick. Strange how things work that way, huh?"

The air in the hospital was cool. Lucy shivered and wished she had a blanket with her.

The elevator hadn't binged once since she'd been out there.

But then, she was at the visitors' elevator and visiting hours were over.

"It's not your fault, Lucy."

"What isn't?" But she knew what he meant. He was talking about Sandy. About exposing her to Wakerby.

"You did what you had to do to put the guy away. You couldn't leave him out on the street."

She could have risked the DNA holding up in court. But if Wakerby had walked? Then what?

"Why do the victims pay so much?"

"Why are there victims at all?"

She couldn't answer that.

"Are you home?" He'd asked where she was. She wanted to know where he was.

"Not yet."

"You're still at the office?"

"No."

"Where, then?" She needed to picture him. To feel him closer.

"I'm driving."

"You went to Walkers's place again."

"I have to understand what drove him to do what he did."

It was like Lionel had said earlier that day. You had to get inside the perp to know how to hurt him where it counted.

And it had to count. Making it count was all they had.

"I'll get to UC on Monday, Ramsey." Walker was driving him. But so was Claire Sanderson. Because he knew Cal Whittier. Because Frank was soon going to be back in the school system. With access to children every day.

Because they'd both met Emma Sanderson.

Because Claire was a precocious two-year-old who deserved to not disappear without a trace.

And neither did Allie…

"I've pulled eight days in a row," Ramsey said.

The man hadn't taken a full day off that she knew of since

she'd met him the previous spring. And they talked several times a week, so she knew a lot.

"On shift."

Okay, that was different. That was current cases, nonstop. In addition to cold-case work.

"I've been ordered to take a few days off."

"I concur."

"I have something to do Sunday, but I'm thinking I'll fly into Cincinnati on Monday. If you're free to meet my flight, we could go to UC together."

Her insides fluttered again. And she couldn't even pretend it was because of the meals she'd missed. "Okay."

"If we get any hits, it could take until Tuesday, which is just about the time you're due for your next meeting with Wakerby, right?"

"You'll go with me?" It was like he was reading her mind. Life didn't usually work that way.

"I don't mind tagging along."

"I'd like you to be there." She'd love him to be there. But that was her business.

"I'll plan to head home on Wednesday, then."

"You'll need a place to stay. You have anywhere in mind?"

He'd stayed at the airport hotel the only other time he'd flown into the area, the day Sloan Wakerby had been apprehended.

"No. I'd like to be someplace in Aurora so you don't have so far to drive back and forth."

The University of Cincinnati was an hour away from Aurora.

"You could stay with me," she said, feeling as if she was jumping off the high dive before she'd learned to swim. "I have an extra bedroom," she quickly added. "On the other side of the house. With its own bathroom."

She held her breath. His answer mattered. It shouldn't. But it did.

Her life didn't have room for it to matter.

"That's fine."

Her breathing faltered. She took a second to let it catch up.

"Let me know what time you get in and I'll pick you up." She sounded almost normal.

It made sense, him staying with her. She was his ride. Their business was together. And cops didn't get paid enough to spring for all of the expenses involved in off-duty investigation.

And none of those reasons were why she'd asked. Or why her heart was pounding.

"I'll text you."

He was going to hang up. Looking around the deserted and sterile vestibule where she sat, picturing the night ahead in the antiseptic-smelling atmosphere, Lucy had a fresh attack of doubts.

"We're going to get them, aren't we, Ramsey? We're going to find out what happened to Allie and Claire. We're going to get the people who take innocent children away from the families who love them."

As she sat there alone, thinking of everything she'd taken on, Lucy was afraid.

"I don't know whether we're going to get them or not." His voice was more mellow than she was used to. He'd had a long week, too. And he was equally alone in the dark. "I just know that I can't stop trying."

There was a certain amount of peace in knowing that you might not succeed. It took some of the pressure off, knowing you couldn't be perfect all the time. And there was peace in knowing that you weren't alone in your aloneness.

"Take care of yourself," she told Ramsey.

"You, too."

"I will."

"Talk later." He disconnected the call.

Standing, Lucy reholstered her phone and went back in to keep trying.

CHAPTER TEN

CINCINNATI MIGHT NOT HAVE the number of elite colleges and universities that Boston boasted, and University of Cincinnati didn't have the reputation of Harvard, but the campus was impressive just the same.

Sitting in the University Pavilion on Monday, waiting for an opportunity to speak with an upper-level records clerk, Ramsey took in his current surroundings, and tried to picture what Jack Colton might have seen twenty-seven years before.

"It says here that UC has 42,000 students." Lucy was reading a pamphlet they'd picked up at the information desk downstairs.

"It's also been rated by *U.S. News* and *World Report* as one of the Nation's Best Top Tier Universities." He'd seen the quote on the UC website over the weekend. "It's a small town, complete with a Main Street."

It was important to stick to facts. To research. And not be distracted by the feminine arm sharing space with his arm on the joined chairs. He'd almost hugged her when she'd met him at the airport earlier that morning.

"It's a public research university." Lucy's familiar voice took on a different note in person. Why hadn't he noticed that before?

They'd driven past the University Hospital complex on their way to this appointment and had parked near the pavilion. They hadn't had a tour of the campus yet.

He needed something to come of the upcoming meeting. He needed something new to go on.

"Did your business yesterday go okay?" Lucy leaned toward him, trying to keep their conversation private in a hallway bustling with people.

Amelia.

"Fine." He'd caulked the toilet. Fixed the drywall. And now where he'd plastered needed new paint. Amelia had made stew and brownies and given him distance as he worked.

She'd had nothing new to add to what she'd already told him about Jack Colton. He had no reason to continue visiting her.

But he'd told her he'd be back.

He could visit with Amelia, but not the people who'd given birth to him? Loved him? Raised him?

That was Ramsey. The guy who looked after strangers but let down those he cared about. And precisely why he wasn't going to acknowledge that Lucy Hayes, the sexiest woman he'd ever met, was someone he could care about.

"How's your mother?" he asked. Not a sexy question at all. In the car on the short drive from the airport, they'd kept the conversation solely on Jack Colton. On the records they were going to request.

Strictly business.

"Back to normal. And a bit whiny because we aren't leaving her home alone anymore. Marie will be sleeping there for the next few months."

"When did she get home?"

"Saturday afternoon."

He'd been polite and asked. Anything more was none of his business. So he glanced at the pamphlet she held. And noticed how dainty her hands looked next to his.

Those fingers hardly looked strong enough to hold a gun, let alone shoot one. But the holster he'd noticed beneath her brown corduroy jacket as she'd climbed out of the car bore testimony to the fact that she'd mastered both the holding and the shooting.

Had those fingers mastered a man's body, as well? Would she know where to grip? How to please?

Or was there something left for him to teach her?

"I told Amber we'd be going to see Wakerby tomorrow."

"Good." Justification for him to be sitting next to the woman who occupied so many of his thoughts.

And made him better at his job, too.

Lucy rested the pamphlet in her lap, atop slender, feminine legs. They weren't long, model limbs. But he'd bet they were long enough to wrap all the way around a guy....

Holy hell.

LUCY HAD NEVER ATTENDED COLLEGE. She'd gone straight from high school to the police academy and then into detective school through the police department. But Monday morning, she felt like a college girl as she walked through campus with Ramsey.

There was something seriously wrong with her. Her stomach fluttered at a brush of his hand. Or a sound in his voice. In just a matter of hours she'd be taking him home with her and—

"This is it," the tattooed young man who'd been leading them to one of the school's two on-campus dining halls turned to say. Simon, in jeans and a UC hoodie, had escorted them at the request of the records clerk, who'd told them that Jack Colton had held a job in the university cafeteria. The clerk had also given them the name and off-campus address of a man who'd once run it.

"Thanks." Ramsey nodded at the young man who continued on his way. "Let's have a look inside, shall we?"

The officer who'd served their warrant was gone. Simon was gone. It was just her and Ramsey now.

And Lucy wasn't focused enough on the case.

"IN POINT THREE MILES, turn right." The sterile voice of her GPS system sounded in the closed confines of Lucy's Buick Rendezvous.

"Not the best of neighborhoods." Ramsey spoke from the passenger seat beside her.

They were on their way to see a man who'd been Jack Colton's boss for the short time he'd been at UC. A retired cafeteria manager, Chester Brown.

"UC isn't in the best of neighborhoods. I was working a burglary battery case a couple of years ago and traced the perp to the University Hospital emergency room. I walk in, trying to look inconspicuous, you know, so all the people in there not feeling well don't get alarmed. Turns out the sick people were the minority, not me. It seemed like the place was crawling with cops. That and homeless folks trying to stay warm and maybe score some painkillers by claiming ailments."

She was rambling. It was better than trying to figure out whether Ramsey was wearing aftershave or cologne. Trying not to get turned on by the scent he'd brought into her car with him.

"I've been to some hospitals in Boston like that."

"Were you born in Boston?" *Not a work question, Hayes. Stick to the work questions.*

"No."

"In Comfort Cove?"

"No."

"Turn right," Bonnie, the name she'd given to the GPS voice, blurted into the silence.

Lucy turned.

"Continue five point four miles," Bonnie added.

Before leaving campus they'd spent an hour in the Rendezvous making phone calls from a list of names they'd gathered from Tammy in records. They had names of people that were part of the UC Bearcats baseball association in 1985, a guidance counselor, a dorm mother. Jack Colton had neither a roommate nor a suite mate, and Ramsey's warrant didn't allow Tammy to provide him with the names of other students who'd had rooms on Jack's floor twenty-seven years before.

They'd reached a total of nine people. None of whom could recall Jack Colton.

"Hundreds of young men came to UC to try out for the team," one gentleman had told Lucy. "There's no way I could remember them all."

"Jack Colton wasn't a troublemaker," she said now. "People remember troublemakers."

"He attended class regularly and had an above-average GPA," Ramsey added, almost morosely.

"If he's not our guy, we'll find out who is," she said. "Any word yet on the evidence?"

A few weeks before, Emma Sanderson had inadvertently led Ramsey to the missing box of evidence from her sister's case. Completely unrelated to the child's abduction, the box had been stolen as part of a plot concocted by Emma's mercenary ex-fiancé to sue the city of Comfort Cove for shoddy police work. Ramsey had been through every thread of evidence with plastic gloves and a microscope. And then he'd sent it to a forensics lab in Boston.

"I haven't heard back from the lab. They're backlogged with current cases."

"In point three miles, arrive at destination."

Current cases had to take precedence. That was a given. But waiting was frustrating as hell.

"Forensic science has come a long way in the past twenty-five years. Something significant might turn up."

Ramsey grunted. Keeping an eye on the road, Lucy glanced toward him. "What?"

"Nothing."

He was watching her. And soon, she'd be taking him home with her.

"What?"

"Just...thank you."

His tone had lowered. Warmed.

So had her insides. Her lips were dry. She licked them.

"Arriving at destination."

Thank you, Bonnie.

"YEAH, I REMEMBER HIM." Chester Brown wasn't quite as old as Amelia, but the black man had to be pushing eighty. If he hadn't already arrived. He glanced at Jack's picture through a screen and without spectacles. "That's Jack Colton."

Ramsey's radar went off. Why did Brown remember a man everyone else had forgotten?

"What can you tell us about him?" Lucy asked. They'd introduced themselves, shown their badges.

Chester had yet to unlock the screen door he stood behind.

Standing on the man's front porch with Lucy, Ramsey sized up Chester Brown.

He lived in a small home, in an older, not so clean neighborhood. A home with a well-manicured, healthy yard, freshly painted black wrought-iron railing and clean window boxes. Chester had on old-as-the-hills brown polyester pants, but they were pressed and clean and without holes. As was his matching plaid button-down shirt.

"I can't tell you anything unless I know why you're asking."

"We aren't at liberty to divulge information from an open investigation, sir." What did Brown have to hide?

Ready to stress the fact that Chester Brown could be found liable in any wrongdoing if he interfered with an investigation by withholding information, Ramsey heard Lucy beat him to the punch.

"We're trying to help clear up a misunderstanding," she said as he continued his scrutiny and saw wide-open, clear brown eyes gazing at him with the honesty of the cautious.

"Jack's in some kind of trouble?"

"Not as far as we know." Lucy's nurturing tone was all for the older man.

Lucky man.

"I don't know that much about him." Chester Brown spoke

slowly, but his voice was strong. Steady. "I managed the cafeteria at UC," he said. "Been retired fifteen years now, but back then there were a certain number of student work positions held open for athletes as part of a scholarship program. Jack Colton came in on a baseball scholarship and was assigned to me."

"You had a lot of kids assigned to you then?" Ramsey looked nowhere but at Brown. The man was a bug under his microscope and he wasn't going to miss anything.

"Five to ten every semester."

"But you remember Jack."

He could feel Lucy staring at him. He brushed off the awareness.

"Yes, I remember him." Chester Brown was frowning now, his tone more reserved.

"I—" Ramsey started in his sternest, don't-mess-with-me voice.

"We'd like to know what made him memorable to you, and anything else you could tell us about him," Lucy interrupted.

Chester looked at her as though searching for something, his expression still concerned.

Ramsey stared.

"He was a good kid—"

"Are you saying all the other athletes assigned to you weren't good kids?" Ramsey interrupted, impatient now to get at the truth. He'd been waiting too long.

"No, sir, that's not what I said." Chester's tone had lowered submissively. The speed with which he delivered the words was exactly the same.

"Jack was a good kid," Lucy said.

"That's right, ma'am." The older man looked her in the eye. "The athletes were only required to work ten hours a week—games and practices excepted. Jack came in asking for extra hours. He was scheduled around baseball practice and class, and still worked twenty, twenty-five hours a week. Never missed a shift. Not once, all semester."

Ramsey was familiar with Jack Colton's work ethic.

"So that's why you remember him?" Lucy asked.

"Partly, maybe, but no, ma'am, not really."

"What, then?" Ramsey blurted. "What makes this guy stand out?"

Chester's gaze didn't move from Lucy. "The boy's heart wasn't really into baseball, not like most of the kids that come through there," Chester explained. "He was good enough to have gotten the offer to try for the team, but he didn't have the… Baseball wasn't everything to him, you know?"

"Yeah," Lucy said, smiling softly.

Ramsey noticed. With a kick to his gut. And a realization that his coworker was handling this interview much better than he was.

He was too aware of her.

"What do you think was important to Jack?" he asked, making a point of softening his tone.

"He wanted to get a college degree," the old man said simply. "He wouldn't take no loans, though. Being in debt scared that boy to death. He figured baseball was the answer. And then he didn't make the team. That's why I remember him. The day they put up the names, and he saw his name wasn't on it, the first place he came was to me."

"That must have made you feel good." Lucy leaned forward as she spoke.

"Heck, no!" There was fire in Chester's voice. Honest fire. "It was horrible! I couldn't do nothing to help him. Next day he drops out of school, packs his bag and catches a bus back to the place he come from. Never heard from him again. Never forgot him, neither. I hope he found a way to get his schooling."

He hadn't. Not as far as Ramsey knew. He was not at liberty to divulge as much.

Probably just as well. No harm in letting the old man hope.

"Can you remember anything else about Jack?" Lucy asked.

"Anybody he was friends with? What he did in his spare time? Any enemies?" Ramsey was back on his game.

"What spare time?" Chester said through the door. "The boy was taking eighteen credit hours, doing homework, practicing and working out six days a week and working for me. He barely had time to sleep."

"What about Friday nights?" Ramsey remembered being eighteen. Nineteen. Twenty. "Were there any girls he had his eye on?"

"There was a girl...." Chester drew out the word, like he was calling up a distant shadow from his memory bank.

Good. Now they were getting somewhere. If there'd been a girl, with a name they could pursue, they'd have someone else to question. Guys tended to get a little sloppy around their girls.

"He never told me about her, but I overheard one of the other guys, one who later made the team, ragging on him for not bringing a girl to the Friday-night mixer. The guys wanted as many girls there as possible and each guy was expected to do his part."

Chester's tone left no doubt as to his opinion of that preference.

"I heard Jack tell the guy that his girl wasn't from UC. I didn't even know he had a girl, and I asked him about her later. He said she wasn't a student, that she was really sweet, but that he wouldn't be able to continue seeing her."

"Because he didn't make the team?"

"No, it was before that. At least a month. He never said anything more about her, and I didn't ask again, but I always figured she was older. And maybe married. Jack was more mature than the rest of those guys. I pictured him with someone older."

"Do you think it's possible that he was seeing one of his instructors?" Lucy asked, frowning.

"I have no idea about that, ma'am. It didn't occur to me at the time, but I guess it makes sense. The boy sure didn't have time to be out meeting folks in the community."

Ramsey thought back to the list of Jack's classes, a copy of which was in a folder in Lucy's car. Instructors were listed by last name only, but they had a staff directory from 1985.

"Well, listen, thanks for your time," he told Chester Brown, pulling a card out of the inside pocket of his suit jacket. "If you think of anything else, give me a call."

The man hesitated, but a few seconds later opened the screen door and took Ramsey's card. He shook his hand, too.

"If you see Jack, tell him I said hello," the older man called as they headed down the walk and back out to the curb where Lucy's white Rendezvous was parked.

"Will do," Lucy called back, turning to smile at the old man.

"Jack Colton's a saint, isn't he?" Ramsey muttered.

He wished he could blame his sour mood entirely on the continual dead ends he was up against in the Sanderson case. While the frustrating lack of a break in the case wasn't helping his demeanor any, it was the fact that he kept picturing Lucy Hayes without clothes on that had him most on edge.

He never had trouble separating work from pleasure. Never had trouble keeping pleasure impersonal, either.

Or keeping mental clothes on women.

His captain might just have been right about him working too many hours without a break.

CHAPTER ELEVEN

IF RAMSEY HAD BEEN a female visiting detective, Lucy would have shown him around Aurora, maybe driven him by the schools she'd attended, taken him down by the Ohio River, perhaps even stopped for a glass of wine and some steak at her favorite riverside bar—not that any of it compared to the unique coastal town on the Atlantic Ocean where Ramsey lived, but apparently hadn't grown up in.

If he'd been female, she'd have taken him to the office to meet Davis, the fourth member of the Aurora Police Department detective squad. He'd already met Lionel and Locken the day of the first Wakerby interrogation.

If he'd been female, she'd ask him straight out where he was born instead of letting her curiosity as to why he wouldn't tell her get the better of her.

If he'd been female, she wouldn't need to lick her lips so often in his company.

"You want to order pizza for dinner?" They were still on the highway—three lanes each way—that was also the main street of Aurora.

"I'd have figured you for salad. Or a frozen entrée." Ramsey's smile eased her tension a bit.

She was making too much of this—bringing him home with her. Everything was going to be just fine.

"I'm not much of a cook," she admitted. "After the day we've had, I'd go for a steak at this little place I know on the shore of Ohio River."

"It's a lot bigger than I pictured," Ramsey said, looking out at the river as they drove.

"It used to be a major tributary, back when all of the coal mines and tobacco farms were using barges to ship their goods. It's actually the largest tributary on the Mississippi River. It runs from Pittsburgh to Cairo, Illinois."

"How long is it?"

"Nine hundred and eighty-one miles. It was on the edge of the Mason-Dixon Line and was a dividing line between the North and the South during the Civil War. But its history dates back to the seventeenth century and beyond."

"You know your history."

"I paid attention in school," Lucy said drily. If they were going home, her right turn was in less than a mile and she had to get over. If steak was their destination, she was fine right where she was.

Ramsey was analyzing the town the same way she'd seen him analyze case files, his eyes focused, his gaze everywhere at once. He wasn't missing anything. His scrutiny felt far too personal. Like he was seeing a part of her that he shouldn't be seeing.

And he was far too impersonal. Like he wasn't fazed a bit about spending the night with her.

Had he ever wondered, even once, what it would be like to kiss her? Or was she the only one losing her mind here?

"Wakerby agreed to meet with me without his lawyer present." She'd had a voice mail from Locken.

The statement won her Ramsey's full attention. "No kidding." He sounded impressed, and she flushed with warmth again. "Let's hope this means something," he said.

Lucy concurred.

"What did you decide on for dinner?" She had to know where they were going.

"That steak you mentioned sounded great."

A table for two on the river, coming right up, she thought, pleased with his choice. And worried about her pleasure, too.

"We can go over the faculty list while we eat," she said.

"I was thinking the same thing."

Trouble was, he probably had been. While Lucy was busy wondering if there was any chance at all that the coming night might bring more carnal knowledge of him.

"How old was Jack Colton when he was at UC? Eighteen? Nineteen?" Lucy was driving again—toward her house, for sure this time. She'd managed to use up a couple of hours of the evening at the restaurant on the river, managed to delay her arrival at her place until after dark.

"About that. He was there twenty-seven years ago and he's forty-six now."

Sandy should already be out for the night with the help of the sleeping pills the doctor had prescribed for her. Just for this first week.

"And already he was fixated on money," she said. Focusing on Jack Colton at dinner had helped center her. Ramsey wasn't going to try anything with her. He wasn't going to kiss her.

She didn't interest him in that way.

She should have thought of Sandy before she'd invited Ramsey to stay with her. She should have thought, period.

"Colton was an only child of older folks who gave him no financial or emotional security. I can understand why providing for himself was important to him." Ramsey was continuing on with the dinner conversation as though they were talking on the phone, not getting ready to have a sleepover.

"Yes, I can, too," she managed, in spite of sweaty palms. "But Jack seems to exhibit more than a normal drive for money. He worked in place of fun, but also in place of sleep—at college and, from what you said, back in Comfort Cove, too."

Headlights came at them, illuminating Ramsey's face as he looked at her.

"Right. Where are you going with this?"

Lucy signaled the turn onto her street, and slowed down. "Motive. What if working all the hours in a day still didn't provide Jack with enough money for him to feel secure? Because if, as it sounds, he suffered from scarcity mentality, then no amount would have been enough. It's not like he was saving for something in particular, right? Or supporting anyone. A single guy, living alone, could certainly have lived on what Colton was making."

"Especially as frugal as he apparently was," Ramsey added. "As you said, he worked all the time, but he didn't own anything of value."

"I'm guessing he had a nice bank account. People with scarcity mentality fear that there will never be enough. No matter how much is there."

"He somehow makes a connection with the black-market baby business and Claire Sanderson becomes another consequence of Jack Colton's fears." Ramsey went with her theory.

Was she off base here? Lucy pulled into her drive and straight into the attached garage, closing the automatic door behind her, trying to get more completely into Jack Colton's mind-set, to let her instincts speak to her.

Her work instincts.

"What do you think?" she asked him, turning off the car. *Think Jack. Talk Jack.*

"It's just the garage, but so far, it's nice." Ramsey smiled.

"I meant Jack's motive." She swallowed.

"I think you could be right." He was all cop again as he looked at her and she wondered if she'd imagined the personal moment. Or conjured it out of an embarrassingly desperate, sudden longing for his body. "I've already looked for black-market baby connections and found nothing," he continued, clearly unaware of where her thoughts had been heading.

"What about Gladys? Jack was in Cincinnati to go to UC. My mother heard about Gladys from an unsavory crowd hanging out by the riverfront in downtown Cinci. Maybe Jack heard of her then, too? And maybe that's why Claire's hair ribbon was at Gladys's house."

Her heart rate was double-timing, and not just because of the man sharing the front seat with her. She was on to something. She knew it.

Ramsey's intent stare told her he felt it, too.

"When the baseball thing didn't work out, he's on a super downer, losing all hope of ever getting out of the poor man's life because he thought his only chance at a degree was the baseball scholarship. He wouldn't go into debt to pay for college, and he thinks he'll never get ahead legitimately without the degree, so he returns to Comfort Cove. He gets the job as a delivery man, which provides him with an easy means for kidnapping and transporting children, and then he sells them."

"If not all to Gladys, then to someone else."

"I'll see if I can get a warrant for Colton's current bank records. Chances are there won't be any dated back twenty-five years."

"Still, a victim of scarcity mentality is often a hoarder, and if we're right about Colton, if he has money that can't be explained, we'll be one step closer."

"And then I need to have another meeting with Jack. I have to make him talk to me."

"And we should speak with Gladys, too. Maybe she'll remember something once she knows that we've made the connection and are going to find out what went on."

She opened the car door, feeling a little panicky. Excitement over the case transferred to excitement over Ramsey. He opened his car door, too, but didn't get out. Lucy looked over. He was watching her.

Jack. Claire. The cases.

"What we have here makes sense," she blurted. "But we

have no proof. Other than that hair ribbon which ties Claire to Gladys's house but doesn't tie Jack to Claire or to Gladys."

Ramsey held up the folder they'd been working on over dinner. "We've got six professors, five of whom are men and not possible girlfriends, but who may know if Colton was involved with a teacher other than one of his own. And one, the female English professor, is still there and is of an age to have been in a relationship with him. We'll go see her in the morning before our meeting with Wakerby. Then we call the other five. And we'll find out everything they know about Jack Colton. Maybe someone saw this guy with Gladys, or someone who knows Gladys, or someone who adopted a baby or wanted a baby or…"

They were out of the car. Lucy unlocked the back of the Rendezvous. Ramsey lifted the hatch and pulled out his carry-on-size suitcase and garment bag.

He'd have personal items in there. Like underwear. Because he'd be stepping out of his in her house.

She was sick. Really sick.

And now it was time to take him—and his luggage—inside.

THE FIRST THING RAMSEY DID when Lucy left him alone at the door of the spare bedroom of her home was close it. Firmly behind him. He didn't look around. Didn't take in his surroundings, didn't note the location of every piece of furniture, every window and door and hinge and lock. He went straight for the bathroom.

He saw the towels on the rack in his peripheral vision. She'd mentioned something about having put them out. Not taking the time to dig into his bag for his toiletries, he pulled off his gun, setting it on the counter just outside the shower, turned on the cold water, stripped off his clothes and stepped into the spray.

It had probably been rude to excuse himself from her company the second they got home. It would have been far worse to accept her offer of a hot-chocolate nightcap and further conversation in the intimacy of her living room with his body hard in response to her closeness.

Tonight, Lucy Hayes's spare bedroom was a hotel room. One that was convenient for her to chauffeur to and from. No more. No less.

He was not her personal guest. Didn't want to be her personal guest.

And she was not one of his casual, one-night stands.

Looking down at himself under the stinging spray, Ramsey wondered how long it was going to take to convince his body of that fact.

HE'D PACKED SWEATS and a T-shirt for sleeping. With his laptop on his chest, Ramsey lay on top of the rose coverlet on the queen-size bed, settled in for the night. Best that he not climb in between the soft sheets. Not tease his libido with images of Lucy Hayes making the bed, or lying on the sheets.

Best that he not give her more work by having to wash sheets and remake a bed when he was gone.

One o'clock in the morning and he wasn't sleeping, anyway. There'd been two other abductions in Massachusetts on delivery truck routes not long before Claire Sanderson had been taken. Both toddlers. Neither had ever been found. Jack had been cleared of any suspicion in those abductions—they weren't on his route, and during the first one, he hadn't even been driving a truck yet.

But maybe there was some other connection. Jack could have come back from Cincinnati, armed with Gladys's information and a plan. He could have originally started as the middleman between the delivery truck drivers and Gladys, and then determined that he could make more money by cutting out the portion he had to pay to the delivery-truck man by handling that part of the job himself. Every piece of that puzzle fit.

Now all he needed to do was prove it.

And find out what had happened to those three children.

He searched the three routes, marking all the similarities he could find, right down to fast-food places from the same chains. It was only two in the morning.

And the phone rang.

Ramsey waited. If Lucy was being called in to work, she'd let him know she was leaving.

Maybe he could ride along. Be of assistance.

And if she wasn't…

He listened for her voice. Heard nothing. And went back to work.

At three, he awoke from a doze and sat instantly upright.

He'd heard something. A shuffle? A…

Cupboard. In the kitchen. Lucy was up.

Settling back against the pillows, Ramsey willed himself to ignore the fact that someone else was in the house. It didn't matter what she slept in. Or if she'd pulled on a robe for his benefit.

Didn't matter if she was having a sleepless night. Or if the phone call had upset her.

She had his cell-phone number. She'd call if she needed him. She always did.

Or…she could always knock on his door.

Pulling the computer to his chest once again, he went back to work.

CHAPTER TWELVE

JACK COLTON'S ENGLISH PROFESSOR, Melissa Beck, had just been starting her career twenty-seven years before. Now she was the head of the English department and, with an eight o'clock class, Lucy and Ramsey figured the best time to get her was before that. Which meant that they were leaving Lucy's house before six in order to make it to UC in time.

They were leaving before Sandy would be up, Lucy thought as she pulled out of her driveway and confirmed that there were no lights on in her mother's small bungalow across the street.

"Is that your mother's place?" Ramsey was following the direction of her gaze.

"Yes."

He didn't say anything more. Didn't ask to meet Sandy. And Lucy was thankful for his lack of interest. She'd learned early in life to keep Sandy off-limits from the rest of her associations.

And to keep her associations off-limits from Sandy. If her mother had any idea she'd had a man spend the night with her, Sandy wouldn't rest until she met him and knew for certain that he wasn't going to take Lucy away from Aurora. Away from her.

"I heard your phone ring last night."

"Oh." She'd felt like an interloper in her own home the night before. "Sorry. I was hoping it didn't wake you." Because what she'd wanted to do as soon as she'd hung up the phone was to knock on the spare-bedroom door and ask Ramsey Miller if he'd...what? Be her one-night stand? Lucy hadn't had sex since she'd slept with her guns instructor at the academy. He'd been a mistake. She'd thought that she and the thirty-year-old bachelor had something. The arrogant jackass had talked about her in the locker room.

"Was it work?"

"No." Two could play Ramsey's game—one word or less when it came to answering personal questions.

But then, he didn't ask personal questions. Until now.

Was he feeling a change in their relationship, too? Was her attraction to him reciprocated? At least a little?

Would he have opened the door the night before if she'd knocked? Invited her in?

Could be he was just making conversation. They had an hour sitting in small confines ahead of them.

"Everything okay?" He was looking out his passenger window. Maybe following the progress of the barge that was making its way slowly upriver.

Sandy had had another nightmare. They'd handled it. "It's fine."

"Your mother?"

"Yes."

His gaze turned toward her. "Was she drinking?"

She never should have told him about Sandy's drinking. It was a part of her life that was between her and her mother and Marie. Outsiders didn't understand. They judged.

But Ramsey Miller had been safely removed several states away, with no cause to ever be in Aurora, or anyplace close to her personal life, the night several months before then when she'd first found out Sandy was drinking again. She'd been tired. And discouraged. And he'd called to tell her that another missing toddler had fallen into Peter Walters's clutches.

They'd both been having low moments and had traded woes. No big deal.

"I don't think she was drinking," she said in answer to his

question. If he judged he judged. He was going back to Massachusetts, anyhow. "She had a nightmare."

"Wakerby induced?"

"They all are, in one fashion or another."

"She has them often?"

They were passing the time it took to drive to their next business meeting. What was it going to hurt to be honest with him? He saw too much, anyway.

And, she reminded herself again, he was leaving.

"All my life. When I was little she used to come into my room whenever she had a nightmare and wake me up just so that she could make certain that I was okay."

Maybe if people saw Sandy's pain, they wouldn't judge her as harshly as her teachers at school had. The guidance counselor in junior high who'd tried to sic child protective services on them. The mothers of schoolmates—potential friends—who wouldn't let their children play at Lucy's house, or, in later years, hang out there, because of Sandy's influence.

"We'd play games. Or watch television. When I was a little older, we'd watch movies on the VCR."

"On school nights?"

"Yes."

"In the middle of the night?"

"Uh-huh."

"That must have made it rough at school the next day."

"I graduated with a three point six." She'd shown the naysayers that she could thrive just fine living with her mother. "My mother lost a child in a brutal fashion," she said, turning onto the freeway that would take them into Cincinnati and back to UC. "It's something she's going to live with for the rest of her life. You don't go through something like that and get over it."

"I'm not suggesting you do."

His tone suggested that she might have come on a bit too strong. Defensiveness where Sandy was concerned was inbred.

"I can't take away the horrors my mom lives with, but I *can* make the worst times easier to bear," she said, softening her tone. "Talking to me, connecting with me, eases her panic. Calms her. I bring her a measure of peace."

"That's a hard cross for a child to bear."

"I turned out okay."

He didn't respond and his silence bothered her. Did he think there was something wrong with her?

Was he judging her, too?

Was that why he wasn't interested in kissing her?

Shaking off the residuals of a lifetime of warding off others' negative reactions to her mother, Lucy thought about Jack Colton. About Professor Melissa Beck. About…

"Have you always lived in Aurora?"

What was with the personal questions?

Did he realize that turnaround was fair play? They had another forty-five minutes in the car and Lucy wanted to know some things about him, too. Just to file away in the box labeled A Guy I Used to Work With.

"Yes, I've always lived here…" she said. "Though I was born in Newport, Kentucky, which is where my dad was living and working until his death."

"He was a cop, right?"

"Yeah."

"Killed in the line of duty?"

"Yep. He was working undercover, part of a drug sting. My dad went for a drop. His dealer made him and came out of the car shooting. I have copies of the newspaper articles about it. He was given a posthumous commendation."

"Was this before or after you were born?"

"Before. Mama couldn't catch a break, you know?"

"Were they married?"

"No. He was recently divorced. They met when he was called in to work a lead on her case—someone turned in a surveillance tape from a bank. The camera caught a woman and child that matched the description of Mama and Allie during the time Mama can't remember anything. It turned out not to be them, but all it took was that one meeting. He made her feel safe. When she was with him, she felt less panicked. And he drank with her. Anyway, she fell for him. Things got out of hand. Mama thinks he would have married her."

"You don't think so?"

"After he died, there was money. It all went to his ex-wife who turned out not to be quite so ex. He was separated, the divorce papers had been filed, but nothing was final."

"Oh."

"Yeah. I was never acknowledged as his child. Mama wanted them to do blood tests after I was born, to prove that I was his and therefore entitled to some of the settlement, but she was threatened with a harassment charge. They said that she was an emotionally unstable woman trying to make trouble for a fallen officer. The guy had kids of his own. Friends in high places. And Mama didn't have money to get an attorney and pursue things."

"Is he listed on your birth certificate?"

"No. She was afraid someone would file charges against her if she did. She let them intimidate her into putting Father Unknown."

"Have you ever tried to find your half siblings?"

"No. Why would I? I didn't know their father. He's no more than a biological set of chemicals to me. Not that there's any proof of that. And I already know I wouldn't be well received."

She and Sandy were a family.

"All my mother ever wanted was to love and be loved," Lucy said, needing him to understand, even while she knew it didn't matter. "She just made some bad choices where the men in her life were concerned."

"What about while you were growing up? Were there men, then, too?"

"One. He finally gave up on her and moved to Arizona."

"Only one? Your mom never dated after that?"

"Nope. After the rape…and then my father… Mama doesn't have much faith in men."

"How about you? Do you share her feelings?"

Did he think she was gay? Was the chemistry that absent for him?

They should be discussing Jack Colton. A guy she most definitely didn't trust.

"I like men just fine," Lucy said, wishing the miles between them and UC would pass more quickly. *I especially like you, Ramsey Miller, and I don't like that at all.*

PROFESSOR MELISSA BECK wasn't sure she remembered Jack Colton. His picture "rang a bell," but she'd had so many students over the years they'd blended together. She most definitely had never had anything but professional relationships with any of her students—was happily married, thank you—and only knew of one teacher/student relationship at UC during her tenure, and that had involved a male teacher with a female student and the two were now married.

"That was a bust," Lucy said as she and Ramsey got back into the Rendezvous. Her stomach was in knots. Wakerby was next.

"Maybe not," Ramsey's reply surprised her. "I've been thinking about this. Colton lived under the radar. He never gave anyone any reason to suspect him of anything. Never drew attention to himself, except as a good worker. What we just heard fits that character type."

"He obviously was a good employee."

"And what better cover for getting away with something illegal?"

Colton's time at UC was probably before his involvement with baby stealing. "You're saying his personality fits the profile."

"Exactly. Or that he was purposely under the radar so no one would suspect him of anything."

"Or remember him."

Again Ramsey's theory made sense. They were closing in on this guy. They just had to keep looking.

And what about Wakerby? Were they still closing in on him? Or was he on the road to getting away from them?

"You want to stop anyplace before we head out to the prison?" They'd had coffee while they'd waited for Professor Beck to arrive, but he was at her mercy so it was polite to offer.

And a stop could distract her for a moment or two.

"What time is our appointment?"

"Ten-thirty." She wasn't afraid of Sloan Wakerby. She was afraid of his effect on her.

The only way to rid herself of fear was to face it. Head-on.

Ramsey settled back in his seat. "I'm good, then."

He smiled at her, an expression filled with concern. And she had fears to face. Not all of them Wakerby related.

"Where were you born?" She'd have liked not to blurt the question so boldly, or with such a lack of finesse, but she was taking care of business now. If she was going to give up her information, he had to give up his.

"Vienna, Kentucky."

He put it right out there. No prevarication. Maybe she'd been going at this all wrong.

She asked where Vienna was and found out that it was a small town in the southern part of the state.

"Did you grow up there?"

"Yes."

"Are your parents still alive?" She felt as if they were playing twenty questions. Except that the answers were far more interesting than any game she'd ever played.

"Yes."

"Still in Vienna?"

"Yes." He was staring out the front windshield, somewhat

intimidating in his navy suit and polished shoes. Funny, his holster didn't intimidate her a bit. The polished shoes did.

"What does your father do for a living? Was he a cop, too?"

"No, a tobacco farmer. He's retired."

She took the ramp for the state highway that would lead to Wakerby's temporary residence until he was sent to prison for the rest of his life. No need for GPS assistance on this trip. She could get to the jail in her sleep.

And she didn't have to think of Wakerby right now, either.

"You grew up on a farm?" Lucy chanced a look at Ramsey, appearing so official as he sat there in his suit with a black portfolio folder balancing on one thigh.

"I grew up working on the farm alongside my father."

Yesterday the man had told her nothing. Today he was giving her his world. Or at least a part of it. What had changed?

"How far is it to the jail?"

"Another half hour or so." Along a stretch of sparsely populated Indiana farmland.

Wakerby had spent time in a house out in this country. So close to Aurora. Lucy shivered.

Face your fears.

"Do you have siblings?" she asked the man who would be traveling back to her house with her, to sleep in her home for one more night.

The man who'd be accompanying her to a wedding in a few short weeks.

The man she'd been tempted to lose herself in the night before.

"I had a sister. She died more than fifteen years ago."

Wow. She hadn't expected that. "I'm so sorry," Lucy said, wishing she could stop the car. Offer him something.

Staring out the window, he didn't look as if he needed anything.

"It was a long time ago."

"Were you close?"

"It was my job to look out for her." Which didn't really answer her question.

"She was younger than you?"

"Older by two years."

He was going to tell her to shut up any minute now. She had a million questions vying for attention.

"Was she sick?" Was that why he had to watch out for her?

"No. She died of an overdose."

His tone warned her that the interview was over. Lucy drove, passing the occasional farmhouse. Horses. Cows. She came to a four-way stop in the middle of nowhere. And drove on.

None of Ramsey's business was her business.

And he was, in the moment, everything to her.

Personal waywardness aside, she was glad that he was going to be on the opposite side of the one-way glass when she was questioning Sloan Wakerby.

Not to keep her safe from anything Wakerby might try while she was with him. Lucy had no doubt she could protect herself against the scum for the second or two it would take for a corrections officer to break in on them if Wakerby tried anything.

She was glad Ramsey was going to be there because when it came to Sloan Wakerby, she was beginning to doubt herself.

That was a first.

"You asked me if I share my mom's negative feelings toward men."

Ramsey Miller's gaze left the road. His silent scrutiny sent her insides trembling.

Face your fears.

"I respect most of the cops I work with, male and female. And the men and women who serve who I don't know, as well," she said.

There was no fear attached to either statement.

"I have faith in my accountant, who is male. And in most

other men I meet on a professional basis, unless they prove that they aren't trustworthy."

Good common sense. Normal. No fear there.

The jail complex was fifteen miles ahead. Wakerby had already been notified of the meeting. He knew she was almost there. He knew that, shortly, he would be alone with her.

He didn't know that she had backup. That Ramsey Miller would be on the other side of the glass.

"I assume you're going somewhere with this?" Ramsey asked, still watching her, and she realized that she'd been silent for a while.

"Personally, I don't have time for men," she said, blurting again. "It's not that I don't like men, or have a thing against men, I just don't have time."

"Okay."

Twelve miles until the jail complex.

Fear.

"No, that's not completely right." Frowning, Lucy swiped back her hair, welcoming the second's worth of cool air to her heated forehead.

She couldn't rely on Ramsey to help her with Sloan Wakerby. Not like this…

"I…don't…trust men." The words were damning. Ugly. Cold. "Not in my personal life."

Her companion's attention switched back to the world outside the car.

"It's okay, Lucy."

"What is?" Where? She needed something to be okay.

"You have no worries where I'm concerned."

She glanced his way. He glanced hers.

And she knew that he was one hundred percent completely wrong.

CHAPTER THIRTEEN

RAMSEY WAS ALONE in the viewing room, with the exception of one officer at the door behind him who was also watching the proceedings between Lucy Hayes and Sloan Wakerby. Another guard stood outside the door that Lucy had just passed through.

Foregoing the row of hard-backed seats, Ramsey stood at the window, holding in both hands the portfolio he'd brought in with him as Lucy got a verbal agreement from Sloan Wakerby that he'd agreed to speak with her without the presence of an attorney.

At the prisoner's acquiescence, she proceeded to nod at the guard who closed the door, leaving her alone with the man who'd raped her mother.

"Nice to see you again, Mr. Wakerby." Her tone told all witnesses to the conversation that she didn't think there was anything nice about the man seated, hands cuffed behind his back, at the table she stood before. It also conveyed, quite clearly, that she was not the least bit intimidated by the man who'd brutalized her mother and abducted her older sister.

Not that Wakerby had any idea who Lucy was, other than a cop involved in his case.

Wakerby's grin was there, but not as apparent as it had been the first time Ramsey had had the displeasure of meeting the sorry excuse for a human being.

The fifty-five-year-old was also sporting a fairly recent bruise over his right eye.

"You been in a fight, sir?" Lucy's tone softened a fraction as she took a seat in front of the man. A move Ramsey would have chosen himself. Wakerby, who was seated facing Ramsey, wouldn't listen to her if she tried to lord it over him.

The prisoner's chin lifted, but there was no other response.

"I'm sorry to see that your reception here isn't all that you'd hoped it would be," she said to the man. "I hear that even in jail there are standards," she continued, her voice almost sweet sounding. "Guys who rape are okay. I mean, everyone knows that the girl was asking for it, right?"

Lucy's pause could have been tactical or it could be that she was choking on her words. Ramsey suspected it was a bit of both.

"But guys who steal babies while they're raping women… now that's looked upon a little differently." Her voice didn't waver at all as she continued. If Ramsey didn't know better, he'd never have guessed that the woman before him was in any way attached to the case she was working.

And he was fairly good at picking up on the unspoken intricacies in people's body language and voice variances.

"Unless we know that you didn't also turn your sick attentions on that baby, you're going to get the reputation of a lower than lowlife, Mr. Wakerby.…"

Lucy's pause this time had to be deliberate. It was perfect.

The woman in front of him might be little and blonde, and sexy-looking in her black slacks and black-and-white fitted tweed jacket, but she had more guts than any officer he'd ever worked with. Himself included.

"What did you do with that baby, Mr. Wakerby?"

The man didn't answer.

"You agreed to meet with me this time without your lawyer present, sir. You can talk to me now."

Still nothing.

"If you did to that little girl what you did to her mother, then, fine, sir, you will pay for your actions. If you didn't, then you should speak up soon, because if people on the inside think you did, the truth isn't going to matter anymore.

"Did you sexually abuse that little girl, Mr. Wakerby?"

Ramsey could only see the back of Lucy's head. She held it straight and tall.

"You jealous?" Wakerby spoke, his gaze penetrating, no smile evident.

"No. I want the truth. I want you to pay for what you did, not for what you didn't do."

The truth in Lucy's words rang clearly. Wakerby might think Lucy was trying to keep him from being unfairly brutalized in jail. Instead, she'd just promised him full retribution for brutalizing her mother, abducting her sister and any other adverse effects that Allison Hayes had suffered because of his actions.

"The truth is, I ain't into babies," Wakerby said. "And I'm done here."

Relief was a sweet release from the tension of the past moments. Lucy had done well.

His next job was to let her know that without crossing the very clear line she'd drawn between them in the car on the way to jail.

"DID YOU BELIEVE HIM?" Lucy's question came as soon as they were alone in the hallway outside the barred portion of the jail building, having just reclaimed the weapons they'd surrendered before entering the visiting area.

"That he wasn't into babies?" Ramsey's words kept her centered on the case, not on the panic surging through her, compliments of Sloan Wakerby.

"Yes." Ramsey was here because she trusted his opinion. And because she didn't trust her own where her mother's rapist was concerned.

"I believed him."

"You don't think he was just saving his ass? Buying my

protection? Because I could have been threatening to let it slip to his fellow prisoners that he'd raped a child?"

"Sloan Wakerby would never let a woman protect his ass." Right. She knew that. Knew his type.

"He was protecting his own reputation," she said, seeing clearly for a moment. "He's not afraid of being roughed up. He's afraid of being seen as something he is not."

"The man feels no compunction for what he did to your mother. Or any other women he may have violated through the years—"

"Because chances are good my mother's not the only one. I know. Amber's all over Wakerby's past, looking for other victims." Amber Locken. She had to call her associate and let her know how the meeting went.

Problem was, she wasn't quite sure how it went. And she couldn't have Locken, or anyone, know that. The one thing Lucy had always been confident about, the one thing she'd never doubted, was her ability to get the job done.

"Sloan Wakerby has Sloan Wakerby's back," she said. "His safety and security comes from his own belief in himself. His weakness is being accused of being someone he isn't—or of a crime he didn't commit. That's one thing he can't tolerate."

"He's also not smiling anymore." Ramsey's words came from directly behind her.

She'd noted the lack of a smile. And chancing that her reading of the situation was accurate, as opposed to wishful thinking, she said, "I'm getting to him."

"Mmm-hmm." Ramsey walked step by step beside her on the way to the car.

She clicked the remote entry on her key ring, unlocking their doors. "I'm not going to get a confession."

"You just got one."

Dropping her purse on the floor behind her seat, Lucy took her time getting in the car. And then, seat belt buckled, she looked at Ramsey. "I got a confession?"

How could she have missed it? What hadn't she seen?

"Wakerby didn't sexually violate your sister, but something about what happened to Allie bothers him. Otherwise, he'd be laughing his ass off at you."

Lucy froze. Too stunned to care that she'd missed something so obvious. "He knows where my sister is," she said slowly. Had she been at this too long to believe that she might actually succeed? "He knows what happened to Allie."

"Yep."

"I…" She didn't know what to say. Didn't know how she felt. About anything. Lucy stared at Ramsey.

"You're too connected to the case for your cop instincts to kick in full swing, or to get a purely professional reading on him. Your personal emotions get in the way."

"You think I should pull out?"

"You aren't in. Not in any official capacity. Everything's in order. Your captain saw to that. And he respects you enough to let you move forward where you must. I'm just saying that you need to go easier on yourself. No one expects you to be on the top of your detective game, here. And even with that, you just conducted a superior interview."

More confused than ever, Lucy started the car, thinking that it was a good thing that she still felt like she knew how to drive.

Everything else in her world was in total upset.

Most particularly the fact that she had a distinct feeling that she'd just been nurtured by Detective Ramsey Miller.

And she'd liked it.

THE FIRST THING RAMSEY DID when he landed in Boston on Wednesday was get on the phone to start the ball rolling for a warrant to seize Jack Colton's bank accounts. He had to provide enough circumstantial evidence to convince a judge that the warrant for Colton's current affairs was in order, although he had nothing but hunches and theories and conjectures based on testimonies from witnesses with twenty-five-year memory lapses to give doubt to their accuracy.

Getting the warrants for the UC records had been easier. Those records pertained to the time period during which the crime had taken place. There was reasonable expectation that they might have turned up evidence that Jack Colton could be a kidnapper and baby dealer.

Still, Ramsey had used his time on the plane wisely. Rather than spending it thinking about his hostess from the past two days, he'd done what he always did when life tried to get messy on him—he'd sunk himself in his work.

He knew his limits. Personal relationships were outside the scope. He failed at them. Every time. Being a good cop, a good detective, was the limit of what he had to offer the world.

By Wednesday afternoon he had the warrant that he needed. And by Wednesday evening, he was in possession of a long night's worth of work.

He showered Thursday morning with the intimate knowledge of Jack Colton's financial affairs.

Lucy was at the desk she shared with Todd Davis early Thursday morning. She was investigating a series of gas-station robberies that had been taking place in Aurora. She'd also put in a call to Lori Givens, the friend who worked in the private DNA lab in Cincinnati. Lori had donated her time to do all of the scientific work involved in setting up the DNA database for all of the babies involved in the Gladys Buckley case.

Lucy wanted some more information on the Claire Sanderson DNA match with evidence stored from the Buckley mansion. What color was the ribbon on which they'd found Claire's DNA? How long was it? Most importantly, what was it made out of? If she had to trace hair-ribbon makers from twenty-five years ago she would. She was determined to give Claire back to Emma—as if by doing so she could somehow ease the ache of not finding Allie.

But Emma and Claire weren't her case.

The person who was siphoning gas from service stations was her problem.

The obvious answer to the gas investigation was that it was an inside job. Lucy didn't like obvious. Obvious was usually a waste of time. But in this case, she'd started there. By Wednesday afternoon, she'd not only cleared all the delivery drivers and station workers, but she'd put in requests for surveillance tapes. And Thursday morning she spent a couple of hours watching eye-glazing videos on a screen at her desk.

By ten o'clock, she had a warrant for the arrest of a suspect: a farmer who had a wife and young kids and not enough money to support any of them, but who also had his own approved, in-ground gas tank on his property. The man had been selling off what others believed to be his own unused gas at lower prices before it evaporated.

No one knew quite how much gas the farmer had been selling. No one knew that it was gas he was stealing, twenty-five gallons at a time in the dark of the night, in order to make enough money to keep his family afloat.

Lucy was having the guy arrested and now he wouldn't be able to help his family at all.

"You got a minute?" At thirty-eight, Amber Locken looked better than Lucy felt at twenty-seven.

Lucy swung around, facing the redhead as she stood beside Lucy's desk. "Of course. What's up?"

"First, good work on Tuesday. Wakerby put in a request to see his lawyer."

The meeting with the captain and Amber first thing Wednesday morning, to report on her meeting with the prisoner, had been short and to the point. Lucy had given the facts and excused herself, not waiting around for the reactions to her report. Or for questions.

"He's going to confess?" Her voice squeaked. She couldn't help it. She was stunned.

"I'm not sure what he's doing. But it's clear you've shaken something loose."

She had to calm down. To remember the job. Not because she gave a whit at the moment about how she looked to her peer—or to her boss, either, for that matter—but because if she didn't stay calm and focused she could miss something critical.

"When's the meeting?"

"Monday morning."

Four days away. So maybe she should pay the man one more visit over the weekend. Just to make certain that he didn't have time to start feeling safe again.

"Thanks for letting me know." The woman was only acting on Lionel's orders, keeping Lucy informed, but she was still grateful.

Amber didn't immediately move on her way. "I had a call yesterday afternoon," she said after a pause. "A woman who claims that Wakerby lived with her for a couple of years. She says she just heard that he's in jail on a rape charge."

Another victim. Lucy braced herself.

"She said that she has a box of his things. She'd been keeping them in the hopes that he might show up again, but now she wants nothing to do with them. She called to ask what she should do with them."

Heart pounding, Lucy held her tongue, waiting. This was Amber's show. "I had them picked up last night and they were couriered this morning. We should have them sometime tomorrow. If you'd like to go through the box with me, I'll call you when it arrives."

"I would really appreciate that, yes," Lucy said. And this time when she thanked her colleague, she smiled, too.

And then she zipped off a text to Ramsey. Just to keep him informed.

RAMSEY WAS NOT IN a good mood when he made it to the station on Thursday. He'd spent the morning looking at a dead body in a hotel room down at the docks—until he found a suicide note. The deceased was a financier from Boston who'd driven to the ocean to end his life after being indicted for misappropriation of funds to the tune of a few million dollars.

He'd tried himself, delivered a guilty verdict and handed down the death sentence all in a day.

Ramsey wondered about the wife and kids, glad that telling the family didn't fall to him. The family were out of his jurisdiction.

Jack Colton wasn't. Ramsey called the man and requested an in-person sit-down, just to go over what the man remembered, one more time.

Or so he told Colton.

The long-haul semitruck driver agreed to meet with him on Saturday, at the end of an East Coast run.

After paying a visit to Colton's former employee, with a request—not a warrant—for Colton's delivery-route logs for the three years he'd worked there, Ramsey set out for a hole-in-the-wall bar not far from the docks, where he could sit in a corner, have a burger and a beer and study Jack Colton's moves twenty-five years before.

Before he was done, he was going to be so far inside Jack Colton's skin, the man wouldn't know where he ended and Ramsey began.

He reached his destination, parked, landed his table, ordered, opened his folder and pulled out his cell. Lucy had texted him. Because his body had responded as soon as he'd seen her name, he'd forced himself to wait to text her back.

You're closing in, he typed in reply a couple of hours later and added, Call if you need me. He read what he'd written. Deleted the if you need me. Reread it. Then deleting, Call, typed, Good job. Read it one last time. Nodded. And hit Send.

Nothing too personal.

She didn't trust men in a personal sense. She trusted her fellow officers. Of which he was one.

CHAPTER FOURTEEN

AT TEN MINUTES BEFORE midnight on Thursday night, Lucy's phone chimed "Carol of the Bells"—her favorite Christmas song, and also her year-round ringtone for text messages.

There was only one person who might text her late at night. Everyone else she could think of who would contact her that late—and there were a number of them—would call.

There was really only one person who'd texted her at all since she'd purchased her new smartphone.

She'd set a police-badge icon as Ramsey's contact ID. It appeared on her screen as she opened her messages.

Lucy set down the phone. She finished pouring the cup of tea she'd been in the process of preparing for herself to take into bed with her.

Other than his brief response to her text, she hadn't heard from Ramsey in almost forty-eight hours—not since she'd dropped him off at the departures gate at the Cincinnati airport Wednesday morning.

She'd expected at least a text letting her know he'd arrived safely back in Comfort Cove. She'd have sent him one if their situations had been reversed and she'd been the one traveling.

Picking up her cup of newly prepared tea, she blew across the steam. The fact that he hadn't called Wednesday night hadn't bothered her. Much. She'd had a few things to share with him, but if he was busy, they could wait. He probably had a desk full of work to catch up on after being away for a few days.

Days he'd partially dedicated to her and her case. Her life.

But tonight, she'd really been hoping to speak with him. What would be in Wakerby's box of goods?

And what news did Ramsey have on Jack Colton's bank account? Had he been able to finagle a warrant to have a look at them?

And did he regret not having kissed her? Did he think of her as a woman at all?

Did he know that she was turned on by him? Was he avoiding her because of it?

Picking up her phone in her free hand, she took her cup of tea, intending to make it to her room before looking at the message he'd sent.

Intending to wait until morning to reply.

But she didn't turn left at the hall to go to her room. She turned right—and ended up in the spare bedroom. The one Ramsey Miller had used. She hadn't been down this way since he'd left. And shouldn't be there now. Saturday morning, when she came in to get the used sheets and clean the bathroom would be the time to be in the room.

Standing in the doorway, she looked around, hoping for a trace of him, something he'd inadvertently left behind. When there was nothing readily discernible, she flipped on the light switch and moved farther into the room—peering over the end of the bed to the other side. No stray socks there. Or even so much as a scrap of paper. No dropped pen or lost tie.

He hadn't left so much as a crease on the bed.

"Carol of the Bells" sounded a second time.

Telling herself that she really was sick, Lucy walked into the bathroom, to see if there was any trash in the small can beside the toilet. Had she imagined Ramsey there? Imagined that they were starting to become friends?

She was a top-notch investigator. She could find evidence of someone's presence when they didn't want to be found.

The trash can was empty.

Either the man flushed his dental floss or he took his trash home with him.

Coming back into the bedroom, she meant to turn off the light and head into her own room where her pillows were already fluffed, her blankets turned down and ready to welcome her for the few brief hours she had to rest.

She turned off the light, but she didn't leave. Sitting on the bed, she smoothed her hands across the covers. She wouldn't pull down the coverlet. Wouldn't let herself sink so low as to lie on Ramsey Miller's sheets.

But she could rest her head, for just a minute, on the pillow he'd used. Setting her tea down on the bedside table, with her cell phone still clutched in her hand, she lay back slowly, as if the pillows would evaporate from her life, as the man appeared to have done.

The pillows supported her weight. And they smelled like Ramsey Miller.

With a deep breath, Lucy lay her hands on her stomach and closed her eyes. Breathing in the essence of a man who made her feel…good. Just for a second, she'd take strength from knowing that he existed. He didn't have to know. No one had to know. She'd be fine. Her old self. In just a second.

"Carol of the Bells" peeled from her stomach. Lucy grabbed the phone from her midsection, wondering why it was there, just as she was remembering where she was.

What time was it?

The LED screen showed two in the morning. Two hours since she'd come into Ramsey's room? She'd been asleep for two hours?

Sitting up in the dark, she opened her phone.

U okay?

The most recently sent text message showed on her screen.

Scrolling with the thumb holding the phone, she read the string.

Possible Colton development to discuss when you get the

chance. The first message that had come in just before midnight had been very closely followed by Let's discuss Wakerby development.

She'd texted Amber's news about Wakerby's request to meet with his lawyer. She hadn't mentioned the couriered box of belongings or her invitation to go through them. She'd been saving that for the phone call she'd been sure she'd receive that night.

He'd texted instead and implied that she should call.

Shaking her head, sleepy, but grinning, she texted back, Fine. Fell asleep. Up now.

Can you talk?

They'd known each other for months and suddenly he was asking?

Of course.

She'd barely hit Send when her phone rang.

"What's the development?" she answered on the first ring. She was going to get up. Head to her own room. Or at least the couch.

In a minute.

"Two things. I got Colton's current bank records. There was nothing from twenty-five years ago."

"That was quick."

"Yeah, well, I was convincing."

He had a good case.

"Have you had time to go over them?"

"Last night."

"And?"

"Nothing. He's a saver, just like you suspected. He's got a couple hundred thousand put away, but based on his income, which I am gathering from regular deposits and tax returns, all I can prove is that he spends wisely. There're no big influxes of money. No big deductions, either, other than the payments he's making on his semi."

"You don't know if that two hundred thousand is from

twenty-five years of working hard and living frugally or from other means," she reminded him, lying back on the pillow that he'd used just a couple of nights before.

She felt decadent. And naughty.

"But I can do the math and see that based on his rate of deposits and spending and saving over the past three years, he could very easily have amassed that amount of money simply from hard work and light spending."

"So maybe he got out of the baby-stealing business too long ago for you to see any indication of it."

"Then what did he do with the money?"

"Same thing he could still be doing with it if he didn't get out of the business. He could be stashing it in an account we can't see."

"Why?"

Motive. Why would a man risk stealing children, selling them and then not use the money?

"For all we know, he does use it," Lucy reminded him. "We see the Jack Colton he wants us to see. The Jack he shows the world. Who knows what he does with the time we can't see? Maybe he has a house in Jamaica. Or a life in Montana! A wife and kids and life that he lives under an alias. If he has a secret bank account, he'd use that account to finance his other life. It's not like it hasn't happened before."

She felt good. Better than she'd felt in a long time.

"Okay, we'll keep that possibility open."

His "we" made her warm.

"You said you had two developments."

"I found something in Colton's work log from the day that Claire Sanderson went missing. He logged in an unusual gas stop. The only time he ever did so, at least as far as the record shows. I'm going through boxes of old handwritten ledgers that probably should have been thrown out years ago except that the owner of the company has a huge basement and keeps everything."

She sat up. "Are you sure? About the gas stop being one he never made before or after?"

"As sure as I can be. He didn't log it again, I can tell you that much."

"Have you questioned him about it? Or what about his old employer? I'm assuming he gave you the records or you wouldn't have found anything."

"He gave them to me. Said he'd do anything he could to help find the missing girl, but that he'd trust Jack Colton with his own kids. I found the discrepancy just before midnight so I haven't called him yet."

"What about Colton? Have you talked to him?"

"He's meeting me at the station on Saturday. Ostensibly to go over what he remembers one more time."

"He still thinks you're just looking at him because of having found out about him from Cal's book?"

"That's all I've told him."

"How's it going on a warrant for his DNA?" They'd discussed Ramsey's chances of getting the various warrants on their way to the airport Wednesday morning.

"No go. Not until I can find something besides theory to support my case."

"Maybe the gas stop will do it."

"I'll get the sample somehow. Offer him a drink on Saturday. Something. Once I get his DNA, I can run it against the evidence we just recovered in the Sanderson case."

"Have you heard back on the Sanderson evidence yet?"

"No."

Investigative work required patience. Loads of it.

She'd been patient on Allie's case for nine long years. Was that why she was having a hard time believing that they were closing in on Wakerby?

Under the cover of darkness, she told him about the couriered box of Wakerby's belongings. Of Locken's invitation to her to be present when they went through it.

"People hold on to innocuous items that connect them to things that they don't want others to know about," Ramsey said softly.

He wasn't telling her what to do. Wasn't implying she didn't know. He was reminding her of what she knew.

Because he knew that in the morning, with Wakerby's things in front of her, she might not be at her best.

At least that's how she took his remark. And she smiled again.

"A magazine with an address label, but the clue isn't the address label, it's a random picture somewhere in the magazine that prompted the person to save it." She'd actually worked on a case where that scenario had come into play a couple of years ago, when she'd been a very junior detective.

"And then there are the accidental things." Ramsey's voice was soft, tired sounding. "A receipt that was left in the bottom of a bag of old socks."

The word *socks* grabbed her. She'd been thinking of that box of belongings in terms of clues to finding Allie. Socks took that box down to a different level, a more personal level.

She didn't want to see Wakerby's socks. Or anything else that brought the man any closer to her.

And she was lying on top of her spare bed because it smelled like a man who'd shown no sign, whatsoever, that he knew she was a woman.

Lucy was off the bed in seconds, picking up her cold tea and making a beeline for her own room.

A BEAT-UP WOMAN, age indeterminable because of the swelling and bruising around her nose, mouth and eyes, was standing outside the office door when Ramsey got off the elevator just after six on Friday morning. He had paperwork to catch up on, reports to write, and had been hoping to get it done before all hell broke loose for the day.

Or, if no new jobs came in, before everyone showed up

and started yawing at each other or someone turned on the television.

Walking past the woman might have been his easiest course.

"Is someone helping you?" he asked, standing there like he had all the time in the world.

"They said I could come up here and wait for a detective." Her words came through lips that were stiff and doubled in size.

"Sure. I'm Detective Miller," Ramsey said, pulling his badge out of his brown suit-coat pocket. "What can I do for you?"

Who in the hell did that to you and where am I going to find him?

"I want to know what would happen to a kid if he beat someone up." She sounded like her mouth was wired shut. But maybe it just wouldn't open. If her jaw wasn't broken it was a miracle.

"Is that what happened to you? A kid beat you up?"

Her chin lifted. Ramsey couldn't tell if it stiffened or not because of the swelling. The woman looked grotesque. Worried.

But not scared to death. "I just want to know what would happen if a kid beat someone up," she repeated, almost as if she'd been rehearsing the line during the time he'd taken to get to work and find her there.

"It depends on the circumstances, ma'am, and the age of the kid, too."

She didn't reply. She wasn't shaking. Wasn't looking over her shoulder, or panicking. He had a feeling she might just turn, get on the elevator and leave.

He couldn't let that happen.

"You're not in good shape, ma'am," he said, stepping closer to her. "Have you seen a doctor?"

She started to shake her head and winced instead. "I'll be fine. I don't need a doctor."

It had to hurt like hell to speak.

"What's your name?"

"Lonna."

"Lonna what?"

"Lonna Baker."

Good. Even if she left, he'd be able to find her. And find out what happened.

"Are you married, Lonna?"

"No."

"Do you have a boyfriend?"

"No."

The ante had just upped. "I need to know who did this to you, Lonna."

"I don't want to press charges." She spoke carefully as though the process was becoming more painful.

"A crime has been committed here. The state could press charges."

Now her gaze, little slits within puffy skin, darted. Now she was afraid.

But not for herself?

"What kid beat you up, Lonna?"

Tears pooled within her swollen eyes, and eventually trickled over the edges of her bruises.

"My kid."

He should have expected that. He hadn't.

He wanted to puke.

RAMSEY CALLED KIM AND THEN sat with Lonna in an interrogation room until the female detective arrived. He didn't offer her anything to drink, not certain that she should ingest anything. Instead, he called for emergency medical services. They arrived just about the same time Kim did.

Half an hour later, he was on his way to meet Randall Davenport, Jack Colton's boss from twenty-five years ago. He took Ocean Drive across town, adding a good twenty minutes to his trip. He had to get out. To breathe fresh air. Comfort Cove wasn't a huge city like Boston. It also wasn't a small town like Aurora. It bore no resemblance whatsoever to Vienna, Kentucky.

Ramsey could process a dead body, male or female, without losing his appetite. Especially if it was a clean shot to the head that did the killing. He could handle guts and gore from bar fights and suicides just fine. Car accidents and even strangulations were part of the job. He didn't think he'd ever get used to seeing women and children abused. It wasn't death that bothered him. Suffering did.

And he had to make certain that Claire Sanderson, dead or alive, hadn't suffered. He knew her family, had an invitation to her sister's wedding. They needed answers—were suffering hugely without them—and it was his job to find those answers.

Randall Davenport, a portly man, invited Ramsey into his office and offered him a cup of coffee. Ramsey accepted the drink in the guise of politeness, of friendliness, not because he intended to drink a sip of it.

"I was not quite thirty when my old man hired Jack Colton," Randall said, leaning back in the chair behind his desk. "Not all that much older than Jack was, which is why I remember him."

Ramsey, with his portfolio resting on his thigh, settled back into the armchair on the opposite side of Davenport's desk.

The room was clean. Organized. With family photos and local awards on the walls.

"You service all of eastern Massachusetts," Ramsey said, reading a sign on the wall.

"That's right."

"Have you always?"

"Yes. My father bought the business from East Coast Meats. They'd started with two brothers. One who processed meat and the other who delivered it. When the one brother died, the one who processed the meat sold off that part of the business. My father bought it—I was ten at the time—and we've distributed for them, exclusively, since day one."

He'd heard of East Coast Meats. They provided beef to all of the restaurants in the tourist district of Comfort Cove. And to places in Boston and surrounding cities, as well. He'd also already known what Davenport had just told him.

He was there to find out what he didn't know. First thing being whether or not Davenport was being straight up with him.

"How serious was your father about the work logs you gave me?"

"Very," Davenport said without a moment's pause. "Reliability is what built East Coast Meats, both in the quality of the meat and the timeliness of its delivery. Meat isn't something that can sit outside and wait for someone to get home. People plan their schedules around the time their meat will arrive so that they can be there to take it in and get it in the refrigerator. If we're late, we make them late. We could ruin an entire day by upsetting someone's schedule, which is not convenient. If we aren't convenient, our customers might just decide to stop in at the local butcher to buy their meat. Even today, if a man doesn't log in, allowing us to verify every delivery, he doesn't work for us."

Amelia Hardy had led him to believe that Jack's job depended on his timeliness.

"Jack Colton made an unscheduled stop for gas the day that Claire Sanderson went missing. I can find no record of him making that stop at any other time that he worked for you."

Frowning, Randall Davenport stood to his full five-foot-eight and reached for the book that was still on his desk from the previous day when Ramsey had been there to collect copies of the twenty-five-year-old records.

Randall turned the pages with the ease of someone who

was completely familiar with them. Ramsey recognized the page when Randall found it. There was a scribble in the upper left-hand corner. Like someone had been trying to get an ink pen to write.

With his pudgy finger running down the page, line by line, Randall appeared to read every bit of information there. He turned back a week and forward a week. Ramsey had done the same thing.

Then he went for another book. For the next fifteen minutes, Randall Davenport spot-checked time pages for all Wednesdays in 1987. And then he went to the basement and came back fifteen minutes later with another book of records.

"I'm looking at finance records, here," Davenport finally told him. "Colton's unscheduled gas stop is logged, with a request for reimbursement. There is no request for gas reimbursement at the end of the day, which was usual for him."

Davenport turned the book around.

"He probably got a truck that hadn't been filled the night before," Davenport said. "We frown on guys turning in trucks before filling them, but it happens sometimes. A guy has somewhere to be, a function that he's rushing off to…"

Ramsey was impressed with the man's record keeping. It rivaled the department's evidence room.

And he was pissed, too. There went his prime suspect. Most likely. Unless he could figure out how the man could steal a two-year-old child, stop for gas, get rid of the child and make all of his usual deliveries, too.

Or…steal the child, stop for gas—a well-planned alibi—make one more delivery with the child in the car and then get rid of the child during his lunch break in time to make all his afternoon appointments on schedule.

Colton would only have to have kept the two-year-old quiet and hidden long enough for one delivery.

Was it so hard to imagine that he'd done so?

CHAPTER FIFTEEN

THE BOX WASN'T THAT BIG. Maybe two feet square. A little bigger than a book-size moving box. It had the name of a popular kids cereal on the outside. Probably picked up free from a grocery store. It was not a box that someone went out and bought.

"You ready?" Amber Locken stood on one side of the island countertop in the evidence room at the station house. Lucy, in black wool slacks and jacket and her power red blouse, stood on the other.

"Yes," Lucy said, staring at the strip of brown packing tape sealing the box.

The handwriting on the top, addressing the box to their care, was obviously feminine. Flowery. Young.

Wakerby was fifty-five. He'd said he didn't go for babies. Just women young enough to be his own baby?

Pulling a utility knife from a drawer in the island counter, Amber handed it to Lucy. "This one's yours," she said.

Surprised, Lucy glanced at the woman who'd brought her up in the business—back when Lucy had been a cop on the beat. Amber was watching her.

"It takes a special woman to be a cop, Lucy. Where men are natural tough guys, we're nurturers. Think of little boys. They figure cutting up worms is cool. They laugh at bodily functions, and consider blood and gore entertainment. Girls, on the other hand, stereotypically, play nurse and house, where they're taking care of people. They like movies with animals in them—preferably horses—and happy endings. They're embarrassed by bodily functions."

Lucy got the point.

"You're a natural at this job. And you deserve this," Amber said, nodding toward the box.

Taking the knife from the other woman's hand, Lucy put the tip of the blade to the tape and sliced with one sure motion.

She was a good cop. She could do this.

THE BEATEN MOTHER WAS GONE by the time Ramsey made it back to the office. Kim was nowhere to be seen, either. Ramsey sat down to write up his suicide from the day before while he ate the cold fried-chicken sandwich he'd bought from the shop downstairs.

Even stale, it was better than the nothing he'd brought from home that morning.

As if on cue—because he was eating bad—his cell phone rang and his father's number appeared on the screen. His first instinct, to push the end-call button and send Earl Miller to voice mail, almost saved him.

"Yeah, Dad, what's up?" He answered the call just before it switched over.

"You busy, son? I waited until lunchtime, hoping I wouldn't be interrupting a meeting or something, but I know that when you're on a case time of day means nothing."

Ramsey bit into his sandwich. Chewing just to be stubborn in response to the voice inside of him that was telling him that he shouldn't eat that stuff.

"I've got a minute," Ramsey said. "What's up?"

"Thanksgiving's next week."

The last swallow of his sandwich stuck in his throat. "I know."

His father always asked. He never nagged.

Or pushed.

"We'd really like for you to come home and celebrate it with us."

His mother must be getting worse. Did Earl think this might be her last Thanksgiving with them?

Heart racing, Ramsey tried to corral his thoughts. His mother was losing her mind. Not her physical health. She wasn't even seventy yet. And she'd always been healthy.

"I can't, Dad."

"I told your mother that's what you'd say. But think about it, would you, Ramsey? It's really important. To both of us."

"I have a wedding to go to that weekend." Until that moment, he'd been dreading the event. Partially because he wasn't sure he could spend any more personal time with Lucy Hayes without her figuring out how much she turned him on.

"A wedding?" Earl's tone changed. "Anyone we know?"

"No. A...victim's sister is getting married. She invited me and another cop."

"Did you get the guy?"

He blinked, fighting against the knot in his chest. If something was wrong with his mother...

"What guy?"

"The one who victimized the sister of the girl getting married."

An image of Jack Colton flashed in his mind's eye. As far as his father knew, the "guy" could have been a "girl." "Not yet, but I'm closing in on him. Hopefully I'll be able to wrap it up this next week."

"When's the wedding?"

"Saturday." Time enough between Thanksgiving dinner and the wedding to make it back from Vienna. "But I'm on call Thanksgiving Day," he said. He'd volunteered. Just like he did for every other holiday. Everyone else, including Kim, had family to be with over the holidays. "Holidays seem to make crazy people crazier," he said, and then wished he hadn't. They made his mother worse, too, but she wasn't crazy.

And he didn't want Earl to think he thought so.

There was a pause on the line. Ramsey could make out the distinct tones of his mother's voice, but he couldn't make out the words. Then Earl said, "How about the week after Thanksgiving? Can you get away then?"

"What's wrong, Dad? Is Mom sick?"

"No."

"Are you?"

"No. We're both healthy, Ramsey. We just had our annual physicals last month. We miss you, son."

And he missed them, too. He just didn't miss the emotional turmoil that coiled around them every time they got together. Even worse was the state his mother was always left in any time he'd been home.

Missing each other was far healthier for all of them.

"I'll see what I can do. If not then, soon," he said, and realized, when he heard Earl's sigh, that his father knew Ramsey wasn't going to be home anytime in the near future.

"How are you otherwise?" Earl asked, and Ramsey felt like more of a heel than ever. His father never called him on his lies, his false promises. He'd never said a word about the fact that it was Ramsey's fault that Diane was dead, either. Not once.

But they all knew that it was.

"I'm fine, Dad. Busier than ever. In addition to my regular homicide duties, I'm working some cold cases. Child abductions."

At least Earl would know that his son was spending his time doing good work, helping people.

Maybe even bringing families back together to make up for having blown his own apart.

LUCY SPENT FRIDAY EVENING with Sandy, giving Marie a break to meet another one of their old high-school friends for dinner. Her mother's caretaker was talking about moving in with Sandy permanently.

"There's no point in paying for two places," she'd said just before leaving that evening. "Sandy's been asking for years, and I'm getting too old to clean so many bathrooms."

Sandy had been asking Marie to live with them since Lucy was a little girl—probably because she'd known that life would have been better for Lucy if another woman, a sober woman, had been there to mother her.

And Lucy had a feeling that Sandy's close call the week before had scared Marie. Sandy, for all of her issues, was the only family Marie had left. And, even drunk, Sandy was a good friend to Marie. She listened. She encouraged. She cared.

"Just one, Luce? A glass of wine won't hurt. Marie's been letting me have one a night. After dinner."

"I'm not Marie."

And after sitting in that hospital waiting room, afraid her mother was going to die, Lucy couldn't bear to see Sandy with a glass to her lips again.

"I've got the shakes, Luce."

"Take a pill."

She didn't look away from the TV game show that they were watching. She was rooting for the young, pregnant brunette. Sandy wanted the blonde newlywed to win.

Neither of them cheered for the thirty-something, handsome man who was the third contestant at the podium.

The blonde won a bonus trip. Sandy smiled. Sat on the edge of her chair. She'd lost weight again and her size zeros were hanging off her bones.

Caught up in the show, Sandy didn't ask again for something to drink until an hour later. The requests came every five minutes or so after that until finally, just past ten, Lucy gave her mother a sleeping pill, watched while the woman changed into her pajamas and then held the covers as her mother settled into her queen-size bed. Grabbing the remote control for the flat-screen TV she'd bought Sandy for Christmas, Lucy climbed on top of the covers on the other side of her mother's bed and settled down to watch a movie she'd seen a hundred times before.

"CAROL OF THE BELLS" SOUNDED halfway through the movie. After quickly silencing her ringtone she glanced at the screen of her phone. U up?

Yeah.

Me too.

She smiled as she typed, No shit.

Hot date?

She read the words a second time. Where had that come from?

But curious, she wrote, No. You?

No.

He was thinking in terms of her with a hot date? Could that mean he viewed her as a hot woman? Or a woman who could get a hot date? A woman who had hot dates?

A woman? Not just a cop?

Lucy smiled again. If she wasn't careful she was going to fall for this guy. And then get hurt.

You home?

She hesitated before typing in the affirmative, loath to lie to Ramsey in spite of the fact that lying to keep her life with Sandy private was as inbred as breathing.

The fact that his next question would be to ask if he could call—though why they'd started checking with each other first she didn't know—drove her reply.

No.

Work?

No. She hesitated. And then, before he had a chance to reply typed, Mama's.

Everything okay?

Fine. Sleeping.

You bored?

Little. Lucy adjusted the pillows behind her and lay back, smiling again. Would he take pity on her and entertain her for a while?

Anything in the box?

The mention of work brought her back to reality, and Lucy wasn't completely unhappy to be able to tell him about the day. She didn't need to, which was why she hadn't called him, but since he'd asked...

Clothes, a razor, deodorant... She knew what kind Sloan wore now and would never, ever be able to pass it in the store again without thinking of him. Damn him.

And framed photo of American flag with some numbers written on back of it.

She sent the message off because of reaching length limits and then kept typing.

Looks like some kind of coordinates.

For what?

No clue. Not yet, anyway. Amber was going to be questioning Wakerby over the weekend, before the meeting with his attorney at the beginning of next week. They'd discussed their tactics together and agreed that they needed to up the heat on him over the weekend, but with the new evidence in hand, it made sense for Amber, not Lucy, to be the one to make this visit.

Lucy was one hundred percent good with the decision.

In the meantime, Spending the weekend with maps. Grocery store where Mama taken. Place by river where found. Areas around and in between. Checking coordinates. If lucky, will be a match.

She'd have started already if she hadn't promised to spend the night with Sandy. And no matter how much she was itching to get started, no matter how good her mother's glass of wine sounded at the moment while she champed at the bit, Lucy was not going to risk doing any work on the Wakerby case in her mother's presence. Or in her home. The chance of Sandy seeing something, having a relapse, was not worth it.

Keep me posted.

Course. Anything with employer?

No extra gas, just different time. Truck likely not full when picked up in morning explains early stop.

Lucy read the text again.

And then typed, Had to turn in gas receipts.

Yes.

Receipt with time stamp could be used as alibi.

Yes. So maybe not dead end.

Agreed, she typed.

Question.

Go.

You ever consider trusting a guy when he's not working?

Lucy started to sweat. ???

Personally, not professionally.

He wasn't suggesting… He couldn't be asking…

Could he?

Depends. She had no idea what to do.

On what?

Was he flirting with her? Did she really want him to? She'd clearly been afflicted with a desire to jump his bones, but beyond that…

The guy.

Oh.

She stared at her phone. That was it? He was going to leave it like that?

She reread their string. Which had started with him asking her if she'd had a hot date. Her stomach had butterflies. Like the salad she'd shared with her mother for dinner wasn't sitting well with her, although she couldn't imagine what, in a grilled chicken salad, would upset her stomach.

Her phone remained still. No messages popping in. Was

he going to throw something like that out there and then just go without even saying good-night?

Why did you ask? she typed carefully and sent.

Wondered. The reply shot right back. Had he been waiting for her to say something?

Lucy shook her head. This is all too confusing. Did you have a guy in mind?

She wasn't breathing properly. And wanted to drop her phone when the reply came back. A good detective knew when she was in over her head.

Knowing was the difference between living and dying.

Yeah.

Who?

Her screen flashed. He'd answered. Lucy got up and went to the bathroom. Down the hall from her mother's room, not the one in her mother's room. She did her business. Finished. Sat on the side of the tub, biting her lower lip.

You'd think she was in high school. Except that she'd never been a ninny in high school. Not even once. She'd been too busy dealing with life to have a single ninny moment.

She thought of Ramsey, alone somewhere in the middle of the night, sending a text and waiting for a reply.

It'd be cruel to make him wait. He didn't deserve that.

She pushed the green button on her phone. Opened up the text message waiting for her.

It was all of one word.

Me.

CHAPTER SIXTEEN

AFTER SENDING HIS LUDICROUS TEXT—which he was going to explain away by the one beer he'd had after work at Bill's invitation several hours before—Ramsey opened the Jack Colton folder.

Halfway through the first couple of pages, he picked up his phone, just to make certain he hadn't missed something coming in.

Nothing.

There was nothing new in the first few pages of the folder, either.

It wasn't like Lucy to walk away from anything. Obviously he'd offended her.

Because he needed her input on the Claire Sanderson case, he picked up his phone, reopened the text conversation between the two of them and typed, Sorry, with one thumb.

She'd warned him. It could appear that he'd ignored her warning. Just what she'd probably expect a guy to do.

For what?

Pushing.

Pushing what?

Not sure.

???

Leave it.

Not a good idea.

He frowned. The whole thing was out of control. What do you want?

To know what you want.

That was easy. Your trust.

You've got it.

Relaxed, he made his second stupid move of the night. Outside of business?

Why in the hell had he done that? He picked up the folder again. And heard his text message tone before he'd focused on the first Jack Colton page.

Yes.

Lying there nude, with the covers halfway up his chest, Ramsey nodded. Squirmed in the bed a bit.

And then said, Good. Night.

Night.

He went back to work with a smile on his face.

JACK COLTON'S HANDSHAKE was firm. He looked Ramsey straight in the eye and took the seat Ramsey offered. The same one Lonna Baker had occupied the morning before.

"Coffee?" he asked, standing by the pot on the counter.

"Yes, thank you." Colton's tone was respectful.

"Cream or sugar?"

"Black."

Ramsey poured himself a cup, as well. Black and strong. He took his time before he sat across from the man and officially started the interview. He needed the time. He couldn't get a read on Jack Colton. Either the guy was as honest and good as he seemed or he was the best actor Ramsey had ever met.

The best criminal. He'd never met one without a chink of some kind.

"Thank you for coming in." With nothing left to do, he sat.

"If I can be of any assistance… I feel horrible about that man, Frank Whittier. I can't sleep for thinking about the twenty-five years he's lost. Those years are on my shoulders. If I'd known…"

Colton's gaze was direct; the moisture in his eyes real.

There were no other suspects. And little girls did not just evaporate into thin air.

Something happened to Claire Sanderson.

And there wasn't a single person involved who was not cooperating completely. Everyone seemed to sincerely want to help. To know what happened.

Someone had to be lying.

His money was on Jack.

"I've had a look at your bank records."

"You what? How? Why?" Jack's brow furrowed.

"I got a warrant."

Ramsey watched every nuance of the other man's countenance, finding his way in.

"You got a warrant." Confusion gave way to resignation in the older man's expression. "Well, I hope you're satisfied with your findings," Jack Colton continued in a voice bearing not the least bit of fear. "I would have turned everything over to you if you'd have asked. I have nothing to hide."

Ramsey wished he had proof to argue that point.

And that was why Colton was there. To give Ramsey his proof.

"I had a visit with your former employer yesterday. Randall Davenport."

"His father was my employer."

"He passed away. Randall runs the business now."

"I suspect it's doing well, then. Randy was a bit squirrelly, with little sense of humor, always one step above the rest of us, but he was also honest and organized as hell. Even more so than his father."

Thinking of the binders lining the walls of Davenport's office, the orderly files in the basement, Ramsey had to acknowledge that Jack Colton was good at reading people.

So he could be good at working them.

Like he was trying to work Ramsey?

"You're right about one thing," he said now, opening his

binder. "Davenport keeps meticulous records." He pulled out the delivery time sheet from the day Claire Sanderson went missing and slid it in front of Jack. "This shows an unscheduled gas stop that just happens to coincide with the time frame of Claire Sanderson's disappearance."

Colton looked over the sheet, but only briefly enough to identify it. "The truck I drew that day came in half empty the night before," he said, his gaze still openly meeting Ramsey's.

"And you remember that? More than twenty-five years later?"

"I remember because it was the morning the little girl went missing. I lost time going back around the block to check on her, and then had to stop for gas."

"I'm just wondering," Ramsey said, leaning forward. "If you noticed the truck was low on gas in the morning, why didn't you stop for gas right away? Or wait until lunch? Why go right after Claire Sanderson went missing?"

Colton blinked. And then said easily, "I did it then because there was an accident stopping traffic and making the light at the intersection permanently red. The only way around the traffic was to cut through the gas station. One of our drivers had just been given a ticket for cutting through a gas station to avoid a red light, and beyond that, in our drivers' safety manual it told us never to cut through parking lots to avoid traffic. I did quick calculations and figured I would spend less time getting gas and leaving via the other side of the gas station than sitting in the traffic. As I just said, I'd already lost time that morning."

The explanation was given slowly, clearly, as though Colton were speaking with someone who struggled to understand.

Or because Ramsey was getting to him?

"You know, Detective, you're all alike. You guys get some kind of mind-set of what makes a criminal and you look at every case through the same eyes. Frank Whittier had been seen with the child in his car, so he must have done it, right?

Because statistics tell that more times than not a child abduction involves a family member or close friend."

Colton knew more than the average citizen.

"And now you find out that I was in the area. I was young, in need of money and driving an enclosed truck so I must have done it."

The profile fit. And the reason profiles existed was because human nature was human nature. Human beings naturally acted in certain ways. And patterns of behavior solved crimes. Successfully.

"Maybe if someone had looked outside the cop perspective, or away from all of the personalities you learn about in detective school, you'd have found that little girl."

Now Colton was pissing Ramsey off.

"You watch a lot of cop shows?" he asked quietly.

"No. Cable is a waste of money. I read. I also wonder, did anyone ever check the big sewage drain just down from that little girl's home? You know the kind that are big enough for kids to stand up in? The kind where you see drug deals being made? That's the first place I would have looked."

Everything inside of Ramsey stilled. The room was encased in cotton, buffering Colton's words so they would not be lost.

"I'm sure they did," Ramsey said, when he wasn't sure at all. He knew those early reports front and back and sideways, too. There'd been no mention of a drainage ditch or sewer of any kind. But the entire area had been searched. Multiple times. By hundreds of people.

"Why would it be the first place you'd look?" he asked as though they were just making conversation.

"Because one day when I was on my route, a couple of little kids were out on a driveway trying to lob a basketball into a hoop that was way too high for them to reach. It caught my attention. Just then one of the kids tossed the ball up—it missed, hit the pole, rolled into the street and down into that ditch. Next thing I know the kid was tearing across the street after his ball. He ran right in front of me. If I hadn't been watching, I could have hit him. I didn't wait to see him come back up out of the pipe with his basketball, because I would have gotten behind schedule, but I never drove on that street again without watching for kids running into or out of that pipe."

Colton should have been a writer. His attention to detail was remarkable.

Or...he was telling the truth.

"I did not take that little girl, Detective."

"Then you won't mind giving us a sample of your DNA, will you? Just so we can verify that you don't turn up on any of our evidence?"

Jack Colton opened his mouth.

Ramsey pulled a cotton swab tube out of his pocket, took the swab, closed the tube, slid it back into his pocket and then said, "I also paid a visit to UC." He wasn't stopping until he knew everything there was to know. Until he had all the answers. He tapped the black portfolio he'd set on the table when he'd come in. Some of Colton's records were there, not all of them.

Jack Colton's gaze narrowed, but the man looked more aggravated than alarmed.

"I had a warrant for your records." Ramsey's coffee was getting cold as he kept one hundred percent focus on his suspect.

"You're digging deep," Jack replied. He hadn't touched his coffee, either.

"I met Chester Brown."

"He's still there?"

"No, he's retired. I paid a visit to his home."

"He's well, then?"

"Seemed to be."

"I'm glad. I liked Chester."

"Then why didn't you stay in touch with him?"

"Because when I lost that scholarship, I had the choice to

let the disappointment sour me, or to move on. I chose to move on. I've spent much of my life fighting against the chip that would like to rest on my shoulder, Detective. Things other people take for granted, I've had to fight for. I've never known the security of unconditional love. Or a guaranteed roof over my head. I never had visits from Santa at Christmastime or home-cooked holiday meals that weren't charity handouts. I sure as hell never had anyone who would help me through college, or buy my first car, or help pay for insurance. I knew a long time ago that I had two choices. I could either feel sorry for myself, wear the chip, hate the world, take what I deserved, or I could stand up to the challenge, work hard, be a decent person and make the most of my life. I chose the latter."

"With the exception of not coming forward the day that little Claire Sanderson went missing. It wasn't such a decent thing, letting Frank Whittier take the fall just to save your ass."

Colton's gaze didn't falter. "No, it wasn't," he said, looking Ramsey straight in the eye. "And that's a choice I regret deeply. But do you really blame me, Detective?" Colton laid both hands on the table. "You've proven my point. This is why I didn't come forward twenty-five years ago. I've done nothing wrong, but you're poking into every aspect of my life, talking to people I associated with, laying doubt as to my innocence. You're investigating me, Detective! Simply because I was doing my job at a time and place where someone else did something hideous."

The man didn't raise his voice. But he was showing emotion. A step in the right direction.

"I'm older now, Detective. And self-employed. I can handle the negative aspects of being interrogated, but twenty-five years ago I was a kid starting out. I had very little savings, no means to get a better education and no parents to fall back on. The only thing I had was my reputation and if you'd done then what you're doing now—which we both know you would have—I could have lost every chance I had at a decent life."

None of which meant that Colton did not take that little girl.

"Chester told us that you had a girlfriend while you were at UC."

"I dated."

"Someone outside of UC."

"That's what I told the baseball team."

"It wasn't true?"

"I didn't have a girl, period," Colton said, his gaze as direct as always. "I dated a couple of girls a few times, but that was it. I knew I couldn't get involved. I had nothing to offer anyone, no ability to support anyone."

Not many freshmen in college thought about supporting their dates.

"I most certainly would not have brought a girl to any of those baseball parties. I didn't date those kinds of girls. And even if I did, I wouldn't subject any girl to the avaricious appetites of those immature, egotistical clods. They didn't know when to say when."

"You remember any of the girls' names? Or anything about them?"

"One. Haley Sanders," Colton said without hesitation. To remember a casual date's name that easily after so many years meant something.

That the girl had made an impression? That Jack Colton was as careful with every single aspect of his life as he was with his money?

"She was sweet, different. More mature than the rest of the girls I knew."

"You remember anything about her? Her parents? Was she a student?"

"I met her outside a movie theater near campus. She was waiting on a date who stood her up. I never met her family. Or knew that much about her. She didn't like to talk about her life. We met up a few times, but I never even had a phone number for her. She always called me, which is how the guys knew she existed. We had a pay phone in the hall on our floor and I wasn't always there to get her calls."

"You hear from her lately?"

"Not since a week before the cuts were announced. Whether I made the team or not, I told her I couldn't continue to see her."

"Why couldn't you see her?" He made himself sound merely curious. And had a feeling the answer was important.

"Because I liked her. A lot. And I could tell she was liking me a lot, too."

"And that meant it had to end?"

"Yes. I was not going to settle down until I had the means to provide."

Right. Colton had already said that.

But he'd seemed to live it, too.

"You've got the means now."

"Yes."

"By the looks of things, you've had them for a while."

"That's correct."

"Then why haven't you settled down?"

"I never met another Haley."

The ring of sincerity in the man's tone almost convinced Ramsey that Jack Colton was telling the truth.

CHAPTER SEVENTEEN

LUCY DIDN'T WAIT FOR Ramsey to call her. No more late-night conversations between them unless there was an emergency that needed immediate attention. Those intimate hours in the dark of the night were far too personal, and reserved for her most private moments.

Saturday, an hour after his scheduled meeting with Jack Colton, Lucy called Ramsey. She was on her way home from Cincinnati—an impromptu trip to see Lori Givens, off the clock, with hopes of picking up the hair ribbon that Claire Sanderson had worn—disappointed and empty-handed. She'd pulled in to get gas and dialed Ramsey while she waited for a pump to clear.

"Miller." She recognized his business voice in the one word.

"You at the office?"

"Yes."

"I won't keep you," she said. "I just wanted to know how things went with Colton."

"I got his DNA."

She smiled at the tiny bit of ego she heard in his voice. "Good for you!"

"I actually have a few things to tell you when I can talk freely. Can I call you tonight?"

No. She'd made a decision. She knew her limits. Had a weakness where he was concerned.

Just like her mother's weakness for alcohol.

"Of course."

She'd always been reticent by nature—she rarely shared anything—and suddenly she was wanting to tell this detective, this man, everything. Every thought. Every feeling.

"I'm on my way to Boston. Following a lead. I pulled over to take your call but was planning to call you when I got home."

The bad mood her dead-end trip to Cincinnati had caused suddenly dissipated.

Nothing was resolved, different or better in any way, but she was smiling.

He'd been planning to call her.

"You're like a fine glass of wine at the end of the day, Detective. You better watch out or I might get addicted."

Lucy's throat was dry again.

"Are you getting fresh with me, Detective?" she said back, in a voice she didn't recognize. At all.

"Depends."

"On what."

"On what you'd do if I was."

"Oh." She didn't know what she'd do. What in the hell was going on? Ramsey Miller had no more interest in a relationship with anyone than she did.

But she was dying to sleep with him. Had she given herself away? Or was he fantasizing about her, too?

"I'll talk to you tonight, okay?"

"Yeah. Talk to you tonight," she said, but he'd already disconnected their call.

LUCY STOPPED IN TO SEE Sandy and Marie. The two women were sitting at the table playing cribbage. Sandy was winning. Of course. Her mother was great at cards. Luckily Marie enjoyed playing and didn't mind losing.

She'd called Ramsey. She'd seen her mother. She wasn't expected at work until Monday. Which left her with the unaccounted-for time she needed.

Time to do what she had to do without having to answer questions. Or listen to lectures about protocol, safety, cop smarts or her lack of professional detachment.

She drove across town, out of town, to the grocery store where Sandy had stopped for baby food that fateful day so long ago. The store had been remodeled, the parking lot repaved, but the basic structure was still the same.

Today's market bore security cameras at every outside corner and interspersed throughout the store, as well.

Parking where her mother had parked, Lucy walked into the store, collected a basket and walked around the store, stopping for a time at the baby-food aisle, looking for diapers. And milk. She continued on through an empty checkout and back outside, without picking up a single item. Pushing the basket with the metal child seat inches from her body, she imagined Allie sitting there, propped up with her blanket because she had just started sitting up completely by herself.

As she stood outside the store, people passed her, going into the store. Coming out. Car tires swerved as they pulled into parking places.

It had been a Saturday, just like this one. Almost the same time of day.

How had Wakerby gotten her mother and a baby into his car without anyone in the busy parking lot noticing?

What had Sandy been thinking about? And when Wakerby showed up, how had she felt? Had she known right away that she was in danger? Had she been stronger then?

Reports said that there'd been debris under her fingernails, as though she'd fought back.

The Sandy Lucy knew would have fallen apart, but had her mother always been that way?

Would a woman with no ability to cope have been able to have a baby alone, and work and care for the child?

Sandy had done so.

And what about Allie?

"Are you okay, dear?" A gray-haired woman, sixty-five or so, stopped with a basket full of bagged groceries on her way out of the store. Her brow was creased with concern as she looked at Lucy.

"Oh, yes, I'm fine," Lucy said, moving over a couple of feet with her basket, out of the way of the door. "I'm…waiting for someone," she said with a smile.

The woman didn't look quite convinced. But she went on her way. Lucy watched her load her groceries into the back of a Cadillac sedan and then waved as the woman drove past.

So how had Allie felt that awful day? Had the baby sensed danger? Had she had any idea that her life was about to change irrevocably?

Talk to me, Allie. Tell me about that day. Take me to you.

Closing her eyes, Lucy focused on the young woman Sandy would have been. On the baby in the cart. She focused so hard she could almost see them there. And she waited.

No huge lightning bolt flashed inside her mind. No voices spoke. But Lucy knew when it was time to move on. Walking out to her car with the basket, she imagined herself unloading groceries. She opened the driver's side door.

Why? Why was that door open with a baby in the cart? Wouldn't Sandy have gone to the passenger's side door first, strapped Allie into her car seat and then proceeded to the driver's side?

They'd found the car with the car seat intact, bearing no fingerprints but her mother's and Allie's, and the driver's door open. Did that mean that Allie was already in the car when Wakerby appeared? Had her mother left her door unlocked as she got into the car? Lucy could picture the man yanking open her mother's door, hauling her mother out of the car, but what about Allie? How did he contain her mother, who would have been frantic to protect Allie if nothing else, and get a child out of a car seat all without attracting attention?

Or had Sandy had Allie in her arms, planning to sit in the driver's seat and from there lift Allie into her car seat?

Had Wakerby come upon her while the door was still open and hauled her, holding her baby, out of the car?

Once he had them both, Sandy would have done anything he said to keep him from hurting Allie. Standing at her car door, Lucy could picture the whole thing. Wakerby had probably pulled up right next to her mother.

"Get in the car without making a sound or your baby dies."

If he'd had Sandy in his grasp, while she had Allie in hers, what would Sandy have done?

She'd have gotten in the man's car.

Lucy got into her own car. Pulled out the map she'd marked that morning with different colors highlighting different routes.

Amber Locken was interested in the numbers they'd found written down among Wakerby's things, too. She was pursuing different theories regarding them and some of the other things in that box, too. Like Lucy, Amber thought the numbers might be coordinates, but she was looking at Sloan Wakerby as a rapist, looking for other rapes that he could have committed. Thinking that if the numbers were map coordinates, they might lead her to another crime. And another woman.

As Lucy drove, she kept young Sandy and six-month-old Allie focused in her mind. Tried to imagine how they might have felt that day. What they might have suffered.

And she watched every inch of the road—in front of her and both sides. She had no idea what she was looking for. Just knew she had to look.

She'd followed Amber's theory and mapped the numbers they'd found in Wakerby's things on an Aurora map, leading from the grocery store. But she wasn't looking for another rape victim.

She was in hell. Feeling the blows to her mother's skin as if they were her own. Feeling desperate. Afraid.

When had Sandy's eyes swollen? At the beginning of her hours-long ordeal? Had she been nearly unconscious, nearly blinded, before the man had raped her?

Or had those blows to her eyes come later? How conscious had she been when her arm had been broken?

Lucy took the shortest route first, between the grocery store and the place where the numbers came together on the area map. The site was less than twenty miles from the parking lot she'd left.

"In point four miles, turn right." Bonnie's voice sounded foreign in the car.

And Lucy didn't see any road upon which to turn.

She slowed, ready to take up one of her regular pastimes and argue with Bonnie, but at the last second, she saw the dirt road to her right. It was hard to believe the strip of tire marks would be on a GPS system, or even on a map.

Lucy inched her way around the corner, watching intently. Right. Left. For a ditch. A mark on a tree. Anything that might give her indication of life, twenty-five years earlier in time.

"Drive point six miles and arrive at destination, on right."

Keeping her car at less than five miles per hour, Lucy approached the unknown. Bare, gnarly branches entangled so tightly she couldn't see where one tree began and another ended, forming a canopy above her. Dried-out remnants of the glorious oranges and reds and yellows of the fallen leaves covered the ground and most of the track upon which she drove. Clearly no other car had been on the road in a while.

She rounded a corner, about three-tenths of a mile from her destination. The road grew darker. She imagined Sandy there, knowing what had to be coming in her near future. Fearing for her baby's life.

Had Allie been crying then?

Had she still been with them?

Had she ever been with them?

In her mind's eye Lucy saw her favorite picture of the sister she'd never known, taken just a week before the abduction. The baby had been dressed in a red dress with white stars and underneath had been white pantaloons. Her cheeks were chubby and so were her arms. They were reaching out toward someone—Lucy knew that someone was Sandy. And the look of pure joy on that baby's face, the smile, had been with Lucy all of her life.

Picturing that baby here, picturing her mother here, knowing what had happened to Sandy, being unable to prevent it, hurt so badly she wasn't sure she could bear the pain. Wasn't sure she could continue.

She couldn't make it better. Not for any of them.

Tears filled her eyes and she ignored them as they spilled over and ran slowly down her cheeks. She couldn't help them, either.

"Arriving at destination."

Oh, Bonnie, do you have any idea where you've brought me? And what happened here?

What *might* have happened there. She had no idea at all if those numbers were coordinates. And if they were, what map they were coordinates for.

But the numbers meant something. Something more than another rape. Wakerby had been adamant about not "doing babies." Had something happened with Allie? Something important enough that Wakerby had written down map coordinates so he could make it back to this spot?

Was there something of Allie's here?

Was this just a memory for him? Maybe one of the few good memories in his life?

Or were the numbers significant in some other way entirely?

Getting out of the car, Lucy wiped her eyes, but couldn't stop the moisture from filling them right back up.

It wasn't completely night yet, but it was dark enough that she had her flashlight out and was shining it in an arc in front of her. She turned, and arced again. And again. Standing completely still, she surveyed the area, afraid that if she moved, she might somehow destroy evidence. She realized that the thought was ludicrous. She'd just driven on the land she was standing on.

And twenty-five years of weather, rain and snow included, would have long ago washed away any evidence that might have been present. She took a few steps. And a few more, her eyes dry now as she concentrated.

She knew what to look for. Anything out of the ordinary. Anything that didn't seem right. Anything disturbed from its natural state.

Darkness was falling rapidly and she was out in the middle of nowhere, presumably on private land, though she'd seen no fences or signs marking it so. Someone had trenched a road out here. Someone had seen that the road made it on a map. Maybe there was a house down at the end of the road. Maybe an address that would have been recorded for postal delivery.

She felt like Sandy and Allie were right there with her, but knew that feeling was more a consequence of the afternoon she'd put herself through than any kind of intuition.

She also knew that the best way to solve a crime was to get inside of it. To be able to figure out what happened, she had to understand what people were thinking. Feeling. She had to know what drove them to do what they did.

Leaves crunched beneath her feet. And something rustled off to her right. She wasn't all that far from Aurora. It wasn't as though there were bears in the area.

There were deer. And skunks and porcupines and…

Had someone seen her drive in? A female all alone? Had they followed her?

Hand on her gun, Lucy continued to look around. Maybe she could have waited to make this trek, but waited how long? Wakerby was talking to his lawyer on Monday. She had no faith that the D.A. would deny a deal. And if a deal was made, Wakerby could be out on bail by Monday night.

Another noise, more than just the wind whistling through the branches, stopped her for a second. She could go back. The car was only thirty feet away. But she was with Sandy all day on Sunday. And Monday she started five shifts—two evening rotations to allow her to be at home with Sandy for Thanksgiving dinner—and then it was off to Comfort Cove for Emma's wedding.

She couldn't wait another eight or nine days to check these coordinates.

She wasn't leaving.

She heard more rustling and almost changed her mind. Until her light passed over a turkey hurrying through the brush toward the road. Presumably to get away from her—the human who'd disturbed its Saturday-evening repose.

Walking on, Lucy shined her light first in front of her and then, turning, behind her, studying every inch of the ground she passed from both angles.

She felt as if she had to pee, but knew she was just scared. About twenty minutes into the trek, she was studying a mound of earth and tripped over a tree root. Her hands came out in front of her, the flashlight flying out of her grasp as she broke her fall, but her left hand slid on the leaves and she came down hard with her chin on another part of the root. Or a different root.

She couldn't be sure. She just knew that her head was spinning, her mouth was bleeding where she bit her tongue and her chin stung. Lying still for a moment, Lucy took stock of herself enough to know that nothing was so severely damaged that she couldn't move.

Slowly, gingerly, she sat up. To face the mound of earth that was now right in front of her. There was something odd about the mound, which was what had stolen her attention to begin with, causing her to miss seeing the root she'd tripped over.

Grabbing her flashlight, and still sitting down, she scooted closer to the mound of earth.

It wasn't new earth. Wasn't disturbed earth. But it was different earth. The entire foot and a half round piece of earth not only hilled up slightly, but it was covered in a thick growth of moss. Not roots. Not the dry, long strands of grass that covered the rest of the earth around her, but moss.

She hadn't seen any other moss in the area and shined her light around just to make sure.

At the same time, she remembered reading once about how things being buried below the surface of the ground affected what grew on top of the ground, which was one reason why topography could change from one inch to the next even under the same sky with the same weather in the same climate.

Dizzy, with a wet and stinging chin—bleeding, she suspected—Lucy figured that she was in over her head. She was supposing based on need, not on fact, or evidence. And she couldn't let it go.

Some part of her recognized that she was losing it as she clawed at the dirt. She knew, on some level, as she felt the dirt and growth beneath her nails, that she should stop. She should get in her car, drive home, take a hot bath and go to bed. Or call someone for help.

What kind of help she wasn't sure. Didn't matter. She had to dig. She had to do this herself.

Didn't matter what her mind told her. Didn't matter if she looked crazy. If she *was* crazy.

She couldn't stop. Her fingers dug. She hurt all over. She was aware of her own cries in the darkness. And she couldn't slow her arms down.

Tasting blood, but driven from the inside out, Lucy continued to dig. She'd tire herself out. Satisfy herself that she'd done all she could do. She'd drive away and no one would ever know that for a short time on a Saturday night in November she'd taken leave of her senses.

Several minutes later, she was still digging, stopping only long enough to take off her scarf, place it over her chin and tie it at the back of her neck. Pulling her gun out of her holster, she used the butt to get through some rock. Something caused that moss to grow, and Lucy had to know what it was.

Maybe an underground trickle of water. A leak in the water table? Was such a thing possible? Probably not.

She kept digging. With both hands. When the hole got too deep for her to reach sitting up, she lay down on her belly. Her cell phone dug into her hip bone. She didn't care. She dug.

The back end of her pistol was covered in dirt. She didn't care. She dug.

Time passed and she had no idea how late it had grown. Or how early it might be. Her head throbbed. Her chin stung. She still tasted blood. And she dug.

She hadn't found anything yet.

She had to find something.

Had to find what made that moss grow.

She was crying. Her tears were dripping off the end of her nose into the dirt. They made her face itch but she couldn't scratch. Her hands were caked with dirt. The tips of her fingers had grown numb. And she just couldn't stop.

And then she did. With her right hand, Lucy scooped down as far as her arm would go, scooping out the next handful of dirt, and scraped her knuckles on something hard. And sharp. And crusty.

A rock, she first thought. Turning her hand, she felt the object with blistered and bleeding fingers. And froze. Lucy's head fell to the earth, catching on the opening of the hole she'd dug, stopping there as her arm hung in the ground. She couldn't pull up the object in her fingers. And she couldn't let go.

She wasn't sure what she held, at least not on a conscious level. Her whole body was shaking. Her heart pounded and she was breathing like she'd run a marathon. After a couple of minutes of lying still, she gave a tug. The object gave way and Lucy brought it to the surface.

A bone.

She'd known. Maybe. The second her fingers felt the aged piece of calcium in the ground.

But she didn't want to know. It was probably an animal bone. Something that died long, long ago.

Maybe even a dinosaur bone.

Sitting up, the piece of bone still in her hand, Lucy stared into the hole. She couldn't dig any farther without a tool.

And through the fog surrounding her mind, she had the thought that she probably shouldn't do anything more, anyway. Just in case this was a crime scene.

She should never have disturbed a crime scene.

Looking down, she stared in the darkness at the fragment in her hand. She tried to loosen her fingers, to see if she could tell anything about the bone—what kind of bone, from what kind of creature—but she couldn't let go. Tears dripped onto her fist. She didn't want to wet the evidence.

With her left hand, Lucy reached for her cell phone. Pushed a button. Listened to the ringing.

"Aurora Police."

"This is Detective Hayes." It didn't sound like her.

"Yes, Detective, I recognize your cell-phone number."

Lucy should know who she was talking to. She didn't.

"Can you please put me through to Captain Smith?"

"Yes, ma'am. Are you all right, ma'am?"

"I'm fine, just—"

The ringing on the line as the dispatcher connected her interrupted Lucy's sentence.

The phone crackled and she jumped. "Smith."

"Lionel? This is Lucy."

"What's wrong? Where are you?"

Oh, God, she didn't know. Yes, she knew. No. No, she didn't.

"Ping my cell, Lionel. I'm in the woods. I have a bone. And my head hurts…."

She got the pertinent stuff out. Then, hanging up, she sat there in the dark, clutching the bone. Prepared to wait.

CHAPTER EIGHTEEN

RAMSEY DROVE HOME from Boston with one thought on his mind. Calling Lucy Hayes. He'd had a long day. An up and down day. A good day in some ways. And still, he thought about Lucy.

He was changing. He wasn't happy about that. But he wasn't fighting it, either. He knew better than to fight the inevitable. Best just to prepare to survive it.

This "thing" with Lucy would be short-lived. She'd made it clear she wanted nothing more than a professional relationship. That's all he wanted or had time for. That was all he'd trust himself to entertain. They lived several states apart. As soon as they solved the cases they shared an interest in, they'd wander off in other directions and lose touch.

But maybe, in the interim, they would share a bed. At least once.

Somewhere over the past days, he'd begun to count on it.

So he thought about her as he reached Comfort Cove, drove straight home, grabbed a juice bottle out of the refrigerator, stripped down and climbed into bed, taking his laptop and cell with him.

Only when he was settled back against the mound of pillows, with his laptop booted up, did he pick up his cell and push the speed-dial button he'd assigned to her. Just for now. While they were working together.

Less than a week and they'd be together. The wedding was only a week away. Could be, this time the following week, she'd be right there in his house. Assuming she stayed with him.

He'd stayed with her....

He wasn't offering her his spare bedroom.

She wasn't answering her phone.

At midnight?

Or at 12:15 a.m. or 12:30 a.m.

She could be on a date. The thought wasn't pleasant, but it wasn't horrible, either. This "thing" between them would be less complicated if she was dating someone.

He called again at one.

So maybe he'd scared her off with his fine-wine comment. For all of her strength and energy and determination, Lucy Hayes was fragile.

Which was why he was getting worried.

He'd give it fifteen more minutes and if she still wasn't answering, he was going to call Lionel Smith, Lucy's captain. If he woke the man up in the middle of the night, it wouldn't be the first time someone had done so.

Thirteen minutes later, his phone rang.

"Hello?" He put a rein on his fear. If she was fine, then everything was good.

"I saw you called. Sorry I missed you."

She wasn't fine. At all. She was talking like she had marbles in her mouth. Or had just been to the dentist. Or something... Sitting up, his entire being on alert, Ramsey said, "What's wrong?"

Had she been crying?

Her mother again?

"I..."

"Lucy?" She was scaring him. "Where are you? Are you okay?"

"I'm home." He started to breathe a little easier.

"And?"

"I took a drive tonight, Ramsey." Her voice wasn't just tired. It was weak. He waited.

"I mapped those numbers from Wakerby as coordinates on an Aurora area map."

With several uncharacteristic pauses and starts and stops, she told him about starting at the grocery store where her mother had been attacked. About coming to a dirt track and trees and looking around.

"I fell, hit my chin. I've just come from the emergency room. I'm not concussed, but I punctured the side of my tongue and have four stitches in my chin."

Her tongue injury explained some of the difference in her speech.

"You fell?"

"Tripped over a root."

Lucy hadn't been watching where she was going? Didn't sound right.

"I…just…went a little crazy, Ramsey. Thing is, I knew it. I just didn't stop myself. I was so determined to find something."

Another pause. Frustrated that he was so far away, that he couldn't do more, Ramsey waited.

"What if we don't break Wakerby? He meets with his lawyer on Monday, and then who knows? We still only have him for Mama's rape. The DNA evidence could be thrown out. Which only leaves Mama's testimony and she's a wreck. Any half-decent defense attorney could cast doubts on her ability to get things straight. He might walk."

"If he does, you'll get him again."

"I can't just sit back and let that happen. I have to look at everything."

"You weren't wrong to look, Lucy. It's what any good cop would have done."

"That's not what Lionel said."

"You've seen your captain?"

"I called him."

"From the emergency room?" He wished she'd have called him. But maybe she'd needed a ride home.

"No. From the woods. I saw this mound. I dug a hole. And…I found a bone."

Fully focused, alert, he stood up, pulled his slacks off the top of the dry-cleaning bag and, one-handedly, put them on. "A bone."

"It's a fragment from a human bone, Ramsey." Her words were starting to slur and he wondered what drugs they might have given her at the hospital. "Lionel's got a uniform team going in at first light with shovels. We don't know yet if this one fragment is all there is."

Pacing his bedroom, Ramsey asked, "What did you use to dig the hole to begin with?"

A bone. She'd found a bone. At the site of the coordinates she gleaned from numbers she'd found in Wakerby's belongings. The woman was good. And far too bold and gutsy for her own good.

"My hands."

"And you dug deep enough to find a bone?"

"I told you, I kind of lost it."

He understood what drove her. He lived with the same forces pushing him from the inside out.

But he didn't worry about himself.

"Could you tell anything else about the fragment? Is it an arm or leg bone? What about the age of the victim?"

"We don't know anything yet and I'm not jumping to any conclusions. Lionel showed up with an ambulance and I had to leave the scene. He met me later, at the hospital, to tell me that he'd cordoned off the area and that the team would be there at first light."

"Did he have anything else to say?"

"Yeah. He's going to take my badge if I ever do anything so harebrained again. And he told me I'd done good work."

She still sounded like she was talking around something, but her voice was gaining momentum. And just a bit of humor.

He sat down on the side of the bed. "How do you feel?"

"Kind of numb. Like I'm outside myself looking in."

"Are you in pain?"

"Stiff, but no. They got some kind of painkiller into my IV before I could tell them I didn't want any."

"Do you have more with you?"

"Yes, but I'm not taking it. I'd rather hurt than have my head feel like fog. Pain, I can deal with."

The fog took away a measure of her control. Her power. He understood that, too.

"Are you there alone?"

"Yeah."

"Has anyone called your mother?"

"No. And I'm not going to tell her what happened, either."

"You've got stitches in your chin," he reminded her. He'd like to see her for himself. To be there just for the rest of the night.

"They're underneath my chin. I'd have to lift my head for her to see them. Besides, they're coming out in four days, she doesn't expect to see me until Thanksgiving day. She knows I'm on shift all week so that I can spend Thursday with her. If the bruising isn't better, I'll wear lots of makeup."

"You've got that well thought-out."

"It's second nature," she said, and took a deep breath.

"What?" he asked, telling himself that he was noticing every nuance about her because he noticed everything about everyone, because he was a good detective.

"I just bit my tongue," she said. "It's swollen and getting in my way."

"You want to hang up? We can talk tomorrow."

"No. Unless you want to. I know it's late."

He should let her rest. He didn't want to let her go. She was hurt. And alone.

"Are you in bed?"

"Lying on the couch. I don't have a television in my room and I plan on taking it easy in the morning. Lionel says he'll fire me if I show up at the station before Monday."

"Okay, you lie there, I'll talk."

"Good, I've been waiting to hear how things went with Jack Colton." Ramsey half smiled and half frowned at the way she sounded with her usual bravado returning, but a thick tongue and painkillers still in her system.

The woman was an enigma. A female version of himself— the parts he liked.

Still, he didn't like her being hurt. And alone. Didn't like the idea that she lived every day with the same dangers he took on.

And he knew there wasn't a damn thing he could do about any of it.

So he focused on work. Just as he'd always done.

He told her about his interview with Colton.

"So what's your take on him? You still like him for doing it?"

"Let's just say I'm not convinced he didn't do it," he told her. He'd been thinking about Colton on and off all day. "He could be telling the truth. All of the signs are there. His hand-shake was firm and confident. He looked me straight in the eye. He only blinked out of sequence once during the entire interview."

"When?"

He remembered exactly. "When I asked him about stop-ping for gas when he came upon the accident."

"What was his answer?"

He told her about Colton using the gas stop to legally cut through the station to avoid traffic and the red light.

"Sounds valid."

"Yeah. He's got an answer for everything."

"Because he's telling the truth?"

"Or because he's smart and he's one step ahead of us. He knows what we're going to ask before we ask and he has his answers all prepared. He's had twenty-five years to work on his stories."

"What does your gut tell you?"

He wanted to know what hers said. "That he might be telling the truth, but your scarcity-mentality theory keeps coming back to me, too. If he's being driven by a base need for safety and security and being chased by the belief that he'll never have enough, he could be capable of saying anything, in good conscience, because he feels justified in doing so since he's never had enough of anything."

"And yet, he has a conscience. Which would explain why he feels guilty about Frank Whittier. His actions created a scarcity for Frank."

"Exactly."

"And his lack of fear of being found out? How do you explain that?"

"He's confident that whatever he's hidden, and where he's hidden it, is undiscoverable."

"I agree. And that means you're going to have to look in the most obvious and least obvious places."

That was when Ramsey told her about the sewage ditch.

"Did you go there?"

"No, I'm doing that first thing in the morning. I intended to go this afternoon, but I got a hit on the Boston case and ended up going into the city instead."

"Did it pan out?" She was sounding tired again, her voice fading.

Ramsey told her about having gone through prison commissary records, focusing on the spending habits of perps who'd been arrested since 2000, looking, specifically, for chocolate-bar purchases. He hadn't found anything significant. Then he'd looked prior to that, honing in on those prisoners who'd been released before August of 2000. And he'd made a hit. A big one.

"I paid a visit to a Boston detective I know, showed him what I had, and they brought the guy in this afternoon—he's been working as a cook in a greasy spoon downtown for the past thirteen years. They tell the guy that they've got a DNA match on him for the August 2000 disappearances, which, by the way, took place shortly after his release from prison."

"They couldn't have a DNA match yet since you just fingered him. The match takes time."

"Right, but they will have it in time for trial. The guy broke. They got a full confession."

"And the girls?"

"He took them to an adoption agency half a block from where he works. They take children, no questions asked. Or they did. They're out of business as of this afternoon. Permanently, if Boston P.D. has any say in it. They claim they were doing a good service. They had statistics that showed how many children who are victims of abuse could be saved if it were easier for parents to drop their kids off, no questions asked, and know that they'd get to a good home."

"Rather than dropping them at a hospital or police station where they end up in the foster-care system," Lucy said.

"Right."

"They're right about that. Just because someone has issues, drug and money problems, youth working against them, doesn't mean that they don't love their kids. They want to know they're in loving homes. Eases their consciences if nothing else. Which is why they keep them when they can't give them proper care. They know that they're loved and hope that will be enough."

Was she speaking from the experience of having grown up in such a home? Or just because of things she'd seen during her years as a cop?

"Well, it isn't right that children can be taken from good

homes and dumped without any records being searched," he said, keeping his focus on the work.

"I agree. Any chance of finding the girls?"

"One has already been located. She'll be returned to her rightful family sometime this next week."

"A family she knows nothing about."

"Correct. And she'll be taken from the only family she's ever known. The parents that she loves."

Sometimes there were no good answers.

"Hopefully her biological parents will allow some kind of visitation."

"They might." He didn't think so, based on the wealthy couple's reaction when they'd been contacted late that afternoon. "And maybe it's in the kid's best interest to have that part of her life gone so that she can start anew."

He left those kinds of problems and answers up to the people who knew better about emotional issues than he did. His job was to serve and protect, not nurture.

"And the second girl?"

"They haven't located her yet. But they feel confident that they will."

"Have her parents been notified?"

"Yeah. I rode along for the notification. They're simple people—he works in construction and she's a beautician—but their whole lives revolved around finding their little girl. She's their only child and they're so grateful she's found. So grateful to know that she's probably safe and well cared for. They can't wait to see her, of course, but mostly they just want her to be all right."

"A good day."

Mostly. Until he couldn't reach her. And then knew that she was hurt and he was too far away to be of any help at all.

"Two more are found, two more cases closed," he said.

"Who would have thought that a penchant for chocolate bars would be a kidnapper's downfall?"

"It's how he lured the girls. He offered them some of the chocolate he always had on him. He kept them happy with it until he turned them over to the agency."

"Who paid money for them."

"You guessed it. He used the money to get back on his feet after prison. Down payment on a place. A car. Some furniture."

"And he'd have gotten away with it, too, if you hadn't been determined enough to research something as innocuous as chocolate."

"Everyone has his weak point."

"What's Jack Colton's? Other than his scarcity mentality?"

"If I knew that, the man would be behind bars."

"So, other than the sewage ditch, what's next with Colton?"

"I'm going to check on that girlfriend he mentioned, Haley Sanders. Depending on what I find, I might need you to follow up."

"Of course."

"And I'm still watching Frank Whittier, and will go back and take another look at what I have on him. I have to find the connection between the two—the time when they met and planned this thing, or met afterward. I've been thinking that maybe Jack saw Frank drive away with that little girl and made a deal with him to keep quiet in exchange for a steady income."

"Which could be why Jack is so believable when he says he didn't take Claire. Maybe the alibi for the time discrepancy is just the truth."

"Frank Whittier hasn't had a bank account that we can find since he left Comfort Cove. And Jack has been independently employed. Maybe some of his regular income has come from Frank," he offered.

"Which leads us back to the question of what happened to Claire. If Frank Whittier took her, what did he do with her?"

Running his hand through his hair, Ramsey had a brief thought of just staying where he was. In bed. He got so damned tired of answers that only led to more questions. And then he caught a couple of hours' sleep and had to go search for answers again.

Before he could come up with an answer he didn't have, Lucy continued. "And the blackmail angle doesn't explain Claire's DNA being in the Buckley home, which, by the way, isn't as clear-cut as we thought. Turns out that Claire's DNA wasn't taken from a hair ribbon, but from a hair found at the scene, probably in the box of ribbons. Anyway, there's no ribbon to trace."

"But the important thing, the connection, the knowledge that Claire was there, is still valid."

"Completely."

"And Jack's our connection between Comfort Cove and Aurora."

"Gladys Buckley had clients from the East Coast. It might be that Jack's time in Cincinnati is only a coincidence. As much as we don't believe in coincidences because they usually mean connections, maybe this time it is just a coincidence."

It was possible. "Is that what you think?"

"No."

"I don't, either." But he was willing to be wrong. As long as Claire Sanderson was found. "I talked to the DNA lab in Boston and was able to get them to move Jack's sample up on the list, but unless he touched something the girl left behind, we won't get a match." He leaned back against his pillows, still wearing his dress slacks.

"So you keep looking at what you've already seen."

Amelia Hardy had invited him over for a turkey dinner when he was off shift on Thursday. Maybe he could take another look at her activity records. Catalog the mentions of Jack Colton. There could be something....

"Something happened to Claire Sanderson, Ramsey. The answer is out there, waiting for you to find it."

Which was exactly why he kept looking.

"Hey, unrelated question for you…"

"Sure, what's up?"

"Are you at all worried that I'm losing it?"

"No." He was worried about her, but not about that.

"I scared myself."

"I know."

"Have you done that? Have you ever scared yourself?"

He was scaring himself right then by the way he was re-acting to her. And the fact that it was the middle of the night, he had to work in the morning and he wanted nothing more than to be on the next flight to Indiana. "Yes."

He had to get her into bed with him. And be done with this. Assuming she wanted to go to bed with him.

He'd never had a problem with that before.

"Pushing yourself like you did tonight is how you know how much you have in you to give." He started to talk to shut himself up. "It's like working out. You go until you drop and then you get up and go some more and somehow the pro-cess makes you a stronger athlete. You were exercising your strength as a detective."

She sighed. "Thank you."

"You're welcome." It was time to hang up. To separate from her and get on with the business of his life.

At least until she was actually in town…

"By the way, are you staying here with me next weekend? When you come for the wedding." He might as well get a start on things. "Since I'm your ride…" The tag-on was his pathetic attempt to pacify the part of him that knew better than to make the offer in the first place.

"I don't want to put you out."

"Turnaround is fair play." He had to offer. Because he'd accepted her offer and stayed with her in Aurora. His mother had taught him manners. "It'll save you the cost of a hotel."

"The hotels in the tourist district are rather expensive." She'd stayed there before.

"There aren't any decent hotels anywhere else in this town." The city had grown tremendously in the past twenty years, but it just wasn't big enough to support an upscale economy hotel for nontourists.

"And I sure can't have you driving back and forth to Boston." She'd stayed in Boston during her first trip to Comfort Cove. She'd rented a car at the airport to drive herself back and forth.

He'd let her do that—even though she'd been in town to help him with a case.

The second trip, she'd rented a car and stayed in the tourist district. He'd let her do that, too, without offering his hospitality.

"We don't know how late the reception is going to go." He continued to kid himself that there was an altruistic bone in his body.

"That's right." She sounded as though she was falling asleep. Maybe, with any luck, she wouldn't remember this conversation in the morning. After the drugs wore off. "Thank you, then. Yes, I'll stay with you."

"Good. Now get some rest."

"I don't think I have any choice."

She sounded like a petulant child and he chuckled. "I'll talk to you tomorrow."

"'K. Night, Ramsey."

"Night, sweetie."

The blood drained from his face. His hands froze.

Where had the endearment come from? He didn't use them.

And Ramsey prayed that Lucy had already been asleep before he'd made that last mammoth mistake.

CHAPTER NINETEEN

LUCY DIDN'T STAY HOME on Sunday. She couldn't risk her mother noticing a light on. Or watching for her car to leave. Or seeing the television flashing through the blind. For the first time in her life, she wasn't prepared to handle Sandy.

Getting up at her normal time, thanks to the alarm clock on her cell phone, she bathed instead of showered—keeping her chin dry—and with very tender fingers dressed in slacks and a crew-neck top and the navy jacket that went with the slacks, slipped on black loafers, strapped on her gun and left the house as usual.

Driving hurt her fingers, but if she gripped the steering wheel with her palms instead of her fingers it wasn't so bad. Not eager to lose her job, she bypassed the station and went down to the river. Something about the Ohio River, even on a cool November Sunday with only the big black cargo barges out on the water, gave her a feeling of strength. The river ran no matter what. Had for many more years than she'd been alive. And would for many years after she was gone, too.

The water put life into perspective.

She pulled into one of her favorite spots—a roadside parking lot with a few picnic tables scattered along the raised bank. She was exhausted. Didn't feel like walking. Or even getting out. She wanted safety. Security. She wanted to be at home without having to answer to Sandy. She wanted to sleep. And so she reclined the seat of her Rendezvous and went to sleep.

Her cell phone woke her. She knew immediately where she

was, but had no idea how much time had passed. A lot, based on the position of the sun in the sky.

The number had a Comfort Cove exchange.

"Hello?"

"Lucy? It's Emma. Sanderson."

"Emma!" She leaned forward, bringing her seat to its upright position. "How are you?"

"Good."

"And plans for the wedding? Are they driving you nuts?"

"Nope. Everything's under control," the high-school teacher said. Lucy wasn't really surprised. Emma Sanderson was the most organized, think-ahead person Lucy had ever met. And she'd thought she was bad.

But she understood. Completely. Emma had to control her environment for her mother's sake. Just as Lucy did.

"I got your RSVP. And Detective Miller's, too. I've put the two of you at the same table for dinner, if that's okay."

"It's fine. He offered to drive so I didn't have to be down at the docks at night."

"Good. That takes care of one of the reasons I called," Emma said, a lighter tone to her voice than Lucy was used to. "Since you're unfamiliar with the docks, I didn't want you down there after dark by yourself. They're safe enough during the day, but it's never good for a woman to be down at the docks alone, and not good for a woman to be alone outside at night, period. I'm arranging rides for all the female guests who are attending alone."

Emma and her mother, Rose, had a lot of close associates from the education field, and from all of the work they did to promote child-safety education. And Emma was Emma. Always careful.

"I'm really glad you're going to be here, Lucy."

"There's no way I'd miss being there. I just wish I had some good news to bring with me. Some closure for you. I swear to you, I won't give up on finding Claire, Em. And neither will Ramsey."

"I know. I take it there's no news on the missing evidence they retrieved? I figured Detective Miller would call if there had been, but…"

"Not yet. It's still at the lab in Boston. I have my lab here looking at the sample of Claire's DNA found in the Buckley home as well as comparing Claire's DNA against a sample from someone of interest, but still no answers there."

"I figured you'd call if you knew anything. I just… With the wedding so close…"

"How's your mother doing?" Would Rose be a blessing at the wedding, or a nightmare?

"Better than I expected. She likes Chris."

"How could she not?"

"He's a fisherman."

Emma and Claire's father had been a fisherman, too. He'd run out on them when Claire came along. And had been killed in a bar brawl not long after—by the husband of the woman he'd just slept with.

"So how about you? Any doubts?"

"Not about Chris."

"What, then?"

"I heard from Cal this morning. He's bringing his father to the wedding."

Frank Whittier. Instinctively, Lucy got excited. A wedding would be a perfect opportunity to observe the only other suspect in the case, to eavesdrop, to see others' reactions to him, to watch him around the mother of the child he possibly stole. She had to call Ramsey.

And then she thought about the wedding. About Emma. And was ashamed of herself.

"Does your mother know?" she asked softly. Rose and Frank had been engaged until Claire went missing, and after the police started looking at Frank, Rose blamed Frank. They'd broken up and neither of them had ever dated again.

"Apparently, though I haven't heard that from her yet. Cal just called. And I…I don't know. I called you."

Lucy smiled. "I'm glad you did." Glad to know that Emma held her in such high esteem. Because Emma filled an empty place inside of her, too. Allie's place? Or the place she imagined an older sister would have filled? "You said your mom knew but you didn't? How did she find out? What did Cal say?"

"Mom and Frank have talked and she agreed that it would be appropriate for him to be at my wedding as long as it was okay with me."

"Is it?"

"I honestly don't know." Emma's tone dropped. "I can remember a time before Claire was gone—I was about four so it must not have been long before that—I was playing Cinderella with my plastic high-heeled shoes and elasticized lace skirt. Frank came in from work just as I was making Cal stand at one end of the living room while I did my model walk toward him. Cal told Frank that I was making him be my prince. And Frank said that a girl as pretty as I was couldn't even think about getting married without a man to walk her down the aisle. He set his briefcase down and offered me his arm and it was one of the happiest moments of my life. Not because I was getting married, but because I somehow sensed that I finally had a full family. I didn't have to be afraid anymore like I had been after Claire was born and our biological father left us."

Lucy couldn't connect the picture Emma painted with the man she suspected of ripping that family irrevocably apart. And she couldn't encourage Emma to invite the man to her wedding, knowing that he might very well turn out to be the cause of all of her heartbreak.

"Do you want him to give you away?"

"No! Of course not. I'm not walking down any aisle and

no one is giving me away. Good Lord, Chris and I have been doing all we can to make certain that Mom knows that I'm not leaving her—she's just gaining a larger family."

The thought of dealing with Sandy were Lucy to ever get married gave Lucy a headache. She didn't know how Emma was holding up so well.

"I just… I loved Frank. And then spent so many years hating him. It's all mixed up, you know?"

Lucy thought about her trek through the woods the night before. "Yeah, I do. And that's the time you have to listen to your heart, Emma. That's all I know. Whether it's right or wrong, it's all you've got. And you'll always have it. If you act contrary to what your insides are telling you, you'll live to regret it."

So she'd dug in the dark until her fingers were blistered and bleeding.

"My heart tells me to tell Cal he can bring his father."

"Then I guess that's what you need to do."

For whatever reason.

"I think I knew that all along."

"I'm sure you did."

Lucy watched a barge make its way slowly up the river. In days past, those barges were the center of commerce in the Midwest. Times had changed, but they still floated. Still delivered.

"How are you doing?" Emma's question brought her focus back.

"There've been some developments on my sister's case." She said what she could, which wasn't much due to the fact that they were dealing with an ongoing investigation. "We made an arrest a few weeks ago." That was really saying too much. Aching, alone by the river, Lucy wished she could tell Emma about Wakerby. Emma would understand Lucy's craziness the night before.

"Does your mother know about the arrest?"

"Yes."

"And?"

Lucy told the other woman about her scare the week before, the night she'd spent in the hospital at her mother's bedside.

"At some point your mom's going to have to deal with what happened. She's not the only woman who's ever been raped. Or even lost a child. She has to take some accountability for herself."

Lucy had heard the words more times than she could count. And always discredited them because the speakers couldn't possibly know…couldn't possibly understand.

But this was Emma. Who did know.

Rose grieved. Emma's life had been hell in many ways. But her mother worked, too. She'd provided.

But Rose hadn't been raped…

"I don't see how you can stand it," Emma said. "It's like she doesn't even try to handle things."

"I guess I'm just used to it," Lucy said, leaning back in her seat to stare at the white clouds in the mostly blue sky. "Once when I was about six, I'd been chosen to be the narrator in a Christopher Columbus play. I had a special suit I had to wear—black pants and white blouse and a vest—and I felt so…important, you know? I could read and I had a piece of paper with my lines on it, but I memorized them all, anyway. I knew everyone would be looking at me and I had to be one hundred percent completely perfect."

"I know what you mean. It's like you have to make up for that which is glaringly imperfect about you. Because everyone knows about that, too."

"Mama was there," Lucy said now, speaking slowly as she relived that day. "Front and center, like she'd promised she would be."

She paused. Emma didn't speak.

"She was so proud of me."

Lucy knew that. Sandy lived and breathed for her.

"And she was so drunk that she couldn't put her two hands together to clap. At the end, we got a standing ovation, and Mama fell over a couple of chairs, causing this crash...."

Her face was hot. Just like it had been then.

"Oh, Luce. I'm so sorry."

"I got over it," she said. "And she tried so hard to make up for it. That was the first time she went into rehab. Marie stayed with me and when Mama got home she was better for a while. She was always there for me, Emma. I never for one second doubted that I was loved. She just couldn't handle the big moments."

Not any of them. Sandy had been present during every important event in Lucy's life, until Lucy had quit telling her when they were. She'd been present—and she'd been falling-down drunk.

Which was one reason Lucy would never dare to have a wedding. But she could still have sex. She was a normal, healthy woman. And Ramsey was all male.

"I'm glad that your mom is willing to have Frank at your wedding," she said, thinking about Emma's situation from a different angle. "It means that she's made a conscious decision to move on."

"I thought so, too. I just don't like to get my hopes up, you know?"

"Yeah, well, the important thing about that is to know when it's time to let hope soar."

She believed what she said. She just wasn't sure that time would ever come for her and Sandy. Her mother wasn't like Rose. Sandy was too damaged to recover.

And Lucy had to know why. What had happened to Allie the day that her mother had been raped?

A SIXTYISH WOMAN WAS OUTSIDE the Sanderson home, with paper spread on the driveway, spray painting something white.

Parked in his sedan down the street, Ramsey watched the regal set of her body, her head, as she went about her task.

Every few minutes she stopped and looked around and then went back to painting.

Ramsey recognized the action. She was watching her back. A common trait in someone who'd been victimized.

The woman was Rose Sanderson. She was fifty-six, not sixty. And still a beauty.

Ramsey had met the woman weeks before, when her daughter's ex-fiancé had threatened Rose's life, among other things. Just as Emma had claimed, Rose was fragile where her personal life was concerned. He didn't want to see her again until he had some answers to give her. He had to know what happened to Claire Sanderson.

Waiting until Rose finished her task and went back inside, leaving whatever she'd been working on to dry on the pavement, Ramsey finally exited his car. He didn't care if the neighbors saw him accessing the sewage tunnel that ran beneath their road, he just didn't want Rose Sanderson to know he was there.

He'd dug up city blueprints and knew that the tunnel he was interested in ran from a mile east of the Sandersons' street to two miles west, where it dumped into an underground city holding device. And it wasn't really sewage. It was a runoff for rain and melting snow. The access Jack had mentioned was a hundred yards down from the Sanderson home and could be reached by jumping down from a retaining wall that ran on each side of the ditch, separating two properties.

Ramsey could easily see how a ball might roll down into the ditch and on into the tunnel. He could also see how a boy might jump down there to play. He doubted a two-year-old girl could make the jump without seriously injuring herself. He doubted she'd even be tempted to try.

But she could have been forced. Or carried.

With a quick glance at his loafers, topped by the brown cuff of the suit he'd put on that morning, Ramsey jumped down the four feet to the bottom of the ditch and made his way slowly toward the storm-sewer opening.

It hadn't rained in a while and they hadn't yet had their first dusting of snow for the season. The water at the bottom of the tunnel was barely enough to keep the cement damp. Ramsey stepped carefully around the occasional puddle.

Jeans might have been a better choice for the day. He hadn't wanted to afford the time to stop back at home to change again before going into the office.

It wouldn't be the first time he showed up to work with dirty feet.

He turned on his flashlight about ten feet into the opening, shining it all around him, taking in the aged, rough cement completely circling him—the graffiti-strewn walls and debris-littered floor. Looking down as his foot crunched something hard, he saw the syringe he'd just smashed. Empty bottles— some beer, some hard liquor—an empty can or two, lay haphazardly around the space. As did chip bags and candy wrappers. He saw a couple of disposable lighters. A cracked pipe. An empty matchbook. Some were soggy. Some hadn't yet been damaged by water. What caught his attention were the empty plastic bags, sandwich-size, the kind with reseal-able openings, bearing white dust. And others, same size, with a telltale green hue.

The tunnel wasn't a place for big-time dealers, clearly. But it was obviously a popular home for small-time users.

He walked west two miles to the end of the tunnel and came up blank. The holding tank that the water emptied into was huge, with a metal grate between the tank itself and the tunnel. Ramsey yanked on the grate. It didn't give, not even a little bit. The only way anyone would have been able to stash a body, of any size, in that tank would have been to cut through that grate. If it had been cut twenty-five years before, it had been repaired. There was no sign of repair, but he'd check back at the office to see if there'd ever been a repair logged. Or maybe the grate had been replaced altogether.

And he wanted to know if the bottom of the tank was ever checked. If the water was tested. If there'd ever been reports of a bad smell in the area. A decomposing body, no matter how small, would emit a noticeable stench. Cataloging the questions in his mind, like a list he could visualize, Ramsey turned and made his way back to where he'd started.

The eastern mile of the tunnel was curiously untouched by graffiti and drug paraphernalia. Instead, he found some toy army men and lawn debris. The end of the tunnel opened out to a little park area between two homes. A somewhat secluded park area.

He might just have found out how someone got Claire Sanderson away from her home, out of the area, without being seen. Had anyone searched the neighborhoods, the areas, a mile from the little girl's home that day? He hadn't read anything about the area in particular. But he would.

Hurrying back to his car, he was already thinking about the files he would start with, the records he would search, including the names of all of the homeowners in the new vicinity. He'd check those records against the city's database of criminal offenders and then move on to the national database.

He might have just found out how Jack Colton only lost four minutes when he took Claire from Frank around the corner from their street, or took her from Frank's car while it was still parked in his driveway after the man had put Claire there and left the car purposely unlocked. There'd been someone else involved. Someone who took Claire from Jack—or Frank—and transported her through the tunnel into a park where he or she disappeared from view before anyone noticed anything amiss.

But even if he'd found his answer, even if he was completely right, he still had no idea what had ultimately happened to Claire Sanderson. He still had no closure for her family.

But if he could prove who took her, he'd be one step closer.

CHAPTER TWENTY

LUCY'S PHONE RANG AGAIN, shortly after she'd hung up from Emma. She'd gotten out of her car and was sitting on a picnic table looking out at the river, reliving her past. The good times and the bad.

She was trying to find herself. Her deep-down heart. The thing that she'd told Emma to listen to. And all she could seem to find was the constant awareness of Sandy. Everything came back to her mother.

To the point that Lucy couldn't seem to get a grasp on where she was. Not physically, but in every other way.

In no mood to be good for anyone, she almost didn't answer the phone. Out of habit she looked at the number on the screen, in case it was Marie.

Ramsey.

"Hello?"

"I wanted to call earlier but hoped you'd be sleeping."

She smiled but didn't feel much. "I did take a nap this morning."

"How are you?"

"Fine. My chin feels like it's got dried glue on it and my tongue's still a bit swollen, but otherwise I'm good to go."

"How about your fingers?"

"I've had blisters before." She'd done yard work for a couple of summers until she was old enough to get a real job. Then she'd worked as a dishwasher for a while during high school. In her effort to get the work done as quickly and efficiently as possible, she'd used the hottest water she could stand and had grabbed knives from the bottom of the sink by the blade a time or two, as well.

No one would have asked Lucy to be a hand model, even before her trek into craziness the night before.

"Emma called," she said before he could ask another question. She didn't consider herself a good topic of conversation at the moment. She told him about Frank Whittier's expected presence at the wedding they'd both be attending that next weekend.

"A gift to us," Ramsey said, echoing her first reaction to the news.

"I just want to make sure that nothing mars Emma's wedding day. If we hear anything or notice anything or even *know* anything, we don't move until after Emma's wedding and reception are complete."

Her adamancy sat kind of odd on her shoulders. She'd only ever protected the job, or Sandy, in such a way.

She wasn't herself.

And she didn't like that.

"I completely agree," Ramsey said easily. "Claire Sanderson has been gone for twenty-five years. Frank Whittier has been a suspect almost all of that time. There's nothing that can't wait another twelve hours to move on, no matter what it is. However, it does mean that I'm going to be working during the wedding and reception."

"Me, too. How could we not?"

"Technically it's not your case."

"I'm not being paid to solve it, that's true. But then, neither are you. It just happens to be in your jurisdiction so you're official." She was half teasing. And completely serious, too. Finding Claire Sanderson was as important to her as it was to Ramsey.

And having Frank Whittier in their immediate vicinity for several hours was a godsend. One that she couldn't let pass if she wanted to.

"I walked the storm sewer this afternoon," Ramsey said, and a shard of fear went through her when she realized that she'd forgotten that he had a sewer to check out that day. One that could lead them to Claire.

"And?"

"I think I know how they might have gotten Claire out of the area." He told her about the east end of the tunnel. About a park he'd discovered at the opening.

"Do you know if the park was there twenty-five years ago?"

"No, I don't, but I suspect it was. The trees are mature. And the houses surrounding it look to be as old, or older, than the ones in Claire's neighborhood. Just better kept. I'm going to check on the park as soon as I'm back at the office. I'm also planning to hire a forensic team, out of my own pocket if the department won't spring for it, to go over that tunnel inch by inch."

A detective didn't make enough money to spend his own funds on an investigation. She'd never heard of such a thing.

"If you do have to pay for it, let me know and I'll help fund the effort," she said. She had savings. And no better way she wanted to spend it.

"I'll know tomorrow when I present my request to the captain."

"Tomorrow's the day Wakerby meets with his lawyer, too."

Another barge inched slowly up the river. She wondered where it was going. Where it had come from. And if the man who was captain of the boat, out on the water on a Sunday afternoon, had family.

"How are you doing with that?" Ramsey's question was softly spoken. Personal.

"Honestly, I'm not sure."

"Elaborate."

"I wish I could." She didn't want to speak—and knew she had to. Her behavior the night before had thrown her completely off-kilter. And if she talked to anyone local, she could end up with a problem she didn't want to have.

She could end up in counseling and off the detective squad.

This wasn't about her professional life.

"Talk." Ramsey's one-word comments hit her where she could feel them. Or maybe it was the fact that he was in her thoughts constantly. And tangled in her emotions, too.

"I can't connect with me." She sounded asinine. Like the drama queen she'd trusted she'd never be. "I don't know who I am, Ramsey. I mean, I'm a cop. I want to be a cop. I'm a good cop. I know I can do my job." She had to make all of that very clear. There were no doubts in her mind when it came to her job.

And yet, last night, she'd done cop's work without acting or feeling like a cop. Which made no sense.

"And I'm Sandy's daughter. I've got that one down. Completely. I don't doubt my ability to be a good daughter to her, to know what has to be done and to do it, no matter what."

"Has anyone cast aspersions on your daughtering skills?"

"No. It's not that." She shook her head. Which made her neck hurt. "I just… I've been sitting here thinking." Lucy chuckled. "I know that's bad…." Because she hadn't been thinking about a case. The given. The known.

"Soul searching."

"Yeah. Lame, huh?"

"No. Uncomfortable, to be sure. And maybe or maybe not productive, but not lame. You had a traumatic experience last night, Lucy. It's human to question everything about it."

"Do I exist, Ramsey? As a person? Me? Lucy Hayes? Or have I become, or only ever been, Sandy's daughter, and now Aurora's cop? Where does the woman fit in?"

"You know I can't answer that for you. But what I can tell you is that your questions, the seeking that you're doing, is perfectly normal. It happens to most of us during or immediately following trauma. It's also exacerbated by medication.

You aren't yourself today so nothing feels normal. Give yourself a few days, a good night's rest. Wait until you're back at work and back into your normal routine, and then ask the questions again. If you need to."

"If I need to. You think they might just go away?"

"I'm saying you might already know the answers, but right now they aren't feeling familiar to you because nothing is."

"You think I'm being hormonal or something? Because I'm female and therefore unable to deal with trauma as well as a male cop would?"

She held her breath, trusting Ramsey to be truthful with her, although the fact that his answer mattered so much didn't sit well with her, either.

"No, I've seen male cops in far worse shape than you're in," he said. "You're acknowledging your doubts, facing them. Guys have a tendency to pretend they don't exist so they just hang around and fester."

Was he talking about himself? Her interest was piqued. And already she felt a tad better.

"You're human, Hayes. And there's nothing anyone can do about that."

She laughed. "I'm okay with being human. That's not new to me, I swear. I figured out the fallible part when I was about six months old." She was talking nonsense. And it felt good. "I'm just not used to… I've just always felt comfortable with myself, you know?" she asked, her voice dropping as shame swept through her. She should be better than this. "Today, I don't feel comfortable."

"If I tell you something, do you swear to me that you won't run scared?"

"I don't run when I'm scared. I figured you knew that by now."

"You're right. I do. And the truth is, I'm not feeling all that comfortable in my own skin right now." He didn't sound like himself, either. "And it has nothing to do with the job."

"Maybe we're both just overtired."

"That's what I'm thinking."

"Okay, then let's promise each other that we're going to put the work aside long enough to get a good night's sleep tonight and reconnect tomorrow."

"Good plan. I concur."

"I'll talk to you tomorrow."

"You can count on it."

The phone went dead and Lucy looked out at the water with a smile on her face.

RAMSEY HAD AGREED TO PUT work aside for one night, to get some rest. He intended to keep his word. But by one in the morning, when sleep still eluded him, he knew that he was going to have to come up with another plan. He got more rest when he worked on and off through the night than he was getting lying there in the dark with nothing to distract his mind.

Rolling over, he lifted his laptop from the other side of the bed and sat up. It only took seconds to get on the secured connection he had that allowed him to access privileged databases and type in Haley Sanders's name.

He looked at driver's licenses in the states of Indiana and Ohio. At marriage licenses, home purchases, birth and death records, divorce records, criminal records and civil citations. He looked for work permits, but didn't find an online database dating back more than twenty years.

He even searched bankruptcy files. Haley Sanders, if that had been her real name, was as much of an angel as Jack described. The woman didn't appear to exist in flesh and blood.

And he had his first real clue that Jack Colton was guilty. The man had lied.

Unless Haley Sanders, who, according to Jack, had been unforthcoming about her life, had lied to Jack about her name.

Either was possible.

He had more questions than answers.

Setting his computer on the pillow next to him, Ramsey lay down and went to sleep.

LUCY WOKE UP MONDAY morning determined to take back control of her life. Her mother's rapist had been arrested. That was good news, not reason to fall apart.

Lionel would deal with the bone she'd found. He'd told her at the hospital on Saturday night that he'd assigned the case to Todd Davis, letting her know that Todd had been ordered not to question her until Monday.

It was a holiday week. And on Saturday morning she was heading to Comfort Cove for two days. She had work to do there—Frank Whittier to keep a firm eye on—and that was good.

Dressing in her favorite, formfitting black suit and white silk blouse, she caked the makeup on a little heavier than usual, slipped into pumps with an inch-and-a-half heel on them, rather than the flatter shoes she normally wore to work, and even stopped for a glass of fresh-squeezed orange juice at the little diner in town before going into the station.

When she ordered, her words came out completely normal and that was good, too.

Wakerby's meeting was at nine. Lucy was at her desk by seven. Todd had cleaned up as usual, leaving no evidence of the bone investigation lying around.

"Hey, Luce, I figured you'd be in early." She turned and saw Todd, cup of coffee in hand, coming toward her. "I'm using Locken's desk today," he said, setting his coffee down on the desk across the aisle from Lucy. "She said to tell you she's with the D.A. this morning. They're on call, at some diner near the jail, waiting to speak with Wakerby's attorney, and you'll be the first to know as soon as she has something."

"Thanks." Lucy smiled. She was fine. Focused. Ready to call Lori Givens, her friend at the private DNA lab in Cincinnati, with another request. Emma was getting married Saturday and she needed a wedding present.

Todd sat down, unlocked the bottom drawer of Locken's desk, dropped his loaded key ring on the desk and pulled out a file. With a flick of his wrist, he tossed it over in front of Lucy.

"What's this?" she asked. But she knew.

Opening the folder, she read the gist of the report. "You recovered enough to know it's a skeleton."

"An incomplete one."

Although he was fifteen years older than her, Todd hadn't been a detective much longer than she had. He hadn't wanted to give up the streets to sit behind a desk. His gruff exterior, a result of all those years in uniform, made him hard to read.

"There's no ID," she said.

"Don't have it yet."

She looked at the report again.

"It's a child." Not a newborn, but less than two, according to bone development.

"Yes."

"Male or female?"

"Don't know that yet, either." He was stoic. Impossible to read.

"Time of death?"

"At least fifteen years."

"Could it be twenty-five years, Todd? Do you think it's Allie?"

His gaze softened as he shook his head. "Honestly, Lucy, no, I don't. I didn't even want to tell you about the body until I knew for sure, but Lionel pointed out—and I agreed with him—that you'd draw your own conclusions if I didn't have a report for you this morning."

"You've put it into missing persons, right?"

"We will as soon as we get DNA back from the lab."

A recently discovered buried body made this a current case. "You expect that yet today?"

"Possibly. Lionel pulled strings, and since this is a new find, it took precedence as a new case. Look, Lucy, there are several missing children from the Cincinnati and surrounding areas that date back fifteen or more years. You know that. You've pulled every single one of the records."

He shared a desk with her. He knew how many files she had yet to go through. Lucy nodded.

"And there's no guarantee that this missing child was even reported," she said aloud. Things happened more often than they wanted to know—parents or babysitters or boyfriends and girlfriends of parents or babysitters who lost patience with a crying child, got a little too rough. No one meant to kill infants. It just happened sometimes. And the next step in that scenario was to get rid of the body, bury the evidence.

"The bones are a little long for a six-month-old baby. And the decomposition reads closer to fifteen years than thirty."

She'd read that, too. "Thanks, Todd," she said. He hadn't said a word about the leave she'd taken of her senses, digging in the woods like a dog. Hadn't mentioned the slight disfiguration of her chin, either. For all of his gruffness, he was a kind man. One she was proud to work beside.

"For now we've got a J. Doe," Todd replied. Not John. Not Jane. Just J.

They made a deal.
SITTING AT HIS DESK, Ramsey swore as he read the text.

"What's up?" Kim Pershing asked from her desk several feet away. Bill was sitting right behind him, too, and Ramsey felt the other man's stare boring into his back. Just because his workaholic mentor had recently succumbed to love didn't mean Ramsey was going to follow suit. His and Bill's personal lives were completely different.

"I'm not sure," he said. But he knew it wasn't good.

"Something to do with one of your missing-child cases?" They shared any and all information to do with current cases. As a team, any of them could be called in to work any of the cases assigned to their squad.

"Yeah," he said, itching to get up and call Lucy. "Out of jurisdiction."

"Something to do with that young lady you had in here a while back?" Bill asked.

"She's a detective," he said, hoping his peers would take the hint and leave him the hell alone.

"So you said."

"In Aurora, Indiana, didn't you say?" Kim asked.

"Yes."

The other woman looked hurt and Ramsey wanted to swear again.

"You give her rain checks, too?"

He couldn't believe Kim had said the words in front of Bill. And didn't want to hurt her further, either. He liked her. Respected her. Enjoyed working with her.

"Nope. But I would have if she'd asked me to do anything outside of work." They were going to a wedding together that weekend, but Frank Whittier was going to be there. They would definitely be working. Everything he and Lucy did together pertained to work.

"You really meant it when you said you don't date cops."

"Yep."

She tilted her head, the red curls falling over one shoulder to cover her breast. "Why is that?"

"Slow morning, Pershing?" Bill harrumphed from behind him.

"What we do here could mean the difference between life and death. We have to stay completely focused." Ramsey answered Kim because he liked her and respected her and he wanted to be able to continue to enjoy working beside her. "Emotions are messy. The two don't mix."

A small smile formed at the corners of her mouth and Ramsey considered himself forgiven for any past hurts where she was concerned. He waited only long enough for the call to come through from the forensic team down at the tunnel—and then he was out of there.

He had Lucy on the line before he'd exited the building.

"What was the deal?"

"Wakerby had information on an unsolved cop murder from thirty years ago. Kept the news to himself to use as collateral if he ever ended up in jail. He told the D.A. what he knew in exchange for bail."

It was worse than he'd expected. Foregoing his car, Ramsey headed around the block and down the street where, a couple of miles farther, the ocean beckoned. "So he's out?"

"He will be. On a bracelet. As soon as they confirm his info. Amber was able to get that much out of the deal. But he's obviously pretty confident he's going to beat the charges or he'd have saved the info for a plea deal."

He'd already reached the same conclusion. "Or he's planning to skip."

The bracelet made it harder, not impossible.

"Either way, it's not good news."

"I just heard from the experts down in the tunnel. The department paid for the search, by the way. The team came up with nothing but theories."

"Anything new?"

"No, just scientific measurements and estimations to lead them to believe exactly as we do that Claire was removed from the area through the east end of the tunnel. The park has been there more than thirty years. It went in before the houses in the area. They took a sample of the water to match against any evidence we might find that was postabduction. Some of the microscopic residue found in that water will be indigenous to that tunnel so anyone or anything that's traveled through it could bear traces of the residue."

"Anyone who's still carrying residue for twenty-five years would also be carrying one hell of a stench."

He laughed. On the job. But quickly sobered. "I think I might have enough to get a warrant to search Colton's home." The day was sunny. Unseasonably warm for mid-November in Massachusetts. And his suit coat was still not enough to take away all of the chill in the air.

"His truck?"

"And all of his belongings."

"What about Frank Whittier? Are you going to try for another out-of-state warrant to get into his house?"

"Yes, but since I know it's unlikely that I'll get approval before the wedding, I'm going to wait until next week to put in the request. The Whittiers think they're free and clear. We stand a better chance of finding out something at the wedding if they continue to feel safe."

"It will be a little trickier to get a judge to issue against Frank since Jack established his alibi."

He walked faster. Harder. Keeping himself warm. "But once I establish reasonable cause on Jack, I can possibly discredit his alibi enough to at least get the warrant."

"You're closing in on this one, Ramsey."

He was starting to feel it, too. But at the moment, he had something more pressing on his mind.

"I've been waiting to hear about the bone."

"They found enough bones in the area to call it a skeleton. Less than two years of age. At least fifteen years postmortem. They don't think it's Allie. We might know more later tonight."

Her words were deadpan. Because she was in complete control? Or so fragile she was clamping down on all emotion?

"I put in a call to Lori," she continued with complete professionalism and absolutely no indication in her pronunciation that she'd had a mouth injury just two days before. "I asked her to run Claire's DNA again and to check it against Frank Whittier's. I just need you to get a sample of Frank's DNA to her."

Ramsey had the sample in evidence. "What are you thinking?" He'd do what she asked without hesitation; he just wanted to be along for the ride.

"That maybe Frank is Claire's biological father. Rose was married at the time Claire was born—naturally she'd put her husband down as her child's father. But what if she and Frank had already been seeing each other? And what if she'd told him, just before Claire was abducted, that she was breaking things off with him, that she didn't want to marry him? She sure was quick to persecute him after the fact—*and* to terminate the relationship. Maybe he'd planned to take Claire all along, but the plan went bad when Cal reported having seen her in Frank's car."

He was still a mile from the ocean and cold as hell. With one hand in his pocket, he turned back toward his car. "But if he was going to go to all of the trouble of stealing his child, wouldn't he also try to raise her?"

"Maybe that was the original plan. He could've planned to hide her away with the intention of hanging around through all the interrogations, playing the part of the grieving stepfather and then, by the time the case went cold and he and Rose were at odds he'd cut his losses, take Cal and go. And meet up with whoever had Claire. If there was another woman, he'd then pretend Claire was her daughter and take the child on as his own—like a stepdaughter. If he wasn't a suspect, no one would be looking at him anyway. It would seem that he'd just moved on with his life. Except that Cal skipped school, saw Claire in his dad's car and told the police before Frank cold stop him."

"He'd have to have a pretty convincing explanation for Cal about why Claire was suddenly living with them and they weren't telling her mother she'd been found."

"Look at how many cases we see where a child remains silent. It wouldn't have been far-fetched for Frank to believe he could scare Cal into silence or convince him that Rose was somehow bad. Or gone. Even killed. In a car accident or something. How would a seven-year-old boy know any differently? Then Cal skips school, sneaks home, sees Claire in his dad's car. He talks to the police before Frank gets to him, and the gig is up. Except that Frank already has Claire stashed away someplace."

Ramsey's blood started to heat up. So much so that he slowed down his pace. "Right. Cal had asked if he could stay home that day. Begged, from the way I understand it. And Frank had been adamant about the boy going to school."

"Yep. The police talked to Cal before Frank even knew that the boy wasn't in school. Before he'd been informed that Claire was missing. Before he could get to Cal to convince him not to tell the police what he saw."

"You might be on to something, Luce. Great work."

"I just got to thinking about what you said about Jack being a blackmailer. What if it's both? What if Frank has his original plan. He waits until Cal leaves for school, Emma's in her room getting ready and Rose is on the phone. Then he takes Claire. Jack sees him with Claire, thinks nothing of it at the time. Then Frank's plan is foiled. Jack sees it on the news, remembers noticing the child and tries to blackmail him to keep silent, and Frank agrees to pay with the caveat that Jack help him hide Claire away until he can figure out what to do. Obviously if he's a suspect, he can't get back to Claire later. He would have known at that point after his plan fell apart, that no one had ID'd Jack's truck in the area."

Ramsey walked, but was no longer seeing his surroundings. "And Jack just happens to know about Gladys Buckley," he takes up. "He hears Frank's troubles and offers to get Claire into a good and loving home. Frank has to think of Cal now, too, about what will happen to his seven-year-old boy if he goes to prison. He figures that at least this way both of his children are being raised in good and loving homes—"

"Or maybe, when Jack approaches Frank he gives him no choice. Maybe part of the blackmail is that Frank turns over

Claire so that Jack can sell her to Gladys, and Frank agrees for the very same reasons you just gave."

"We may be on to something here, Lucy."

"I think so, too."

"I'll get the sample on its way to Lori within the hour."

"I'll text you the address and let her know it's coming."

"Good."

"Okay."

Things were getting awkward. His butt was cold. And he was low on patience.

"I'm looking forward to seeing you."

"Yeah, me, too."

He still felt awkward. Worse, he didn't mind feeling awkward if she'd look at him the way Kim Pershing did.

And that was why Ramsey hung up without saying another word.

CHAPTER TWENTY-ONE

LUCY KNEW THE SECOND that she walked into work on Wednesday and Lionel, Todd and Amber Locken all watched her come toward them that something bad had happened.

"What?" she asked, dropping her purse on the top of her desk. Todd wasn't supposed to be there. He wasn't on shift. She was.

"Come into my office, Lucy," Lionel said.

Like an automaton she walked into his office, not sure who was following her. Just Lionel?

It was Lionel and Todd. Todd was the last one in the room and shut the door behind him.

"Have a seat," the plainclothed captain said.

She did. And wondered why they hadn't just had whatever conversation they were about to have in the squad room. It was obvious Amber Locken knew what was going to happen, and she was the only other one on their small team of four.

Lionel stood behind his desk. Todd sat beside her. All neat and proper like. Protocol was protocol.

Her gray pants weren't her favorite. She should have worn her favorite.

Lionel picked up a file.

The whole morning had turned into a slow-motion film.

"What's up?" Her voice sounded surprisingly normal.

Lionel hesitated. She had a doctor's appointment in an hour, to get her stiches out. If Lionel didn't hurry up, they might have to postpone this little meeting until after lunch.

Lucy was just thinking that she liked the sound of that

when Lionel interrupted her with, "We identified the body you found."

"And?" She was fine, sitting there. All professional and fine.

"It's Allie, Luce. I'm so sorry."

She nodded. It was okay. Really. Not sure if she spoke out loud, she nodded again. She'd been prepared for this moment for a long time. The chances of Allie being found at all, after being gone so long, were minuscule. That she'd be found alive even less so.

She opened her mouth to speak and nothing came out. Coughing, she tried again and managed, "Cause of death?"

"Hard to tell for sure, but…are you sure you want to know this?" Lionel asked. And then, sitting down, he said, "Of course you do. The skull was broken, severely crushed."

"He bashed in her head."

"Someone did."

"He did it," Lucy said, clearly, succinctly. "He is going to pay for this, Lionel."

"I'm already on it, Luce." Todd spoke for the first time. "We're bringing back all the dirt that surrounded the body. We're going to go through every single grain until we find some of that bastard's DNA. If he scraped a finger and left even a small piece of skin or a drop of sweat on any of the bones… You sweat when you dig. Chances are some of it dripped. We're cleaning the bones now. We'll find something."

"We're thinking maybe the rape took place in the same area. If we could question your mother we might…"

Lucy shook her head. "Not now at any rate." She'd just lost Allie. She wasn't going to lose Sandy, too.

"How sure are you that the bones are Allie's?" They didn't have her sister's DNA. And Allie hadn't broken any bones prior to having been abducted. There were no identifying marks or any dental records.

"We matched the DNA from the bone samples to your

mother's DNA. Which they had for the rape case. The match isn't conclusive, but there are enough similarities to make a legal positive ID."

She nodded again. Unless Sandy had had another baby who'd been buried in those woods, the body she found was Allie's.

"You did amazing work on this one, Lucy. You're a good cop." Lionel was clearly at a loss for words. But if she heard *those* words again, she was going to puke.

She was tired of hearing what a great cop she was.

She wanted to be more than a good cop.

What she'd wanted was a happy ending to a lifelong quest. She'd wanted her mother to be healthy. She wanted to find the joy that everyone else seemed to take for granted.

And they'd just nipped that one in the bud.

"MILLER? THERE'S SOMEONE OUTSIDE asking for you." Bill's voice came from behind Ramsey late Wednesday morning. His associate was coming back into the office from a home-invasion call.

"Who is it?" Ramsey asked, not looking up from the list of phone numbers he was perusing. Jack Colton's personal cell-phone calls. He was in possession of a warrant to go through the man's truck and apartment, too. He just had to find him, first.

And didn't like the fact that he couldn't. Colton wasn't answering his cell. Ramsey didn't believe for one second that that was a coincidence.

"Cal Whittier. He says you know him."

Bill didn't know him. Because Cal was one of the cold cases Ramsey was pursuing on his own time. He kept up his share of the team work. And his team left him alone to do the rest without complaint.

Ramsey had thought, a time or two, that Bill might have

been willing to help him a bit with the cold cases, on his own time, too. He might have asked, if he hadn't met Lucy.

"I know him," Ramsey said, putting the pages in front of him back in their folder, and locking the information in the top drawer of his desk. He grabbed his navy suit coat—the only suit he hadn't dropped at the cleaners that morning—off the back of his chair, tightened the tie he'd loosened, tapped on Bill's desk as he passed by and went out to greet the son of one of his prime suspects.

"Lucy, you're sure you're okay?"

Amber stood beside Lucy's desk, her eyes filled with more compassion than Lucy had ever seen.

"I'm fine." She was writing up a report on the dig from the other night. The discovery of the bone.

She'd tried to call Ramsey, but he hadn't picked up. And that was just as well.

Todd had gone home and Lionel was in his office with the door closed, which left the two women alone.

Pulling her chair over, Amber sat down at the side of Lucy's desk.

"Listen, there's a fine line between having what it takes to do the job, and going nuts to do the job."

Lucy didn't want to hear it. She was not going nuts. And if Amber thought she was going to convince her she had a screw loose, then she could save her breath.

"You're a woman, Luce. You deal with things differently than a man would. That's okay. It doesn't make you any less capable as a cop."

Where, a second ago, Lucy had been ready and able to speak her mind loud and clear, she suddenly couldn't speak. She looked at Amber and prayed that she wasn't going to cry.

Amber's hand covered hers. "We've got a tough gig here, holding our own with the men whose ability to do the job isn't questioned beyond physicals and test scores. If we show emotion, we're weak."

If Lucy showed emotion it scared Sandy to death. Unless it was hurt feelings from liking a guy who didn't like her back. Or fear of the first day of school.

"But the truth is, Lucy, what makes us a valuable asset to the team is the differences we bring to the investigations. You, in particular, your ability to understand people, to get inside and know what makes them tick, that's a real talent, Lucy. Most of us just guess based on personality profiles and experience, which is all good, but you…you've got an edge on us that makes any team you're on lucky to have you."

She listened. And she believed. She just wasn't sure how much she cared at the moment.

"But if you lose your ability to feel, your femininity, the nurturing that comes so naturally to you, you're going to lose that edge."

Maybe. And maybe that was as it should be. Maybe she wouldn't always be a cop. Maybe she just didn't know who she was at the moment.

She'd let her mother down. And she'd let herself down. She wasn't going to bring Allie back. She wasn't going to be able to save Sandy, as she'd always told herself she would do. She couldn't give her mother a happy ending. She wasn't ever going to know who Sandy had been before the rape. Before she'd lost Allie.

"You're at a crossroads, Lucy. One that most female cops come to at some point or other. You either shut down and eventually lose what made you a good cop to begin with, or you learn how to be a cop and a woman at the same time."

It wasn't Amber's words so much as the honest and warm look in the woman's eyes that reached Lucy.

"What was your crossroads?" she asked.

"I answered a call for a baby who wasn't breathing. The mom called it in. I listened to the 9-1-1 recording—she was frantic. I got there. The baby was blue, but worse, she had these marks around her neck. I was sick to my stomach and needed to console the mother, and then I realized she didn't even see that her baby had been hurt. It didn't take an hour to build the case. The mother, probably in a postpartum depression, tried to quiet her own newborn daughter by grabbing her around the throat. She held the baby, rocking her, crying, begging her to be okay, and I had to collar her."

"Did the baby live?"

"Yeah. And miraculously without brain damage. She's in second grade now and excelling in every way."

Another happy ending. "That's great!" Lucy said, truly happy for the little girl, and for the mother, who'd acted out of illness but whose daughter meant everything to her in the world.

"Yeah. She's living with her aunt and uncle. They're her legal guardians since her mother's in prison for assault and battery on a minor."

"But you said she was suffering from postpartum depression...."

"The jury returned a guilty verdict and the judge gave her fifteen to life. And the night after sentencing, when I left the courtroom, was my crossroads. I am a woman. I don't have children of my own, but I hope to someday. As that poor mother was taken from the courtroom, sobbing for her baby, I wanted to die knowing that it was partially because of my testimony that she was going away. I'd done my job well enough to get a conviction."

"What did you do then?" Lucy asked.

"I went to a bar, got drunk, met a man who was more than willing to hold me, went to a hotel with him intending to have mind-numbing sex and ended up spending the night sobbing in his arms. I'm a good cop. I'm capable of getting the job done. And when the case is heartbreaking, I cry."

She would never have guessed it.

Amber Locken cried.

CAL WHITTIER, DRESSED IN JEANS and a button-down shirt under a long-sleeved blue sweater, hardly resembled the man who'd been with Emma Sanderson that day she'd brought in hair ribbons containing her sister's DNA providing the means to prove, one way or the other, if Claire Sanderson had been one of Peter Walters's victims.

The man who stood before him, holding a brown paper sack rolled down from the top, was relaxed. At ease. His eyes met Ramsey's with a peace that was noticeable. His hair was longer, too.

Ramsey looked for a wedding ring on the other man's left hand and noted there was none. Had his fiancée, who was the single mother of a ten-year-old boy, wised up? Did she know that Cal was covering for his criminal father?

"I brought you something, Detective," Whittier said, holding out the bag. "I was going to give it to Emma, but Morgan insisted that you might be able to use it. And this morning, when I asked Emma, she said the same. I don't think it'll help, but if it does, then I am with them one hundred percent in wanting you to have it."

Leary, Ramsey took the bag.

"You and Morgan set a date yet?" Ramsey asked.

"January 18," the professor replied with a smile. "Society weddings require a bit of time to plan and prepare for."

"I wouldn't have figured you for a society wedding." Whittier was the most private man Ramsey had ever met.

"I'm not. And neither, incidentally, is Morgan. But if that's what it takes to keep the family intact, and to get her old man to walk her up the aisle and give her over to me, then I'm game."

So they were still engaged. And had her family's blessing.

Would the Lowens still be as willing to put on the big public bash when the fiancé's father was called out for abducting a little girl?

And why didn't Ramsey feel any better about knowing that the wedding would soon be off?

"What's in the bag?" he asked, holding up the brown paper.

"Claire's teddy bear."

What? Ramsey peeled open the bag and looked inside. He'd have pulled out the brown bear—something Claire had, reportedly, refused to have out of her sight—if he'd had gloves on.

"How did you get this?"

The bear had been found in Frank Whittier's car after Claire had gone missing. Everyone in the family had reported that Claire had been trying to feed the bear breakfast the morning of her disappearance. And then the bear had turned up underneath the seat in Frank's car.

It had been logged in as evidence, but it'd been missing from the box of forensic evidence that was stolen and later recovered from Emma's ex-fiancé. The evidence that was, at that moment, at the DNA office in Boston waiting for further testing.

"I guess you could say I stole it," Cal said, his face serious. "When Claire disappeared, they brought us all down here to the police station."

Cal had been here, in Ramsey's building, while Ramsey had been a child running around on the farm in Vienna, Kentucky.

"They put me in a room," Cal said. "They gave me French fries and anything else I wanted to eat. They brought in a counselor. And they asked me questions about Claire and my dad."

Ramsey had read about the meeting in the writings he'd confiscated from Cal in August. And in police reports.

"The container of evidence they were collecting was on the counter," he said. "I saw Claire's bear there. And when I was left alone for a couple of minutes, I took it. I was scared to death, for her and for me and Emma, too. I thought about how

Claire wasn't afraid as long as she had that bear. And I guess I thought that if I kept the bear safe for her, she'd come to get it. And in the meantime, Emma and I would be safe, too."

The elevator binged and the doors opened. Kim got off. She gave Cal a curious look, smiled at Ramsey and went on into the squad room.

"I hid the bear in my jacket, brought it home with me and have kept it hidden ever since."

Ramsey frowned. "Your father never knew you had it?"

"Nope. No one did until I showed it to Morgan. And then, this morning, to Emma."

"Has Frank seen it?"

"No."

"Is he here with you?"

"No. I came early because Emma and Chris have asked me to officiate their wedding and I had to get a single-use certification to do so. My father and Morgan are due in on Friday."

"You said you showed the bear to Emma. Have you seen Rose, as well?"

The professor hadn't visited his one-time almost-stepmother during his last visit to town. From what Emma had told Lucy, Cal hadn't yet forgiven Rose for turning on his father.

"Not yet. We're having dinner tonight." Cal didn't seem all that eager.

Because Rose had done him a great disservice? Or because, even now, he knew that his father had done the worst disservice to Rose?

"Will Sammie be coming with Frank and Morgan to the wedding?" Morgan's ten-year-old son reportedly adored both Frank and Cal.

"No. He's spending the weekend with his grandparents. With Frank and Rose seeing each other for the first time since we…left Comfort Cove…we just figured Frank deserved a bit of time to deal with things without having to keep up appearances for Sammie's sake."

Maybe Cal Whittier knew that there was a chance his father would be arrested upon his return to Comfort Cove and he hadn't wanted Sammie to witness that.

But Ramsey was beginning to believe that Cal really was what he seemed. A good man who only wanted to do what was right.

A man who'd been a seven-year-old child the day Claire Sanderson had been abducted. One who truly did not know if his father had anything to do with the little girl's disappearance.

Had the older man played his son, just as he was playing the rest of them?

Thanking Cal for the package and telling him he looked forward to seeing him on a much happier occasion that weekend, Ramsey returned to the squad room with one thought in mind.

To get the bear to the lab for testing against the sample of water taken from the storm sewer near Claire Sanderson's home. And to have it checked for prints, too. By most accounts, the bear had been in Claire's possession when the kidnapper had grabbed her.

Ramsey could almost promise whose prints they'd find.

Of course, Frank Whittier would claim that his prints were on the bear because he'd lived with the little girl, had picked it up to tuck it into bed with her. Or some similar, logical explanation.

But Frank's days of skating the law due to too little evidence were almost through.

Cal Whittier had delivered his father to the police twenty-five years before. And he might have just unwittingly done so again.

And this time, the police weren't stopping short of a conviction.

CHAPTER TWENTY-TWO

LUCY TRACED HER FINGER OVER chubby rosy cheeks. Those big blue eyes…they held nothing but joy. Allison Elizabeth Hayes. That image had always been her strength, her drive. She felt that her sister had been calling out to her to take care of their mother and never to stop looking until she'd found Allie.

At home in her bedroom, she sat cross-legged on the floor with a small wooden box open in front of her. Inside were the only photos they had of Allie. Sandy had been poor and single, without close family, when she'd had Allie. Back in the day when people had to not only own a camera but pay to have film developed.

After the rape, Sandy had rid herself of everything that reminded her of the daughter she'd lost. She couldn't cope with the reminders. Her doctor had suggested that she pack them away until the grief and anger passed. Sandy had given them away instead. Only these few photos had survived. They'd been in Lucy's possession since she was four. She'd seen her mother going through the box and crying, with a fifth of liquor in her other hand. That night, after Sandy had passed out, she'd taken the box into her room and hidden it.

Sandy had never asked her about the box.

Lucy had never fessed up to what she'd done.

Ironically, here she was, twenty-some years later, sitting on her own bedroom floor, just as Sandy had been that night, looking at the same pictures, with the same agony eating away at her.

The only difference between then and now, between mother and daughter, was the bottle of booze. And the truth.

Tears dripped down Lucy's cheeks, wetting her new scar, before dripping off her chin. Her stitches were gone. The swelling was gone.

Had it only been four days since she'd found that bone?

Allie's bone. She'd held her sister in her hand.

She'd promised herself she wouldn't cry. She wasn't going to lose control again. She wasn't going to end up like Sandy.

And looking at that picture, the sweet little face, the companion she'd carried in her heart her whole life, she sobbed a bit more. Allison Elizabeth Hayes had been an innocent baby who'd brought joy into the world. How could anyone extinguish that joy?

Why?

Maybe, if she knew what had happened…if she could understand—

Her phone rang, startling her, bringing her back from that long-ago day in the woods. She was home early. It could be Sandy having noticed her car….

She couldn't talk to her mother in this state.

It was Ramsey.

"Hello?" She tried her best to sound normal.

"You called. Are you crying?"

Lying seemed pointless. "Yeah. They identified the body. It was Allie."

She wasn't fighting the news. Wasn't even shocked.

She didn't know what she was.

"Oh, Luce, I'm sorry." And then, "Lord, I wish I was closer."

The emotion she heard in his normally even tone wrapped around her, and she cried a little harder.

"I didn't know her," she said. "How can I love someone I never even met?"

"She was your sister, Lucy. You loved her memory, if nothing else."

With her favorite picture of baby Allie in her lap, Lucy traced the cheeks again. "All my life I've felt as though Allie was out there someplace, speaking to me, giving me the strength to take care of Mama and get to her so that we could all be together again. It's like both of them were counting on me, and when I'd look at Allie's picture, I'd feel the joy emanating from her, and I'd know I could come through for them."

She wasn't sobbing anymore, but the tears hadn't completely stopped falling. She wiped her nose, looking down at the box.

"It's why I kept looking, never letting up, because I could hear her calling to me. Where other girls had best friends and confidantes, I had Allie. When I was younger I'd talk to her sometimes, like she was really there. Yet in truth, Allie was never out there. She was never more than a six-month-old baby who died way too soon. I didn't have a big sister calling to me all these years, giving me the strength to go on."

"Your own strength kept you going."

"Then why do I feel so bereft? Like I just lost my best friend? My lifelong companion?"

"You know I don't believe in much I can't see, or eventually prove, but I don't discredit the chance that you've had that companion all these years, just as you say. They say that aside from flesh and bones we all have spirits—something that lives on after our bones return to the earth. Maybe it's not Allie's body that's been calling to you, Luce. Maybe it's her spirit. And maybe she led you to her bones the other night so that you could stop looking for her. Maybe it's her way of telling you its time to get on with your life."

She hadn't thought it possible for anyone to ease the agony in her heart. She'd been wrong.

"You really think so?"

"I know that there's more to life than bones and death."

"God, I hope you're right."

"I don't believe you imagined what you felt."

She didn't, either, not deep down. But to think she had to let go…

"If what you say is true, then I haven't lost anything, really, have I?" she asked. "I mean, if Allie's spirit has been talking to me all these years, it's not like she's going to suddenly abandon me. Because she's no worse off today than she was twenty-five years ago. And I don't need her any less, either."

"The only thing you've lost is the hope of seeing her in the flesh in this lifetime."

"I really had counted on that," she said, pulling the box of photos onto her lap, cradling it. "Crazy, huh? I'm a cop. I work cold cases. I know more than most that I had little chance of seeing Allie alive. But I still believed I would. I really thought we were one of those miracle statistics and that that was what she was telling me."

Sniffling, she studied the baby's photo.

What happened to you, little one? What do you need me to know?

"How's your mother?"

"Drinking, but not heavily yet. She'll be drunk tomorrow." She'd spoken to Sandy on the way home, telling her that she'd been to the grocery store and would be over first thing in the morning to help with Thanksgiving dinner preparations.

She had a pie to make later that night. Her mother, largely, did the rest.

"I figured, with Allie—"

"Oh, I'm not telling her. At least, not yet," she said, putting the pictures back in the box, closing the lid and tucking it into the bottom drawer of her nightstand so that Allie could watch over her at night. And calm the bad dreams. Just like Lucy had always done for Sandy.

"The holidays are always hard enough. It would do her in to have a double whammy. And there's no reason that she has to know right away. Why take away another week or two of hoping for her? Todd is going to need to interview her at some point regarding the place where we found Allie. I'll need to take her out there, see if she remembers anything. But not today.

"Wakerby is already out on bail and until they have enough to bring him in on—"

"It's okay, Luce. I understand. You don't have to justify anything to me. I'd have made the same decision. Especially with tomorrow being a holiday."

Lucy stopped at her living-room window and looked over at her mother's house. The television was on. She could see the screen through the sheers. Marie drew the heavy drapes at night, but she always opened them during the day, insisting that daylight was a balm to Sandy.

She was probably right.

"I'm being selfish," she announced, watching that window. She wanted to be as devoted as Marie. She'd tried. She just couldn't cope with Sandy 24/7. "I'm not telling her right now because if I do she'll have a relapse and I'll have to cancel my trip to Comfort Cove."

She wasn't going to miss Emma's wedding.

Nor a chance to see Ramsey.

"I think you should come early."

"I'd love to, but…" she answered automatically, without forethought.

"You've had a rough few days. You need some time to grieve, to process, without worrying about your effect on your mother. You shouldn't be dealing with this all alone. Especially after today."

After she'd found out that Allie was really dead, he meant. Because she was. She was never going to get to meet the big sister that she'd been loving all of her life. Tears came to her eyes again and, leaving the window, she blinked them away.

"I don't know if I can get my flight changed." Spend more than one night with Ramsey? In her weakened state?

She couldn't think of anything she wanted more.

Or less.

"I'm sure you can for a price. Comfort Cove sprang for the storm-sewer forensic team, which frees up the capital you offered…."

His tone held humor. And insistence.

"I'll call and see what I can do. Lionel told me I could take whatever time I needed."

"I'm being selfish, too, Lucy."

In the kitchen, she used her free hand to pull out a pie plate. And a mixing bowl. She had cans to open—pumpkin, evaporated milk. She needed sugar and eggs and a pie shell.

"I want you here."

Could she get through this time by leaning on him? Just a little bit? And come out unscathed?

She pulled out the big glass mixing bowl that Sandy had got for her when she'd first bought the place. Everyone had to be able to make cookies in the middle of the night, she'd explained.

"I had a visit from Cal Whittier today."

Lucy stopped still, midway between the counter and the refrigerator. Was Cal finally ready to tell them the truth about his father? Was seeing Emma again, having her back in his life, more important than running and hiding? The thoughts flew so quickly, she hardly heard Ramsey's next words.

"He brought me a package."

"What package?"

"Claire Sanderson's teddy bear."

"The one that was missing from the box of evidence? But…Cal didn't have anything to do with the box's disappearance…."

Frowning, she leaned against the counter, trying to find a way past the muck in her own life to get into the case.

"He took it out of the evidence box the day they brought him in for questioning twenty-five years ago. He's had it ever since."

"And he just turned it over to you? Just like that?"

"Emma sent him in. He brought it to give to her."

"The kidnapper's prints might be on that bear."

"I know."

"We're one step closer."

"I know. Like I said, I need you here."

For work. He needed her mind. Her support. Her tireless energy when it came to the case.

Good. That she could give him.

"I'll get my flight changed. Do you have a preference between tomorrow night and Friday morning?"

Sandy would be passed out by dark.

"The sooner, the better. If you're here in time, I'll take you to Amelia's with me."

"I'll text you my times."

"And I'll put some sheets on the bed in the spare room."

The spare room. He wasn't expecting her to share his bed. Not that he should be. Still, the confirmation was a little... disappointing.

SHE COULDN'T GET A SEAT on a flight until Friday morning. Not because of cost, but because there were no seats available out of Cincinnati. Figuring it was for the best that she not land at night, anyway, giving her and Ramsey nothing to do but go home without work as a diversion, she texted her flight times, made her pies and went to bed.

And before she went to sleep, she thought of Allie, just as she always did. Not the baby her sister had been on earth, but the adult spirit her sister had always been. She closed her eyes and in a whisper said, "Thank you."

THE LOCAL, COMFORT COVE P.D. lab dusted the bear for prints. The stuffed toy had leather insets on all four paws, a leather face and plastic eyes. All of which had at least partial prints.

Frank Whittier's among them. Cal's were there, too. And Emma's, which they'd documented when she'd been in to give them Claire's DNA. They found others, probably Rose Sanderson's. Claire's. And one, unidentified, clear print on the back right paw.

Jack Colton's? They had his DNA, not his fingerprint. Not yet. And the man still was not answering his phone. He hadn't used his bank card in the past couple of days. Nor had his rig been spotted along America's highways.

If he was on a run, how was he paying for gas?

Reading the lab report that had just come up Thursday morning, the thought of Jack Colton buying gas reminded him of the gas-station robbery case Lucy had worked on recently. She was at her mother's, probably preparing dinner. Would Sandy have the wherewithal to make it through dinner?

Had Lucy ever had a happy holiday in her life?

He'd had plenty. And then he'd quit having holidays.

THE DAY WAS JUST LIKE EVERY other holiday at the Hayes home. Sandy started out full of energy and forced cheer, insisting that they observe all of their traditions—from starting with a glass of egg nog and breakfast casserole to singing their first Christmas carol of the season as they stuffed the turkey.

After the bird was in the oven, Sandy played only Christmas music until New Year's, even though she couldn't listen to any of it and stay sober.

She tried, though. Every year she insisted that she'd make it. That she'd give Lucy a traditional and happy holiday season. The stuff memories were made of.

She had plenty of memories. A lot of good ones containing her mother. Even some holiday ones.

Over dinner, they listened to "Carol of the Bells" and the rest of Sandy's favorite Christmas CD, all bell songs.

Other years, when Marie was there, they listened to Barbra Streisand's Christmas album, too. Marie was in Cincinnati for the day, this year, serving dinner in a soup kitchen. She'd be back by nightfall, freeing Lucy to go home and pack and get some rest before her early morning flight.

"Mama? Remember that witch's costume we made?" she asked as Perry Como's version of "Silver Bells" played in the background.

"You were in seventh grade," Sandy said, the words only slightly slurred as she chewed and smiled at the same time. She was still just drinking wine, which was a good sign.

"Remember how we spent a whole evening looking at patterns and choosing fabric?"

"You were so eager to learn. You were the best helper in the world, Luce. You always have been."

"I like being with you."

Sandy's eyes filled. But then she took a sip of wine and continued. "We put starch and cardboard behind the fabric in the hat and it didn't droop like all the other witches hats we'd seen," Sandy said. "And flannel underneath the black linen skirt and bodice so you'd stay warm."

"I remember the black streaks you put in my blond hair. I was the best-looking witch ever," she said, wishing they had more pictures.

"You won first place in the costume contest at the junior high."

Sandy had been drinking then, but she'd had it under control.

"The dressing and Waldorf salad are perfect," Lucy said, gorging herself. And thinking of Allie's spirit watching over them.

She'd tell her mother about Allie. It was the right thing to do. And maybe, if Sandy had answers, she'd move on. She'd fall apart at first, sure, but with closure her mom could get out of the valley of pain she'd been living for Lucy's whole life, make peace with the past and move forward into the future.

If she had nothing to hang on to, maybe...

As she ate and relaxed and talked with her mother, and as Sandy slowly got drunk, as they continued on with tradition and watched *Miracle on Thirty-Fourth Street*—the original version—Lucy knew what was happening.

She was no longer hanging hope on Allie's return to bring her mother back to her. But the hope that she'd one day have a healthy, sober Sandy in her life had not died. It was reshaping itself.

Finding a new version. One that might just have a chance of coming to fruition.

It was almost as if Allie's spirit was at work, helping her to see that the future didn't depend on the past.

CHAPTER TWENTY-THREE

RAMSEY MILLER WOKE UP Friday morning with a new lease on life. He felt as if he'd survived a storm. He guessed, in a sense, he had.

He'd made it through another holiday.

Dinner with Amelia at eight o'clock the evening before had been lovely. She'd made a turkey and all the trimmings, just like his mother used to. She'd asked about his parents—if he had any, where they were.

The odd thing was, he'd told her about them. About Diane. About his own culpability. About his mother's subsequent withdrawal from life.

He was a boy again, believing he had something good to offer, although how Amelia helped him feel that way, he had no idea.

And when he was through, he thought maybe he'd imagined the whole thing. Maybe Lucy was right. They were just tired. Overworked. Near the end of years-old cases. They weren't themselves.

As his voice had faded away, Amelia had told him that he had to go see his parents. Before the year was out.

She was clearly disappointed in him, too.

He'd promised to bring Lucy to meet her.

He'd called his folks from work earlier in the day because calling from work gave him an excuse to not be on the phone longer than the time it took to wish them a happy Thanksgiving and tell them that he loved them. He was the only detective on duty, which they knew, and the holidays had a tendency to bring out the crazies.

Those crazed with grief or loss or aloneness. All maladies that were exacerbated by occasions centered on family celebrations.

He'd had a relatively easy day of it in Comfort Cove. The uniformed guys got the standard domestic violence and disturbance calls.

He'd had to go out on a possible murder, but it turned out that the ninety-year-old man hadn't been murdered by his much younger, obviously distraught wife. He'd died of natural causes. At least, Ramsey was certain that the medical examiner was going to return that determination later in the day.

In the meantime, he'd investigated the scene, collected evidence, talked to the new wife and older children, taken statements from witnesses and told everyone not to leave town. And then, after dinner with Amelia, he'd come back to the office to write up his report on the incident.

And now, a few hours later, he was up and full of energy. He'd put clean sheets on the bed in the seldom-used room across the hall from his bedroom. It was going to be a good day.

LUCY GOT OFF THE PLANE ready to go to work. A full day on the job, dinner someplace in Comfort Cove—maybe at the place in the tourist district where Emma Sanderson's fiancé, Chris, played piano on Friday nights. Not that he'd be playing tonight since it was the night before his wedding.

And then a short night's sleep before—

"Hi." Ramsey was there, standing by the luggage carousel, looking gorgeous in a gray suit with a white shirt and red tie, his sandy-colored hair long enough to touch the tip of his collar and kind of windblown. But it was the warm glow in his green eyes, focused straight on her, that froze the professional greeting on her lips.

"Hi." She turned for her bag, giving her face time to cool down. "I'd have just done a carry-on but I have my dress and shoes for the wedding, and my garment bag doubles as a suit-case and was too big...."

She was embarrassing herself.

He stepped up to her, close enough that their bodies were almost touching, close enough that she could feel his heat and every breath she took was an inhalation of his musky aftershave. Bending over, he lifted her face and Lucy closed her eyes, ready for the kiss that was probably wrong, but that she'd known, in some part of her being, was also inevitable.

Who were they kidding?

They were healthy adults. Who liked each other and didn't have a significant other. It was natural that they'd experiment, satisfy the curiosity and be done with it.

But her curiosity wasn't satisfied.

Opening her eyes she saw him bent over her farther, to get a good look at the disfigurement on her chin.

"It's a nasty jag," he said. "But they did a good job stitch-ing you up. Looks healthy, and there won't be much of a scar."

"It's not like it's going to show," she said, back on track. They weren't experimenting. There would be no kissing be-tween her and Ramsey Miller.

"I'm just glad that it's healing."

"It itches." She saw her bag. Went for it.

Ramsey grabbed it just as she was about to lift it off the carousel.

He carried it to the elevator, into the parking garage and put it in the back of his car.

Fine. The necessary personal stuff was done. Now they could get to work. She wondered who would be in the office. Bill Mendholson? She'd met him once. Liked him.

"You hungry?"

"Not too bad." Her flight had been too early to think about breakfast. But she'd eaten a ton the day before.

"Have you had breakfast?"

"No."

"I took a chance that you wouldn't and waited. We can stop anyplace you'd like. Or we can go back to my house. I fry a mean egg. And I brought home the lab report on Claire Sanderson's teddy bear."

"You don't have to be at the office?"

"I flew solo yesterday so I'm off today."

"And tomorrow?" They had the wedding.

"Yeah. I'm off until Monday."

So was she. She also wanted to see the Sanderson file. Even if all they had was theory, she wanted to be able to give Emma at least a slim line of hope on her wedding day. Hope was everything.

As she'd learned when she'd temporarily lost hers.

"Breakfast at your place sounds great," she said. "I brought some things to show you, too." The Wakerby file, which now included all of Todd's information regarding Allie. They had to find a way to tie her sister's death to the bastard who'd killed her.

RAMSEY HAD NEVER BEFORE had a hard-on while frying eggs. Thankfully the suit he was wearing hid the evidence, and experience told him that as soon as he focused his thoughts, the embarrassing reaction to Lucy Hayes in his home, sitting at his dining-room table going over his files, would dissipate.

"Here, take a look at this," he said, pulling a binder from the far corner of the table and putting it on top of the report she was currently looking at. A copy of what he'd written late the night before regarding his ninety-year-old dead body. They were going to go over the Sanderson file together while they ate. "I asked Amelia Hardy if I could take a look at her activity journal and she insisted that I bring it home with me."

Opening the pages, Lucy was soon engrossed enough that he was able to get eggs and toast onto plates and in front of them at the table. He managed napkins and forks and glasses of juice, too.

He didn't manage to rid himself of a great desire to take the woman at his table into the bedroom, hold her in his arms and block out the world for a while.

"It says here that immediately prior to Claire's disappearance, Amelia was living in Boston."

"That's right."

"So she doesn't know if he had someone at his place then or not."

"Correct."

"He and Frank could have met there and we'd have no way of knowing that."

"Yep."

She waited for him to sit and then started right in on the eggs and toast. "Before we look at what we have, I think we should pretend that Frank and Jack are out and see if there are any angles we're missing. Let's make certain that we aren't just on this path because we need answers and can make cases that sound strong."

So they spent breakfast coming up with other theories, using the tunnel, and not. And reached dead ends for every single one of them. If the perp had been completely unknown, wouldn't Jack have noticed? Wouldn't Frank? Wouldn't Claire have cried out? And the police had combed the area at the time of the disappearance. There was no sign of anyone who didn't belong in the area, not a stray footprint. Not a car or a bike or anything.

Which was why Frank Whittier had been the only suspect all these years.

"But Jack had been there and the police hadn't known that," Lucy pointed out.

"Because his presence wasn't anything unusual in the neighborhood."

"So let's look at everyone else that 'belonged' in the area. Could any of them be our perp?"

By rote, he went over every resident on the block, naming names, alibis, job descriptions and family situations.

"There's no motive here at all," Lucy said, half an hour after the food was gone.

Getting up from the table, she gathered the dishes and moved to his sink.

Ramsey followed her. "I'll get those."

"Like hell you will, Detective," she said, grinning at him. "You cooked, I'll clean up."

Mostly because his body was all out of whack again, due to the saucy grin she sent him and the way she'd said *detective,* Ramsey leaned back against the cupboard and let her do her thing.

THEY WORKED FOR AN HOUR after breakfast. Going over reports again, looking at different angles. Making calls to check on updates from Lori Givens at the Cincinnati lab, to the Boston DNA lab that had Claire's box of evidence and Jack's DNA sample. To the Comfort Cove lab to see if there were any answers back yet on the storm-sewer water sample. To Ramsey's office to see if anyone had called in any reports on Jack Colton's location.

And then it was just the two of them at Ramsey's dining-room table with reports they'd been over numerous times. And a whole day stretched in front of them.

Lucy felt like a schoolgirl on her first date.

But she wasn't on a date.

And she hadn't been a schoolgirl in a long time.

What she was was a grown woman who was tired of being out of sync. Of not feeling or acting like herself.

She'd been thumbing through Colton's phone records, looking for Ohio and Indiana phone exchanges—any connection that might lead them to Gladys Buckley. Ramsey was leaning over her, to check on a local number.

And she couldn't stand it anymore.

"Look, I have to be honest here."

He stood back, his hands on his waist. "Okay."

"I'm... Do you ever think about...us...you know... personally?"

His eyes narrowed. "Personally, how?"

"Man and woman."

He glanced away. And she had him. When he glanced back, he knew she'd made him. "Obviously, the answer to that question is yes. I'm a man. We have thoughts. It would be pretty much impossible for me to spend time alone with a woman as gorgeous and sexy as you are and not have thoughts."

He thought she was gorgeous and sexy? He'd had thoughts?

She was a cop. A detective with a mission. Sandy's daughter. She wasn't free. As long as her mother was alive she wouldn't be free....

"You have nothing to worry about with me, Lucy. I swear to you. I'm in complete control here. I won't ever act inappropriately where you're concerned."

"What makes you think I'm worried?"

"That look in your eyes."

"I was thinking about the fact that even if I wanted to start something with someone, I can't because my first obligation is to my mother. Not that I want to. I'd never be good at a relationship. I can't keep my mind off the job long enough to remember to pick up my own laundry. Can you imagine how I'd be taking care of someone else?"

"You take care of Sandy. And always have."

He had her there. Still...

"You said you wouldn't ever act inappropriately."

"That's right. I can't deny having...urges. But I assure you that I can control them. Always."

Allie was dead. The two dimensions in her life were feeling

Allie's void. And the man standing two feet from her brought a third dimension that she needed. Just to get her over the hump.

"What if I wanted you to behave inappropriately?"

He didn't move noticeably. But the change in him was obvious to her. "Do you?"

"I think that…if we'd just act on this…thing…satisfy the curiosity, solve the mystery, then we could be done with it and move on."

He took a step forward, watching her intently. "This…thing… Mind elaborating?"

"You have thoughts. So do I. I'm not a man, but I'm human. I have feelings…thoughts…too."

His sudden ear-to-ear grin, surprised her. "I turn you on."

"Yeah."

"Oh, lady, you have no idea how glad I am to hear you say that." He pulled her up out of her chair.

"You are?"

"I've been sitting here wondering how in the hell I was going to stand the sweet torture of having you here for the next two days without you figuring out that I was…"

"Hard?"

"Yeah. You noticed?"

She smiled and licked her lips because they were dry and it occurred to her that she'd just subliminally invited him to have his way with her.

"I'm a good cop. Trained to notice things. Changes," she said. Could she help it that his fly was in her line of vision now and then?

He moved closer. He really was going to kiss her. And Lucy put a hand up against his chest.

"I'm using you, Ramsey."

"I know."

"It's just…it's like Amber said, this is my crossroads. I have to get through it. And I need to feel something good to do that."

Pulling her closer to him, he said, "You have no idea how glad I am that I'm able to bring you that good feeling." He pressed his groin against her, lightly. And it made her want to spread her legs right then and there.

"I'm not real experienced," she warned. "There's only ever been one other guy."

"Then here's a pointer for you for the future—a lack of experience is a turn-on. You say it like it's a bad thing."

He leaned in, his lips so near she could see variances in their color. And she wanted to feel them on hers, against her, so badly she almost wept. She'd cried all her tears.

And they still felt so close.

With her hand against his chest again, she said, "And we aren't…we're just satisfying curiosity, getting the inevitable over and done with, right?"

"I'm not going to expect you to marry me in the morning," he said, his smile warm. And sexy, too.

"Okay, then. Can you please kiss me and shut me up?"

He did. And he did.

And Lucy didn't feel like herself at all after that.

HE'D BEEN MARRIED BEFORE. He knew what it was like to hold a woman in his arms and feel the need to protect her. He'd had his share of one-night stands and understood about pleasure for pleasure's sake. He liked having sex and considered himself good at it, at being an unselfish lover.

With Lucy he was a freshman. A virgin stumbling over his first threshold. He'd never held a woman and forgotten everything but the need to bring her every bit of joy possible.

He'd never had sex without thought before.

One minute he was standing in his dining room, smiling at a beautiful woman he was about to make love with, and the next minute he was lying naked with her on top of his unmade bed, completely spent and not sure how he'd gotten there.

He remembered bits and pieces. That first kiss in the dining room. He didn't remember the second. He remembered stumbling down the hall with her. He'd taken off her suit jacket. He couldn't remember who'd taken off his. Or where it had ended up.

If he didn't know better, he'd think she drugged him. But he'd been the one to prepare breakfast. And she'd been no-where near his kitchen beforehand.

"I've heard it said that women like to talk afterward, but men don't."

"You know better than to stereotype, Detective." His voice sounded unfamiliar. Husky.

"Do you mind if we talk, then?" She was half lying on top of him, her head nestled into the curve of his neck. He held on to her, not ready to let go.

"No, I don't mind." He'd prefer conversation to the mental byplay he'd been engaging in.

"You were married before, right?"

Not the conversation he'd been expecting. "Yes."

"What happened?"

"That's not something I can sum up in a few words."

"Try."

He wasn't sure what to say. And he didn't want to move her. He didn't want to get up.

"It's just that…you know why I am how I am. My mom and Allie and all. The way I grew up. Why the work I do is so important that I put it first in my life. I want to understand you, too."

His marriage didn't have anything to do with who he was or why he did what he did. That was for sure.

"My marriage ended because I was married to the job. She got cold."

"So whatever drives you happened before that."

He just figured out another reason he'd never slept with a cop before. Or had more than a professional friendship with one.

But it was Lucy in his arms. And he liked having her there.

"I do what I do because I think I'm good at it and because I think I make a difference."

"Mmm-hmm."

He *was* a good cop. But she was probably the better interrogator of the two of them. She knew when to push. And when to wait.

And he knew her well enough to know that once she had questions, she didn't stop looking for the answers until she had them. All of them.

He didn't want her looking.

"I'm married to my job because I won't ever marry again. I won't have a family."

"Why not?" He couldn't see her face, for which he was thankful, not that his view of the ceiling was helping matters much, but the tone of her voice told him that she was concerned. For him.

"Just as I'm good at my job, I'm not good at the family thing. I stick to what I'm good at and that way no one gets hurt."

"Because one woman wasn't happy being married to a cop?"

"Marsha has nothing to do with it."

"Then who does?"

He started to push her away, intending to get up. Lucy rolled on top of him, resting her chin in her hands on his chest, and stared up at him.

"I care, Ramsey."

"I didn't ask you to care."

Her expression fell, but she was a hell of a lot classier about the situation than he'd just been. She was off the bed and dressed before he'd managed to do more than pull on his underwear.

"I'll wait for you in the kitchen," she said. "And you're absolutely right. I apologize. You didn't ask and I shouldn't have pushed. And…thank you for satisfying my curiosity. You are a better lover than I'd even imagined. I'm glad I had the experience."

It was the nicest kiss-off he'd ever had.

CHAPTER TWENTY-FOUR

LUCY TRIED TO BE ANGRY with Ramsey for being such a guy. She tried not to be hurt at his curt rejection.

Failing at both, she went back to work. Until they had their answers, they had to keep looking. There was no such thing as a perfect crime. And bodies did not disappear into thin air.

She was back at Jack's phone records when Ramsey walked into the room ten minutes after she'd left his bedroom.

"I'm sorry I pushed," she said before he had a chance to get close enough to sit down. "I don't want any of this…today… to get in the way of what we do best, and do so well together."

She didn't want to lose her friend over a roll in the hay, as incredible as it had been.

Or over hurt feelings, either.

When he sat down without saying anything, Lucy feared that it was already too late. She'd already ruined things.

"I had a sister."

He knew that she knew that.

"Her name was Diane."

Lucy closed the folder on Jack Colton. And looked at her hands, clasped together on top of it, giving Ramsey as much space as she could. Then she held her breath.

"She was two years older than me and the sweetest girl I've ever known." His voice spoke from far away. "Our small village was like a ghost town after the tobacco industry tanked. People bugged out left and right, shops closed, homes were boarded up. Until all that was left were a couple of thousand hearty people and a few stores. What used to be a happy thriving town, where folks called out to one another in the square and you were never short of a smile, turned into a commune of worried faces and petty arguments. Except for my sister. She loved Vienna. She loved the small-town life. She was always helping out, insisting that we'd all bounce back. She was determined to get married and have a hoard of children to instill new life into Vienna."

She already knew the ending to this story. She just wasn't sure how they got to it. Or what Ramsey had to do with it.

"But not me. I was bored and unhappy and used every excuse I could find to get out of town. Our high school closed and we were bussed to Greer, a neighboring town that had always been twice the size of Vienna and was still growing and thriving, and I started hanging out with all of the kids there, rather than the kids I'd always gone to school with."

He paused and Lucy looked up. He had his suit back on—complete with red tie knotted perfectly at his throat. And he was watching her.

"I'm giving you useless information instead of telling you what you really want to hear about."

"I want to hear all of it. It's your life, Ramsey."

"I was a senior in high school when I introduced Diane to a friend of mine, Tom. He'd seen Diane around school and wanted to meet her. I had a crush on his older sister and after they'd been seeing each other for a while, Tom set up a double date. We were going to some parties in the next town. It was spring break, so things could get kind of wild, and my parents made me promise to stay with Diane the entire time.

"But Tom's sister wanted to go for a drive in her daddy's new convertible. She wanted me to take her out to the lake. Diane was having fun at the party we'd stopped in at and told me to go on ahead. She said it was embarrassing to be on a date with your kid brother watching your every move.

"I left. That was the last time I saw Diane alive."

Her breath stuck in her throat, Lucy watched him. She'd been afraid he'd been leading up to something like this.

"What happened?"

"Tom gave her some pills. She'd never done drugs before. He had, but apparently didn't know what he'd gotten hold of. By the time we made it back to the house, they'd both been rushed to the hospital. They died later that night, within an hour of each other."

"It wasn't your fault."

"Yes, it was. And if I'd had any doubts about that, the look in my mother's eyes when I saw her the next morning dissipated every last one of them. They'd given me explicit orders not to leave my sister. I disobeyed them."

"I'm sure your mother doesn't blame you."

"I'm sure she does. With good cause."

"Have you talked to her about it?"

"No. Mom's in the beginning stages of dementia—though, to my knowledge, there's been no official diagnosis. I'm sure it's been brought on by depression."

"What happened to Tom's sister?"

"I married her."

"Marsha was Tom's sister?"

"Yeah. We clung to each other that first year or two after Diane and Tom died. She felt as responsible as I did. The party was at the home of a friend of hers. Tom was her younger brother. She was the reason we'd left the house to begin with."

"All of which was perfectly normal behavior for a girl and boy your ages."

"It was also wrong."

"Diane was a big girl, Ramsey. She told you to go. She chose to take the pills."

"She had no idea what she was taking."

"I understand. It was a horrible, ghastly thing that happened. And I get that you wish you'd done things differently. All I'm saying is that you couldn't possibly have known what was going to happen. You didn't do anything that any other boy your age wouldn't have done. And…well…I'd trust you with my life. Personally or otherwise."

She had her answer. She understood why Ramsey spent his life trying to save lives. To protect and serve. He was trying to buy himself back from hell. To earn back his own self-respect.

His eyes glistened. He didn't say a word. So she did.

"You said your folks are still in Vienna. Do you see them often?"

"No. I went home regularly for a while, but every time I go it sets Mom back and my father is left there alone to deal with her."

She reached for his hand, whether it was the right thing to do or not. "I guess we both know how much a woman suffers when she loses a daughter, don't we?"

Ramsey gave a short nod.

And they went back to work.

THE EXPERIMENT HADN'T WORKED. Satisfying his curiosity had not in any way lessened Ramsey's desire for Lucy. To the contrary. Every time she moved, a hand to pick up a folder, a tilt of her head, his body responded. He hadn't found distance. He'd become connected to her so that every part of her felt as though it was part of him, too.

This wasn't good.

It didn't affect the work, though. As long as she wasn't moving.

Ramsey was on his computer, logged in to the Comfort Cove P.D. when he saw a message come through.

"Hey," he said. "We got an answer back on one of the numbers in Colton's phone records. It's one of those prepaid cells."

"Which makes it untraceable. Why would someone be calling him on a number that can't be traced?"

"Could be someone who can't afford a regular cell phone, but it's curious, isn't it?" He went back to the phone records to check when the first call came in from the number in question. "He received his first call from that number last Tuesday, at 2:55 p.m."

"Right after we were at UC asking about him."

His blood was racing in a way that was familiar to him. He was on to something big. The break in the case was coming.

"Someone we talked to notified Jack."

"And that could explain why he was so calm and prepared when you interviewed him last weekend. My money is on the professor," she said. "That Beck woman."

"I was thinking Chester Brown."

"Then we go back to both of them."

He agreed. "Unfortunately, we're in Comfort Cove. With a wedding to attend tomorrow." Maybe she'd suggest that they miss the wedding. Emma would rather they find Claire than watch her get married. And Ramsey would rather be working than anything else.

Especially now. He was teetering on the brink of something disastrous, now that he knew Lucy in a personal sense, and the only way to circumvent the inevitable, to protect himself and everyone else, was to bury himself in work.

"You could try calling the number," Lucy said, Amelia's book open in front of her. But her attention was on Ramsey. "See if someone answers."

"We risk tipping them off to the fact that we're on to them if we do that."

Colton didn't yet know that Ramsey had warrants for his personal belongings. He only knew about the financials.

"So we phone Professor Beck and Chester Brown and tell them we're doing a follow-up call."

She wasn't letting him off the wedding hook.

"Wait a minute, Ramsey, look at this." Lucy slid Amelia's book over beside his laptop, which he moved to make room so he could see where her finger was pointing.

"Amelia says she got an extra preemie blanket made for

the church's blanket drive for the neonatal intensive-care unit at Boston General because she'd been woken by Jack's raised voice," she said. "She thought she'd heard him say something about a baby. Later she'd asked him about it and he'd said that he'd said *maybe*. He apologized for waking her up. He'd been talking to someone he worked with who'd been out drinking and wanted to know if Jack would come pick him up and give him a ride home. She made the note because when she heard the word *baby* and couldn't sleep for loneliness creeping in, she calmed her heart by making the blanket. She finishes the entry by saying that God always takes care of those who take care of others."

He was reading as she was speaking.

"I'll bet Jack did say *baby*, Ramsey."

Ramsey was sure of it. Calling the station, he put out an APB on the man. And when he hung up, Lucy was just ending a call, as well.

"That was Lori Givens," she said slowly, frowning.

"From the DNA lab in Cincinnati?"

"Yeah. She says she found something. It sounds really important."

"She didn't tell you what it was?"

"No." Lucy shook her head, her blond hair more tousled than usual. "She said that it's going to be pertinent to your case, and since you're the lead, she feels that you would want to make sure that all protocols are properly followed. She's sending the results to your work fax number. It must have to do with Frank Whittier, Ramsey. And that sample you sent her."

He picked up his keys. "Then let's go."

WAITING IMPATIENTLY WHILE Bill greeted Lucy effusively, Ramsey tried not to notice the other man's admiring glances toward his pseudo partner, or to care. Bill was crazy in love with Mary, and Lucy was not Ramsey's to claim.

He'd slept with her. Past tense. And they'd agreed, going in, that it wouldn't mean anything more than it had in the moment.

But instead of having her wait at his desk while he grabbed the fax off the machine on the other side of the room, he sat her with a cup of coffee she didn't ask for in the break room that doubled as an interrogation room, closing the door behind her.

No telling who might walk into the squad room. Kim. One of the other, younger detectives on the squad. He didn't need Lucy distracted right now. They were getting ready to close a twenty-five-year-old cold case.

Or at least close in on it.

Finding the perp didn't automatically mean that they'd find out what happened to little Claire Sanderson.

After shutting the door behind Lucy, he went straight for the fax. With proof that Frank Whittier was Claire Sanderson's biological father, he could prove motive for him taking her. With the new, previously undisclosed evidence, he could arrest the man on grounds of impeding a criminal investigation. And it just so happened that Frank was going to be in town later that day. Which meant that he wouldn't have to extradite him.

Timing was everything.

He slid the fax cover sheet underneath the actual data page and briefly glanced at the headings, before going straight for the results.

Frowning, he then read the heading in full. It didn't make sense. He pulled the cover letter back out, and read the message that Lori Givens had sent him.

And stood there.

Good God in heaven.

FRANK WHITTIER'S PLANE should have landed. Lucy waited impatiently for Ramsey to get back with the official word from Lori regarding Frank's sample. Fully confident that all things happened as they were meant to, she knew there was no mistake that Lori's call had come in on the very day that Frank would be in Massachusetts. They wouldn't have to wait to have him extradited. They could bring him right in.

This one couldn't wait until after Emma's wedding. Lucy had faith that Emma would agree with her. If Frank had taken Claire, Emma would most definitely not want the man at her wedding.

Tapping her finger on the table in time with her foot on the floor, she wondered what was taking Ramsey so long. She didn't want the coffee he'd poured. A little juice would be nice, though.

There were paper cups on the counter by the refrigerator. If Comfort Cove was anything like Aurora, there'd be juice in the refrigerator to go with those cups. And a place to drop change to help replenish the juice when the supply was depleted.

She waited another couple of minutes, eyeing the cups and the refrigerator and then got up to help herself. She'd just poured the juice into the cup—cranberry, not the orange she'd been expecting—and still hadn't had the sip she'd been craving when Ramsey opened the door.

Cup halfway to her mouth, Lucy froze. "Ramsey? What is it?"

He was haggard-looking. His cheeks were drawn and his color wasn't good. Heart pounding, she didn't move.

"Sit down, Lucy."

"Tell me what's happened." It wasn't the fax. No matter how badly they wanted Frank Whittier, a case wouldn't make Ramsey look as if he'd seen a ghost. He'd been gone too long.

"You need to sit down."

It was Sandy. She'd left Ramsey's number with Marie as a backup. Her mother had found out about Allie. She'd killed herself. She… "Tell me," she said, her voice too loud. "Tell me, now."

"I don't know how."

"Tell me!" The shrill tone couldn't be her. But there was

no one else there. Just the two of them. In a little room with a closed door blocking out the rest of the world. Her juice sluiced over the sides of her paper cup.

"Did Lori Givens show you how DNA matching works?"

She didn't give a damn about Lori right now. "Yes," she bit out. "When we were working on the Buckley case. I asked her to explain it to me."

"And you gave her a sample of your DNA to use for the lesson."

"Yes!" So what? Who the hell cared. "Tell me what's going on, Ramsey!"

She had to know. Couldn't take any more. Her limbs felt weak, but she wasn't going to take this sitting down.

They kept their station too hot.

She couldn't lose Sandy.

"We found Claire, Luce." The elation that should have accompanied his statement wasn't there. He sounded…lost.

Claire was dead, too. The knowledge settled on Lucy with a certainty that weighted her to her spot. They were going to have to tell Emma that her little sister hadn't made it.

And by the look on Ramsey's face, the little girl had suffered.

A lot.

"Where was she?" she asked. Still standing. Still holding her juice. There was no room in the moment for movement. Of any kind. Claire took everything they had.

"She's here." His eyes were warm. Settled on her. And vacant, too. As if he was seeing something she couldn't see.

"Here? In Comfort Cove?" She'd been here all along? Buried not far from her home?

It wasn't the statistic they'd been hoping for. Poor Emma.

As Ramsey nodded, Lucy felt the loss for her friend just as she had for herself earlier in the week. The loss of hope.

"Where?"

"Right here."

He wasn't making any sense.

"Where is she buried, Ramsey? Did she at least get a proper grave? Tell me she wasn't thrown in a hole in the ground like Allie was!" She wasn't in control.

"She's not buried. She's alive."

Her chest burned. And hurt. "She's alive."

"Yes." His stare was intent. He was telling her something. And she wasn't getting it.

"Here."

"Yes."

"Where, here?"

"In this room, here."

She looked around. There were only the two of them standing there. He was losing it.

"Where, Ramsey? I don't see anyone else in here with us."

"You're her, Luce. You're Claire Sanderson."

Her glass of cranberry juice fell to the floor.

CHAPTER TWENTY-FIVE

SHE WAS SITTING ON A CHAIR, bent over, with her head face-down in her knees. How she'd gotten there, how long she'd been there, Lucy didn't know. A hand rested at the back of her neck, holding her. Activity flurried quietly around her.

"Get them in here." That was Ramsey's voice. Right above her. She was glad he was there.

Dots of red stained her ankles between her dark slacks and shoes, and stained the floor, too.

"Okay, back up. I'm sorry, Detective, we'll need you to move."

Black bulky shoes appeared in her line of vision. With blue cotton pants on top of them. A leather satchel, big and with a medical marking on it, appeared next to the feet. Her arm was taken, a band wrapped around it, and Lucy closed her eyes again.

She wasn't her problem right now. Someone else would take care of it.

WHEN LUCY OPENED HER EYES again she was lying flat, stretched out on something cold and leather. Looking around, she noticed the refrigerator where she'd helped herself to juice.

Her mouth was dry. Had she ever had that sip of juice?

She'd been waiting on Ramsey. Where was he?

"You're awake."

He was there, at the end of the sand-colored divan that had been along the far wall of the break room in the precinct room of the Comfort Cove detective's squad room.

"Yeah. What happened?"

"You fainted. But your vitals are fine. If you hadn't woken up in the next minute or two the EMTs were going to take you in. I asked them to wait. But they're right outside if you want to go."

"Go where?"

"The hospital."

She shook her head. It felt fine. And so she sat up. "I'm not sick. Am I?"

"No..." He drew the word out.

Lucy saw the cranberry juice spattered on the floor and the cupboard behind which she'd stood. She looked up slowly. Through the squad window she recognized curious, though comfortingly concerned, faces. Two EMTs. Bill Mendholson. Kim Pershing. Captain Winston, Ramsey's boss.

And she shuddered.

Ramsey scooted closer, wrapped one of his big strong arms around her shoulders. "It's okay, sweetie." His chin touched the top of her head.

"No, Ramsey," she said, feeling dizzy again. "I don't think it is."

"We've called the department psychologist," he said. "She's on her way up."

"I don't want to see a shrink right now, Ramsey." She had this huge wall in front of her. And behind her. She was trapped between the two of them. All that existed was this room. Her. And Ramsey.

"Okay. You're the boss."

She nodded. Yes. She was the boss. She liked that.

They sat there. Ramsey holding her. People watching. And she started to cry, hiding her face in his chest. "I don't know what to do," she said through her sobs. "I don't know what I'm supposed to do right now."

"Just sit here a minute, sweetie. We'll get you some juice

and then see how you feel. One step at a time, okay? For now, let's just sit a minute."

She could do that. She could sit. As long as Ramsey was holding her. But…

She made herself stop crying.

She felt weak when she cried.

Sniffling, she said, "You keep calling me 'sweetie.'" And started to cry again. "It's because you don't know what to call me, isn't it? I'm not Lucy to you anymore."

He didn't say anything and the part of Lucy's mind that was working guessed that he hadn't been coached that far in the brief time he'd had with whoever was telling him how to handle her.

Beyond that, she couldn't think. Couldn't comprehend what Ramsey thought. What he'd said.

"I'm here for you." The emotion in his voice touched her. She didn't want to feel. And she couldn't stop the feeling from coming, either.

"I'm scared."

"I know, sweetie. But you aren't alone. I'll be here with you every step of the way."

Pulling back, she looked at him. "Will you, Ramsey? Will you really? You'll stick this out?"

He hesitated and then, looking her straight in the eye, said, "Yes. I give you my word."

She believed him. Whether he believed himself or not.

THERE WAS A KNOCK on the door.

"I don't want to move." Lucy said what she was thinking, but she knew she couldn't stay wrapped in the safety of Ramsey's embrace forever.

She heard the door open. "Detective, can I come in?" The voice was female. Even. Calm.

"Dr. Zimmerman." Ramsey's chest rumbled beneath her cheek as he spoke. He didn't move.

The door closed, a chair scraped, and Lucy knew that if she didn't want to be hauled off, she was going to have to pull herself together.

"Lucy?" The doctor's voice wasn't far from her. And Lucy pulled herself out of the last safe harbor she might ever know. Sitting up, she looked over at the doctor, expecting to see pity in the other woman's eyes. Instead, she saw intelligence assessing intelligence.

"You've had a shock."

"Yes."

"You remember what Detective Miller told you just before you fainted?"

"Yes."

"You want to talk about it?"

"No." She took a deep breath. "But I guess I don't have much of a choice, do I?" With a glance toward the window, Lucy noticed that everyone but the EMTs had faded away.

Dr. Zimmerman shook her head. Lucy figured the woman was old enough to be her mother. And then had the crazy thought that she'd have to stand in line if she wanted to apply for the job. The doctor had a little bit of gray showing through her dark hair, and she wore a dress that Marie might have worn.

"I'm not sure what to do." She repeated what she'd told Ramsey. "I mean, practically speaking, do I just get up and walk out of here and change my driver's license?" The damned tears started again on that last word.

"No." Dr. Zimmerman smiled softly as she shook her head again. "I think the best thing is for us just to sit here and chat for a few minutes. Would you like Detective Miller to leave us alone?"

Ramsey was still sitting next to her, but he was no longer touching her.

"No." Her answer was unequivocal. Ramsey was the one

person she wanted around. No one else felt real to her. In any life.

"Okay, then let's talk about this morning."

Right. She'd already lived through that. "You know how the discovery came about?"

She shook her head.

"You gave a sample of your DNA to a woman named Lori Givens…."

"My friend from the DNA lab in Cincinnati. Or rather, Lucy's friend."

"You are Lucy Hayes. Don't for one second think that you are not."

"But I'm not really, am I?"

"Yes." Dr. Zimmerman's nod was emphatic. "You are also, by birth, Claire Sanderson. Our job, or your job with someone else if you'd prefer another therapist, is to help you bring the two together."

For the first time since she'd woken up, Lucy felt just a small bit of familiarity. Like she had something she could grasp.

She felt a smidgen of relief.

The horror wasn't gone. Nor was the fear.

"You aren't going to lose yourself," Dr. Zimmerman said.

"I feel like I have. Like I'm nobody, dropped into this room from outer space or something."

"I'm not surprised."

Tired of feeling like a fly under a microscope, she turned to Ramsey. "Tell me what Lori told you."

There could still be some mistake. Her first course of action was to find it. And then she'd think about the world that was pressing at her mind.

"She meant to run Claire's DNA against Frank's, but she'd put his in her private database, the same place she had yours. She set the machine to look for a match and got a phone call. When she turned around she saw that she had a match for the Claire Sanderson DNA sample we got from Emma. But it wasn't Frank, which made no sense to her, and then she saw that she'd set the search for the entire private database, not just Frank's sample. She ran a second match with just the two specimens—yours, which you donated for your DNA lesson, and Claire's, which we sent to her. She got an identical match a second time."

"She's sure it's my DNA and not a second sample of Claire's?"

"Yeah, she's positive. And this also explains the DNA from the Buckley mansion that we thought was Claire's. It was yours. From when you went there undercover."

"The match that came through after we got Claire's DNA from Emma."

"Right. The original sample of Claire's DNA from the Buckley home was taken from a piece of hair found in the box of hair ribbons."

"Not on a hair ribbon." She could focus on the case. That felt normal.

"Right."

"I spent a bit of time in Gladys's home. Amber had coached me. She wanted me to use my time there to do an unofficial search of the place, to see if I could find anything. I looked through those hair ribbons."

"Our best guess is that when you were there undercover you shed a hair that made it to Lori's lab with the rest of the evidence that was later recovered from the scene."

"What are the chances of that?"

"There's always that one small thing that ends up being the key to the truth." Ramsey was talking to her the same way he always did. As if they were equals. Professionals.

"So she didn't test my DNA sample against the one we sent of Claire's from the ribbons Emma brought in? She only tested it against the sample we found of Claire's DNA at the Buckley mansion?" It was her job to look at all the angles. To find the holes in logic that the D.A. would look for. Because the defense attorney would be sure to find it, too.

"No. She ran them both."

"So according to my DNA, I'm Claire Sanderson." She could say the words. She couldn't fathom what they meant.

"Yes."

She looked at Dr. Zimmerman. "What are my chances of coming out of this with my mind intact?"

"That depends on you," the woman said, her expression serious. "Right now you're coming out of a state of shock. That's normal. The future depends on your ability to accept all of the emotions that will be coming at you as you go forward."

"Accept them."

"Let yourself feel them, Detective. Experience them and they'll lose, at least in part, their ability to harm you. Push them away and you risk the chance of being emotionally displaced for the rest of your life."

She couldn't feel anything.

"I'm not going to lie to you," the doctor said. "You've got a tough road ahead of you."

Her whole life had been a tough road.

AFTER SPENDING ABOUT half an hour with Dr. Zimmerman, Lucy took the doctor's card, and with Ramsey's arm around her shielding her from the people milling about his squad room, they left the Comfort Cove police headquarters.

Stepping out into the day, sunlight blinded her. But she liked the feel of it on her skin. She wasn't cold. But she wasn't warm, either.

She didn't know what she was. Or who.

Dr. Zimmerman had told her that questions were going to bombard her. She was to let them come. To take them one at a time. And some of them not at all. She was to let go of anything that was too overwhelming and visit it again later.

Ramsey saw her into his car like she was an invalid. She

felt sick. Not physically, but she felt the way she did after having had the flu. Completely out of sync and weak.

"I thought we'd drive out to the ocean. Sit for a while."

He was pulling out of the station.

"I'm not going to hold you to your promise to see me through this, Ramsey. From what Dr. Zimmerman just said, it could be a long haul."

"You got someone else in mind to fill my shoes?"

She looked over at him. He was giving her his "don't mess with me" stare. "No."

"Then how about you let me do it?"

"Okay. And I'd like to drive out to the ocean. Thank you." They turned into the street, and then around a corner.

Everything looked exactly the same to her as it had that morning. She saw it all as Lucy Hayes would. Not as Claire Sanderson would.

"Ramsey?"

"Yeah?"

"Could we please drive by Rose Sanderson's house?"

Maybe she'd see that as Claire Sanderson would.

He glanced her way, but didn't hesitate when he said, "Of course."

RAMSEY WASN'T BIG ON EMOTION. His job required compartmentalizing—putting things, emotional things, in boxes and keeping them there. He couldn't get shook up over every dead body. Every loss. Or weep over the injustices.

But he couldn't get his heart away from Lucy Hayes. He ached for her. All over. She sat beside him, straight and determined, and he could sense how close she was to falling apart.

He didn't know how she was coping well enough to look out the window. To talk rationally. If he'd just found out that he wasn't Ramsey Miller...

And not only had she just found out that her whole life was

a lie, she also had to somehow accept the fact that she was a woman she'd just spent months looking for.

Most of the ramifications of the news hadn't hit her yet. Dr. Zimmerman had had a talk with him while Lucy had used the restroom before they left the station house. He'd added the doctor's number to his speed dial in case there was a problem.

But as long as Lucy could deal with the shock herself, the better off she was.

"You want to stop and get that prescription filled?" he asked. Dr. Zimmerman had advised her to take sleeping pills for the next couple of nights.

"No. I'm not going to risk…" She stopped and he glanced over to see her wide-eyed, lost look.

"What?"

"I'm not Sandy's daughter."

It was starting already. "Not biologically."

"I don't have her propensity to addiction."

A good thing. He waited a minute, and then asked, "Do you want me to stop for the prescription, then?"

Tapping her thumb against the door jamb, Lucy said, "No." And added, "I don't want to take them, Ramsey. I don't like that foggy feeling in my head. And I especially don't want it right now. This is hard enough, finding any sort of clarity, without making the struggle worse."

He wasn't sure, but it seemed to him that what was happening was that Lucy was already starting to sort through what she thought about herself, and what she knew, deep down, *was* herself.

And somehow, no matter what her name was, she'd come out the other side of this ordeal a whole person.

If ever he'd been amazed at another human being, it was in that moment. And if ever he'd fallen in love, it was then, too.

HER FOOT STARTED TO TAP. In tandem with the finger still strumming a beat on the passenger door handle.

They turned a corner. "Stop!" She shouted the word.

Ramsey slowly pulled over to the side of the quiet street. He put the car in Park, but left it running. "You recognize something?"

"I've been here before," she said, her stomach roiling, her breath coming in spurts. "I've been here before, Ramsey. I don't know where I am, but I've been here." She was babbling. Looking around frantically. Crying.

"Where am I?" Her gaze landed on him and she sounded like a lost little girl.

"You're around the corner from Rose Sanderson's house."

She sniffed. Gathered her composure. "I don't like this corner."

He knew the statement mattered. Knew, too, that he'd have to call Bill and get him to start checking out Jack's route, Frank's route on the way to the school, against the corner he was parked at. He'd already made arrangements for the other man to take over the Sanderson case. Ramsey could no longer be impartial enough, removed enough, to bring this one home in a way that would convince the D.A. and secure the conviction they all needed.

"You want to head to the ocean now?"

She shook her head. "No. I want to see Rose Sanderson's home."

Dr. Zimmerman had told him that Lucy was the boss. With trepidation, he put the car in Drive and rounded the corner.

CHAPTER TWENTY-SIX

SHE'D NEVER SEEN THE HOUSE on the corner before. She'd swear it. "Are you sure this is the street?" Lucy asked Ramsey as he turned the car onto the street he'd indicated as Rose Sanderson's.

"I'm sure."

It looked…old. Her earliest recollections were of the house she and Sandy had lived in before they'd bought their bungalows across the street from each other when Lucy graduated from the academy. It was old, too. But not in a neighborhood as run-down as this one.

"You said Rose Sanderson is a principal in a high school."

"That's right."

"And she was a teacher before that?" The woman was a name to her. A job. Lucy had never met her.

"Yes."

"And she can't afford anything nicer than this?"

"She won't leave this neighborhood."

Understanding dawned instantly to the cop Lucy was. The mother of a missing child was still living with the hope that the child would come home. And she had to be there if she did.

And then she remembered that she might have already known that about Rose. She couldn't remember for sure.

"She has the same kitchen table in her kitchen, too," Ramsey said. "It's where the family had their last breakfast together, the morning Claire disappeared."

Her back itched. And her arms, too. She looked at Ramsey.

"You mean, me, right? Before I disappeared?" The words rang so loudly in the car, they made her ears hurt.

She stared at Ramsey.

Slowing the car, he stared back at her.

"Yeah, that's what I mean."

He'd stopped. They were at a curb in front of a house. She didn't feel anything at all. They could have been in front of any house in any neighborhood she'd ever been in. "This is it?"

"No. I didn't want to take a chance on Rose being home from school so I didn't park out front. That one's it."

She followed the direction of his finger to a white house across the street and kitty-corner from the one in front of which they sat. With newish paint, nicely done landscaping and front steps that weren't crumbling, the house was inarguably the most attractive one on the block.

Lucy studied it. As a cop. Looking for clues. She went inside the case, just as she always did. Thought of the reports she'd read. The interviews.

Tried to picture witnesses and suspects and…

"Ramsey?" Her voice wavered.

"Yeah, Luce, I'm right here."

"Emma Sanderson. She's my sister, Ramsey. She's my big sister." She was looking at him, but couldn't really see him through the big pools of tears in her eyes. She couldn't see him in her mind's eye, either. "It wasn't Allie who was calling to me all these years. It was Emma!"

RAMSEY GOT A CALL from Bill Mendholson shortly after he and Lucy arrived at the seashore. They were sitting in a roadside park just outside of Comfort Cove. During the tourist season, the park, with its cliffside location, was a popular lookout point. Today, in spite of the glorious ocean sunset, they had the place to themselves.

"It's Bill, I have to take this," he told Lucy, who hadn't said ten words since they'd left Rose Sanderson's home. She'd cried a little. Softly. But otherwise she'd sat quietly beside him. He was about ready to call Dr. Zimmerman.

"Miller." He picked up the call, getting out of the car so that he could speak openly without risking upsetting Lucy.

When he heard the passenger door open, he knew that he'd sold her short. She came up beside him as Bill said, "We got a hit on Colton. He's in Aurora. Just paid for gas with his debit card."

Ramsey quickly told his mentor about the UC interviews. He told him to get uniforms out to watch Brown and Professor Beck. And to cover the Buckley place. "He knows we're on to him."

"We've got someone in Boston, meeting Whittier's plane. It was delayed."

Ramsey would have liked to have been there for that one. But the end result could have gotten the case thrown out of court. He wouldn't have made a good arrest.

"Put someone on Cal Whittier, too," Ramsey said. "I'm fairly certain he's innocent, but he's also loyal to his father. He's staying at the Coastside."

"We sent someone over while Lucy…I'm sorry, Claire… was still unconscious."

"Her name's Lucy," Ramsey said, taking his cue from Dr. Zimmerman.

When he hung up from the other detective, Ramsey could not avoid the look in Lucy's eye. She wanted to know everything.

And so he told her.

Her face went blank. She was looking at him, but not seeing him. Ramsey's stomach started to burn.

"You said Jack's girlfriend at UC was Haley Sanders."

"That's right." And then he knew, too.

"Sandy Hayes. My…not mother. Haley Sanders. Sandy Hayes. He couldn't have her. He couldn't name her. But he couldn't desert her, either. Haley Sanders is Sandy Hayes.

He transposed her names—and came up with a variation of Sanderson. Even then, his guilt was coming through. Haley Sanders. Sandy Hayes."

"Jack Colton's weakness."

"Why didn't we get it sooner?"

"Because we were too close to the case."

"My mom…Sandy…she got me from Jack. All this time… she knew I was stolen, that another woman was grieving for me just as she grieved for Allie. I should have gotten that before now, huh?"

She stumbled and he held her up, bringing her body up against his. "Or…" he said, leading her back to the car. "It's as we thought and he found out about Gladys Buckley, sold you to her, who gave you to Sandy." He didn't know what to do except bring her focus to the case. "You said that Gladys was rocked by the story of your mother's rape. The loss of her daughter. And that your mother later contacted her. Maybe she didn't contact her looking for Allie, but was in contact with her to get you. Maybe when Frank called with a toddler, instead of a baby, she thought of Sandy and made a quick pass-off."

"So my mom…Sandy…*doesn't* know that I was abducted?"

This wasn't just theory. Wasn't just a case. "I don't know, Luce."

But he was going to find out.

"Do we have to go just yet?" They were in Ramsey's car, still at the ocean. "There's nothing we can do and Bill's obviously going to keep you updated to the minute." Ramsey had spoken to the other detective again, filling him in on the possible Haley Sanders/Sandy Hayes connection.

"You come before the case, Luce. We'll stay here all night if that's what we need to do."

She had no idea what she needed. She couldn't access herself deep enough to find out. She just wasn't ready to go back to town.

The clock in the car said it was four-thirty. "Is that right?" She pointed.

"Yeah."

"Lori's call was just three hours ago?"

He nodded, his arm draped over the back of his seat, letting his hand rest on the back of hers. He played with a piece of her hair. It felt good.

"Legally, am I Claire Sanderson or Lucy Hayes?"

"I'm not sure. Your Lucy Hayes birth certificate is obviously false, but you've got a social-security number and driver's license as Lucy. That might stand as an official name change. If not, you can always have it legally changed."

She was glad.

"Remember what Dr. Zimmerman said, Luce. Take things one step at a time. You have no idea how you're going to feel about your name, or any of this, in the coming days. Your feelings will probably change a lot."

"I know. The roller coaster she talked about. I'm just supposed to ride it for a while." She'd always hated roller coasters. Saw no sense in scaring herself silly when there was plenty to get scared about just by being at home.

"I want you to stay with me."

She wanted to go to sleep. But knew better than that, too. She wouldn't even rest her head against the back of the seat. Oblivion was too tempting, and all she had was herself now. For the first time in her life she had to come through for her.

"I *am* staying with you."

"I mean, for the next little bit. While you ride the ride." He sounded like he was prepared for a fight. "Dr. Zimmerman said that you shouldn't be alone. She also said that you were going to have to take a bit of time off from work. She plans to write a report to Lionel."

If she'd thought about it, she'd have been expecting as much.

"Okay."

"You'll stay?"

"Yes." She gazed out at the ocean. It was inviting her to sail away to a place where she could just be who she was inside, all by herself, and not have anyone need to know anything about her. "I'm not stupid. I know that I shouldn't be alone—and most particularly not alone near Sandy. Whether she knows about the Sandersons or not, I am not her biological daughter and she knew that much. I need some time to assimilate that information."

She sounded like an automaton—even to herself. And that scared her as much as anything else.

And then she said, "If she doesn't know…if she thinks I was legitimately adopted, this is going to kill her." Her throat closed. And she looked at Ramsey. "I love her.…"

This time she was in Ramsey's arms before she started to cry. "I know, sweetie. It's a mess. But you're strong. And smart. And it's for the best that you know the truth. I really believe that."

She heard him. She wanted to believe him. Mostly she just wanted him to go on talking so she wouldn't be able to think.

IF ASKED, RAMSEY WOULD HAVE SAID, hands down, that he would never be able to offer emotional support to someone in Lucy's position. No one asked him. And he found himself doing what had to be done.

He sat quietly with Lucy when she needed silence. He talked with her when she needed to talk. When she needed movement to divert her from the panic, he drove. And when she needed to be held, he held her.

And somehow, in the doing, in helping Lucy stay with him while she found her grounding point, he started to find a piece of himself again.

She wasn't Diane. Or Marsha. Or anyone else he'd known. And he wasn't the old Ramsey Miller who would act without forethought to those around him. That Friday, as he experienced hell with the woman who'd broken the barriers around his heart so gently he hadn't even felt the break, he wasn't putting himself first. And didn't think he could have if he wanted to.

Which knocked him off the selfish-bastard pedestal he'd put himself on. Not that it mattered.

The thought just occurred to him as he drove, Lucy sitting quietly beside him. And by early evening, when they were nearing Comfort Cove city limits, he had another random thought. He was his father's son.

And just as Earl Miller was there for his wife, no matter what the future held, Ramsey Miller might be able to come through for Lucy, too.

At the moment, there was no other choice. She might be a woman with two families, but for now, she shouldn't live with either one of them. Which meant that he was all she had. According to Dr. Zimmerman, her best shot was to take both relationships slowly—the separation from Sandy, and any reunion with Rose and Emma—to work on being comfortable with herself first, and then open herself up to the needs of others around her.

So he would do what he had to do.

"I read a poem once." Lucy broke the silence in the car. Darkness had fallen and he was beginning to worry about her. Nights were always harder in times of fear and stress. And he knew that, for her in particular, they were much worse.

"Tell me about it," he said, slowing down to thirty-five miles an hour as he entered the city. Tourist district first, he figured. To let her reacquaint herself with people in a more jovial setting.

"I can't remember the poet, or the poem. I just remember one line. It said something about being someone who could go through hell the night before and still have what it took to get up in the morning and feed the children."

He slowed as he came abreast the bar where Chris Talbot

usually played on Friday nights. They hadn't talked about the wedding yet. He figured he was going to call someone in the morning and say that Lucy had the flu. Or something else that would get them out of appearing, or being visited.

"I've always wanted to be that person," she said. "I think I'm one of those people who can go through hell and still be able to get up and feed the children."

He smiled. And knew in that moment that the woman beside him was an angel.

And that she was going to be just fine.

DINNER TIME HAD COME and gone. They hadn't eaten since breakfast at Ramsey's house. He had to be starving.

"You want to get something to eat?" she asked, wondering how on earth she was going to keep anything down, but knowing she had to if she was going to have the strength to feed the children.

"I can grill some steaks back at the house, put some potatoes in the oven. There's stuff for a salad."

She actually felt a grin coming on. And when it surfaced, her face was so stiff it felt like it cracked. "Sounds like you were prepared for a visitor," she said.

"I was." His warm glance thawed her enough that she knew the night ahead was probably not going to be easy. She was starting to feel again.

"But we can eat out if you want to," he offered. "If you'd rather stay out."

"I'd rather be at your house. I like it there." There was no way she was going to be able to keep up any kind of appearances at this point. "And while we're at it, can I just say that I want to sleep in your bed with you, too?"

"I'm glad to hear that. I envisioned a long night camping out on the floor in the spare room because there was no way I was leaving you alone tonight."

Another crack in the ice.

She knew how ice worked. Once it cracked, the warm air got inside and then the solid chunk started to melt from the inside out.

CHAPTER TWENTY-SEVEN

RAMSEY'S PHONE RANG JUST as they were pulling onto his street. "We've got Frank Whittier in custody. I'm not telling him about Claire, for now. I can give you until tomorrow to find out how Lucy wants us to handle this. But be warned, the family isn't happy."

He didn't give a rat's ass about the Whittiers at the moment. He felt a twinge of guilt when he thought of Emma, but he knew that, in the end, she'd understand.

And if she didn't, she didn't deserve Lucy for a sister.

"The big news is Colton," Bill continued. "Is Lucy there?"

"Yes, she's right here."

"You think she's up to listening or do you want to fill her in later?"

Looking at the woman sitting beside him in his car, in his driveway, Ramsey didn't hesitate. "Hold on," he said into the phone, and then asked Lucy, "Bill has a report on Colton. You want to hear it now?"

"Yes." Her answer was unequivocal, just as he'd expected it would be.

With a push to his phone, he said, "You're on speakerphone, Bill. Go ahead."

"Hi, Lucy," Bill's voice softened.

"Hi."

"I wish the news was better...."

"It's okay, Bill, I'm prepared for whatever it is."

Ramsey wasn't sure about that, but he knew that if anyone could be prepared on such short notice for life-altering change, it would be Lucy Hayes. And the doctor had said she was the boss.

"Colton's in custody. We picked him up at Sandy Hayes's residence."

Lucy's sharp intake of breath filled the car, and possibly transmitted to Bill, too.

"Go on," she said a few seconds later.

"You were right. Haley Sanders and Sandy Hayes is one and the same. She fell in love with him during their brief time together at UC. She got pregnant. When she told Jack, he broke up with her. But he sent her money every single week."

"Jack Colton is Allie's father?" Lucy spoke. He shared the thought.

"Yes. Sandy called him a month or so after the rape. Told him about the attack and that their baby had been abducted—"

Lucy sat forward. "She has no memory of what happened to Allie?"

Ramsey wanted to disconnect the call. He watched Lucy, looking for any sign that this was too much for her. She didn't seem to notice him.

"She *didn't* remember, and it was pretty much touch and go, emotionally. Apparently Colton, on hearing of his daughter's abduction, grew up quickly. He took complete responsibility for the child's disappearance, saying that if he'd been there it wouldn't have happened. And he took complete responsibility for Sandy. Which was why, when he realized we were on to him, he went straight to her. Seeing him, coupled with seeing Wakerby so recently, probably jolted her memory. She was pretty much incoherent but was able to tell the authorities what had happened to Allie."

"Wait," Lucy said again, her tone demanding. "What happened to Allie? How did she die?"

"She was crying. Wakerby hit her to shut her up."

"Mama saw him kill Allie?"

"She was holding the baby up to her chest at the time.

Which is why the injury to the baby's skull was in the back of her head. It's also when Sandy's face got bruised. A psychiatrist from the hospital was called in. He believes the blow to Sandy's face and head, combined with the trauma of seeing her baby daughter killed, triggered the amnesia."

"Oh, my God." Lucy's eyes filled with tears. She was rocking back and forth. And Ramsey took the call off speakerphone.

RAMSEY HAD GRILLED THE STEAKS. He was eating his slowly. Lucy picked at her potato and looked at the salad. She was going to eat some of both. She just had to get used to the smell first. Let it convince her that she really wanted to eat.

"I have to know the rest," she said. He'd suggested one glass of wine might do her good. She'd agreed and sipped at it.

"Eat something and I'll tell you."

"That's how you bribe a child." And she sounded as petulant as one. She felt a bit petulant.

"You're drinking wine on an empty stomach."

He had a point. So she put food in her mouth. Chewed and swallowed. Enough times so that Ramsey started to talk.

"Colton was sick with guilt when he found out what had happened. He blamed himself for leaving Sandy alone to fend for the baby herself."

"I blame him, too."

"After Marie called, telling him about Sandy hanging out in downtown Cincinnati—looking for Allie—he brought her to Comfort Cove to live with him."

"That's the girlfriend Amelia never got to meet because it was during her semester in Boston."

"Right."

Lucy nodded.

"She was drinking too much and getting worse by the day and Colton couldn't afford to put her in rehab or get her any real help. They had no insurance. While she had Allie, Sandy had had assistance, but since the baby was gone..."

He paused, looked at her. Lucy put another bite of potato in her mouth. Chewed. Swallowed. And thought about a Pavlovian dog who acted automatically for the desired response.

She couldn't think about Sandy. Or her poor baby.

"Jack was afraid to leave her alone, so he started taking her with him on his route. He'd make her hide in the back anytime they got close to a delivery so no one would report him. On that Wednesday—"

"The one when I was abducted?" There. She'd said the words. They were out there. Between them. "Skirting the issue isn't going to make it go away," she said as Ramsey stared at her.

He nodded. Took a bite of meat. And then said, "That day, Sandy saw you outside by yourself as Jack drove past your house on his way to the neighbors'. She was frantic, saying that you were going to be hurt. That you'd run out into the street, and fall down into the storm sewer."

"Jack was giving us a clue when he mentioned that sewer."

"Yes, he just didn't realize it would lead us back to him."

"That child. It was me?"

"Yes."

"Okay. Go on."

He hesitated. She put potato in her mouth. Chewed. Swallowed. It didn't feel all bad in her stomach.

"She jumped out of the van while it was still moving. Jack was frantic by then, too, thinking he was going to lose his job and any ability to support them or get her the help she needed. She made a deal with him that if he'd just let her go up to the house and make certain that someone took notice of the child, then she'd get back in the van and not make another sound."

Setting his knife and fork down, Ramsey sipped from his glass of wine and then said, "Colton agreed. He couldn't lose time waiting for her to go to the house, or go with her, so he told her that she could go up to the house, make sure the child was safely inside while he made the delivery, and then she was to meet him at the corner when he came around the block.

"Instead, when he came back around, there she was standing with the child in her arms."

"Me."

His gaze was intent. And then, picking up his knife and fork, taking them to the steak in front of him, he said, "Right."

"He panicked. Didn't know what to do. And she gets in the van like nothing is wrong. The change in her was miraculous. She was the girl he'd known in Cincinnati. And Jack didn't have to worry about finding the money to get her help."

"What about me?"

"He's been sending monthly money orders to Marie ever since."

Which was why she'd never known about any money coming in to Sandy.

"Marie knew I was abducted."

"Yes."

"Jack has been supporting us my whole life."

"Yes. He's also spent the past twenty-five years eating himself alive over the Sanderson family losing their child. At first he told himself that Sandy was right. Here they'd had a baby murdered, when Sandy had been a great parent, and there were parents who cared so little about their children that they left them to wander the streets alone."

"I was in my front yard. Hardly out wandering."

"The best we can figure is that you followed Cal out the door when he left for school. He said that you always made a fuss when he left."

Right. Cal Whittier. Emma's brother. The Sanderson case.

"What about Cal reportedly seeing the child in his father's car?" she asked, and realized, when she saw Ramsey's frown, that she was doing it again. Shutting off.

"I'm like a faucet, huh? On and off. On and off."

He covered her hand with his and the ice started to melt again. "You're doing great, Luce. And in answer to your question…Sandy saw someone driving down the street right after she grabbed you up. So she dived into Frank's car with you. She tried to keep your head down, but you popped up and she didn't want to make you cry, which would have been when Cal saw you in his father's car. And when you dropped your teddy bear. As near as we can tell, Cal was sneaking into the backyard while Sandy snatched you, because she did it when Jack made the delivery two doors down, and Cal used his truck to hide behind."

"I didn't cry?"

"Apparently not. Jack said that you clung to Sandy from the very beginning. Like you recognized her and were meant to be hers. At least, that was the way he chose to see it."

Nodding, she put down her fork. Picked up her wine. "This means that Sandy is a kidnapper." Think about wallpaper. Or table linens. Think about paperwork. Target practice.

"Yes."

"She's in custody?"

"For now. I suspect that she's going to make an insanity plea and be admitted to a mental-health facility."

Lucy nodded again. Sandy probably should have been put in a facility a long time ago. And she might have been. If Lucy hadn't been a child at the time.

"SHE'S ASKING TO SEE YOU, LUCE."

They were still sitting at the table. There was still wine in her glass. Ramsey had cleared the plates away. And Bill was on the phone.

"Not now."

"Agreed."

He finished with Bill and she asked, "If I'd said I'd see her, would you have taken me in?"

"Yes. But I'd have told you that I didn't agree with the decision."

"Good. Because I'm relying on you to help me see what I might miss."

"That's what we do, right?"

"On cases, yes."

His look was not at all professional. "It's what we do, Luce. Period."

She believed him. And would have told him so, except that this time her phone rang.

"Sandy's got my number," she said, before pulling her phone out of its holster. It was the only holster she was wearing. Sometime between walking into the Comfort Cove Police Department and waking up on the divan, she'd been relieved of her gun.

She didn't ask about it. Ramsey didn't say anything about it, either.

But she knew protocol. She'd get her gun back when she passed a department physical—which, in her case, meant a therapy session.

"Bill wouldn't let her call," Ramsey said as Lucy looked at her phone.

"It's Emma Sanderson." The case. The job. She looked at Ramsey. The phone rang a second time.

"Frank's in custody," he reminded her. "Bill said the family's upset."

She looked at her phone.

"She doesn't know…" Ramsey said. The fourth ring sounded.

"Shouldn't Frank be free now? Since they have Colton? Frank Whittier had nothing to do with my disappearance."

She'd said *my.* As the word sounded, her heart missed a beat.

Frank Whittier was once almost her stepfather. A fifth ring sounded.

"Bill said he's giving us until the morning to tell the family. Colton hasn't been extradited yet. No charges have been formally filed."

"Hello?"

"Lucy? It's Emma Sanderson." Something within Lucy lay down to sleep as soon as she heard that voice again. Something she'd been holding up for a very long time.

"Hi, Emma." She was speaking with her sister. Her big sister.

"A Bill something or other is assigned to our case now," Emma started in.

"Because Ramsey's going to your wedding. He's no longer impartial."

"I know. That's what they said. This new detective arrested Frank, Lucy. Cal's very upset. My mother is back to being certain that Frank is responsible for Claire's disappearance. She's beside herself, Lucy. Chris is with her, but I need to know if you can find out what's going on. I didn't know who else to call. I figured, maybe, since you're going to be in town tomorrow, there'd be something you could do. Detective Miller would know something, wouldn't he? Even though he's no longer on the case?"

"You want me to ask him?"

"You said he was picking you up at the airport in the morning and…I just don't know what to do, Lucy."

The words, a mirror to her own, broke through the numbness Lucy had been fighting all day. Tears were streaming down her face and she hadn't even realized it.

And she knew what she had to do.

"Can you bring your mother and meet us down at police headquarters?"

"In the morning, you mean?"

"No. Tonight. I'm in town, Emma. I flew in this morning." She hoped to God her sister couldn't tell she was crying.

"I'd rather come without Mom. I'm telling you, she's a mess."

"She needs to be there, Emma. I'll explain when we see you."

"It's bad, isn't it?"

She had no idea what it was. It just was.

"It's messy, Emma, but we finally have some answers."

"You found Claire."

"Just come to the station."

"Tell me if she's alive, Lucy. Please. Don't do this to me."

Lucy was in way over her head. But she heard the plea coming from her sister's heart. She remembered how it felt, before they'd told her about Allie.

Poor baby Allie. Who wasn't her big sister, after all.

"Lucy?"

She looked at Ramsey. He'd been listening to the conversation and, shrugging, mouthed, "It's up to you."

"She's alive."

"Oh, my God. Oh, my God!" The first was a cry of relief. The second a scream. "And she's here? In Comfort Cove? Are you serious? Oh, my God!"

The woman who'd always been so calm, so controlled and willing to settle for almost nothing was suddenly screaming in Lucy's ear.

"Calm down, Emma," Lucy said in as much of a professional voice as she could muster, but she wasn't going to last much longer. She couldn't hold back the sobs.

Ramsey slid the phone from her shaking fingers. She heard him say, "Emma? Ramsey Miller, here. Your sister is here in town, but she just found out today that she isn't who she thought she was. She's got another life, another family that she's loved as her own for the past twenty-five years…."

"She doesn't want to see us." The elation was still in Emma's tone, clear over the speakerphone. "It's okay, Detective. I can handle that. I know it'll take time. Mom and I have been working with missing-children cases my whole life. I'm just so glad to know that she's alive. That she's okay." Emma was sobbing now. "Just so glad."

Lucy heard Ramsey finalize plans to meet Emma and Rose at the police station. He suggested that Cal Whittier might come along, as well, but emphasized that the initial meeting with detectives would be with only Rose and Emma.

She heard him ring off.

She was in the bathroom, throwing up potatoes.

"YOU DON'T HAVE TO do this."

Lucy stood with Ramsey in the squad room, waiting for Emma and Rose Sanderson to arrive. The guard downstairs at the door had already called up to say they were on their way.

"Yes, I have to do it, Ramsey. We both know I do."

"Not tonight, you don't."

She'd brushed her teeth. Run a comb through her hair. Washed her face and put on fresh makeup. She was still wearing the suit she'd put on at home in Aurora that morning.

What would they think of her?

How much did their opinion matter to her?

"Something I learned a long time ago," she said, listening for the elevator bell to chime out in the hall. "When you have something tough to face, it's best to just get it over with, whether it be a shot, a paper to write or bad news to tell."

"You've faced more than your share today."

"And getting this done tonight is going to make it easier to get up tomorrow." At least that was her theory. She hoped she was right.

Ramsey nodded and she knew that as long as he was standing there with her, she'd be okay. If she collapsed, he'd catch her.

She wanted to hold his hand. But needed to think that she was there as a professional.

"In the next few minutes, I'm going to be meeting my mother," she said aloud.

Bill and Ramsey exchanged glances. "I'm just making sure we all understand what's going on here," she said.

The elevator binged. Both men turned to look at her. "You're sure?" Bill asked.

She'd have said yes, but couldn't get by the lump in her throat. So she nodded.

CHAPTER TWENTY-EIGHT

"DETECTIVE MILLER?" ROSE SANDERSON went right by Bill Mendholson. "My daughter tells me that you have news regarding our missing Claire?"

Lucy watched the well-dressed, elegantly beautiful woman enter the squad room and approach Ramsey. She was crying, but she did that gracefully, too.

Emma, dressed more sedately in jeans and a white button-down blouse with a navy blue sweater that matched, came up beside her mother and gave Lucy a hug.

"Thank you for being here," Emma whispered.

Lucy hadn't expected the hug. Her arms flew out automatically. She held on to Emma's body—slim like hers, but taller—and when the other woman would have pulled back, she couldn't let go. She just couldn't let go.

"Detective?" Rose's voice wobbled. "What do you know about our Claire?"

Lucy couldn't open her eyes. She was afraid if she did, that beautiful woman was going to take one look at her and run the other direction. She was going to claim that it had all been a great mistake.

She wasn't ever going to accept the woman that Sandy Hayes had raised.

"Lucy?" She heard Ramsey.

"Mrs. Sanderson, why don't you step over here for a minute." Bill's voice came closer. "We have some pictures we want you to look at."

A part of Lucy wondered what pictures they had. There

were no pictures in the Sanderson file. Bill led Rose to a small viewing room next door.

"Lucy?" Emma pulled back. There were tears streaming down her face, and, Lucy realized, down her own, as well. "Is it that bad?"

"I don't know, Emma," she whispered, a little girl again, looking up to her big sister. "I've been asking myself that all day."

"You've known all day? Have you seen her, then? Talked to her?"

Ramsey was right there behind here. Ready to hold her up.

"It's me, Emma. I'm Claire." It wasn't planned. Rehearsed. It just happened.

Emma stumbled back and Lucy's heart dropped. She'd had all day to prepare. She'd known that she wasn't what they'd expect their little Claire to be....

"You?" Emma stared. Aghast? "But—"

"Please, can we all step into this room and have a seat?" Ramsey didn't give Lucy a chance to respond to his raised voice as he rapped on a window and motioned to Bill. With a hand on her arm, he led her into the little room where, only that morning, her life had changed so drastically.

With Ramsey's guidance, Lucy was the first person in the room. He showed her to a chair at the table and saw her seated. Standing with his hands on the back of the chair beside her, he had Rose take the seat across from Lucy. Emma sat down next to her. Bill stood just behind Ramsey.

"Do you mind if I take this?" Ramsey asked. Bill shook his head.

"Mrs. Sanderson, I'm sorry for making you wait to hear this. There's just no easy way to bring everyone together."

Lucy looked at the other woman because it was easier than seeing Emma, who knew her, and knew the truth.

"I understand, Detective," Rose said. "Just please, is Claire alive? Is she well? Can you tell me—"

"Yes, ma'am," Ramsey spoke clearly. Concisely. But the last word was barely discernible for the animalistic cry that Rose emitted.

She didn't say a word, though. Biting her lip she continued to give Ramsey her full attention. He continued. "I can tell you that we've located your daughter. She's been properly identified through DNA records."

Lucy heard Emma's gasp. Ramsey probably did, too, but he didn't even pause.

"She's alive and well. And for the past twenty-five years, she's been living another life, with another family. She just found out today that she is not who she has always thought she was."

With tears running down her face, Rose said, "Oh, poor baby. My poor, poor baby." Her gaze turned to Emma. Lucy continued to watch Rose. "Did you know, Em? They found our Claire."

"I know, Mom." Emma was clearly crying.

"Okay." Rose folded her hands on the table and sat forward. "What do you need us to do now?" she asked, smiling, still crying, but focused, too. It was astonishing, how the woman could take control and fall apart all at the same time. "Tell me what she needs, Detective. Time, I assume—that's a given. And then what? I assume she has her own place, but if she doesn't, she can stay with Emma or me."

"With Emma?" Lucy spoke for the first time since she'd come into the room. And Rose seemed to finally notice her sitting there.

"Yes," the woman—her mother—smiled at her. "I'm sorry, I don't believe we've met...."

Her voice drifted off and all the color left Rose's face. "Oh," she said. And Lucy wanted the floor to open up.

"Oh!" Rose said again. And then, "Oh, my..."

Her hands, trembling visibly, moved slowly across the table as Emma said, "Mom, this is Claire."

Rose's mouth fell open. She stared. And then, with tears streaming from her eyes, she jumped up and was around the table. Ramsey was no obstacle to her at all as she pushed by him and reached for Lucy. "Oh, my baby. My Claire." Her fingers ran lightly over Lucy's face. They were so soft, Lucy could hardly believe they were adult hands. And they were wiping away her tears.

"Emma, come here, love," Rose said, putting an arm around Emma and pulling her close. Lucy knew they were a real family—Emma and Rose. She understood. And then, somehow, she was with them, encircled by their arms, as both her mother and her big sister held her so tightly she somehow knew that she was never going to fight another battle alone.

"YOU'RE COMING HOME WITH ME," Rose said half an hour later. She was sitting on the divan between her two daughters, holding both their hands. Ramsey had just told Emma and Rose about Jack and Sandy. It was Emma who told her mother that Lucy had grown up in Aurora, still lived there and had only arrived in town that day.

"I'm sorry, Mrs. Sanderson," Ramsey said, not to be pushed aside this time. "But she's coming home with me. For the next few days, at least. That's not negotiable."

Rose frowned. "Is that proper, Detective? I mean—"

"I think Ramsey and Claire are falling in love, Mom. I've been hoping so, anyway."

"I'm here!" Lucy said, holding up her free hand. And Ramsey wanted to hug her in the worst way. "And Ramsey's right. Dr. Zimmerman, the therapist who helped Ramsey pick me up off the floor this afternoon—almost literally—advised that I needed some transition time. I'd already planned to stay with Ramsey when I thought I was just coming to attend Emma's wedding, not to become her sister."

She looked tired. And strangely afraid, too.

"I understand," Rose said. "And I won't push. Too much. I've waited a long time to bring you home," she said to Lucy.

Lucy wasn't saying much—she just nodded. And Ramsey knew that she'd had enough.

It was time to get her out of there and take her home.

THE WEDDING BETWEEN Chris Talbot and Emma Sanderson was an emotional affair—starting hours before the actual ceremony.

Ramsey and Lucy had agreed to meet the family at Emma's house just after noon. Cal and Frank Whittier were going to be there, as well. The overall consensus was that it would be best if everyone met before they all showed up for a wedding attended by scores of fishermen and their families.

Chris and Emma met Lucy and Ramsey at the door. The four of them had spent some time together shortly after Ramsey had first contacted Emma about the missing box of evidence from her sister's case. Ramsey had figured this meeting would be the easiest part of the day ahead.

Until he saw Emma and Lucy, after a night apart, greet each other with a hug that looked like it was never going to end, and another spate of tears.

He'd expected to be up with Lucy most of, if not all of, Friday night, but she'd been so exhausted that she'd fallen asleep in the car on the way home from the station and had barely woken enough to know that he was carrying her into bed when they got home.

Surprisingly, considering he had a woman in his bed all night for the first time since his divorce, Ramsey had slept straight through the night, too.

"You're the first ones here," Chris said, his long hair trimmed and tidy.

"How was she last night?"

"Emma? A nutcase. And I loved every minute of it. She's

had too many chains around her for too long. I can't wait to see what the woman does now that she's free to live!"

Ramsey grinned, figuring Chris Talbot was going to have his hands full.

"How's Rose?" Ramsey liked the woman. He'd probably have liked Sandy Hayes, too, if he'd known her heart as Lucy had.

"I hardly recognize her," Chris said. "I'm looking forward to seeing what the future brings."

"Just so long as it's not little Talbots anytime too soon, huh?" Ramsey asked.

"No, I think I'm looking forward to those, too."

"Talk about a transformation…"

"Yeah, well, watch out, man. I get the feeling you're about to see what loving a Sanderson woman can do to a guy."

Ramsey smiled, playing along. Even if for the day. Lucy needed him right now. It didn't mean she'd need him in the future. Or even that she'd want him.

One step at a time, Dr. Zimmerman had told her. He figured it was good advice for him, too.

CAL AND FRANK WHITTIER ARRIVED shortly after Lucy and Ramsey did. She was nervous as hell about meeting both of them. They'd been paying for her disappearance for the past twenty-five years.

She should have known better than to worry. Her heart should have known. Cal walked into Emma's home, took one look at Lucy and walked right up and grabbed her into a hug so tight her feet left the ground.

"Goodness, girl, you have *no* idea how good it feels to have you home."

There was that word again. It kept creeping up. Rose wanted to take her home. Ramsey took her home last night. Cal was glad to see her home.

She wasn't sure what home was.

But she wanted to find out.

"It's good to be home," she told the man who was almost a complete stranger to her. These people remembered her. She had no memories of them at all.

The man standing behind Cal had to be Frank Whittier. He approached her slowly, looking at her with the oldest pair of eyes she'd ever seen. And the kindest smile.

"Daddy?" The word came out without thought. Without her even realizing she was going to speak.

The room grew deathly quiet. She could feel the silence as much as hear it. Everyone was staring.

She was Lucy Hayes, the one who always knew how to fix things, the one who took care of everything, and she had no idea what to do.

She stared at the older man in front of her. And he smiled. "You remember me, Claire Bear?"

Her mind flashed. Like a camera went off. She was a little girl. Looking really far up and she saw that smile. She saw those lips move and heard her special name. "Claire Bear."

"That's me," she said aloud. "I had a teddy bear…"

"Yes, you did," Frank said, grinning from ear to ear. "I'm so glad I lived to see this day." He just stood there, with empty arms, this man that she somehow sensed used to carry her around wherever she wanted to go.

What she wanted to do right then was hug him. So she did.

BY THE TIME THEY ALL GOT to the wedding, Lucy was exhausted. She also had something she wanted to talk to Ramsey about—several things, actually, but she started with one.

"Would you still think of me as you did when we were working together if I was called by a different name?" They were standing on the deck of the wedding boat, away from the last-minute preparations, to give her a much-needed breather.

"Now that's a difficult question to answer," he said, his

brow raised as he assessed her. She couldn't tell if he was being serious or not.

So she played along. "Why?"

"Because I don't think of you now as I thought of you when we were just working together, and it has nothing whatsoever to do with what you call yourself."

"Oh." Her face got hot again. She hated when it did that. And loved the familiarity of feeling like herself.

"Then let me rephrase that," she said. "Would you still think of me as you do now if I changed my name?"

"You are who you are, Luce. It doesn't matter to me what we call you. What matters to me is having you in my life."

Turning at the rail, she looked up at him. "You mean that."

"I do."

"Then I have to tell you something."

"What's that?"

Life had shown her one thing for sure. There was no time for holding back. Things could change in an instant.

"Through all of this craziness, even with remembering Frank and starting to identify with Claire, you are my constant. I want to get to know my family. I desperately want to be a part of them. But everyone is saying *home* to me, wanting to bring me home, and the only time it rings true at all is when you tell me you're taking me home."

"And as crazy as this sounds, I've realized, through all of this, that you're my home, too."

"What do you think it all means?"

"I'm not sure yet. I mean, like Dr. Zimmerman said, we have to give you time to assimilate, acclimate." He wrapped his arms around her hips, pulling her up close to him. "But what I think it means is that one of us is going to have to move. It's hard to be home when there're hundreds of miles between you and there."

"My home is here, Ramsey. In Comfort Cove. It's where I was born."

"You might change your mind—"

"No." She shook her head. "I already talked to Bill, this morning, when he called while you were in the shower. He asked Captain Winston if there's any possibility of a detective's position opening up in Comfort Cove."

Ramsey grinned. "And?"

"He said he was certain that whenever I was ready to go back to work, the Comfort Cove Police Department would have a place for me."

She was going to have to see Sandy. To come to terms with the love she still felt for the woman who'd stolen her life from her. But there was time for that.

"I have an idea," Ramsey said, his gaze warm and open as he held her.

"What?"

"Why don't you and I get married and then we can just call you Mrs. Miller and be done with the whole name thing."

Mrs. Miller.

A week ago, she'd have said she was never going to be "Mrs." anything. But, if she'd been honest with herself, she'd also have said she was in love with Ramsey Miller.

"Don't you think it's a little soon?" she asked.

"Do you?"

"No."

"Then…"

"Are you proposing?"

"Yes."

"Then, yes. I think you and I should get married." Not because of how she felt today. Or last night. Or even yesterday morning. But because of how she'd felt before she'd ever left Aurora.

"I love you, Detective Miller."

"And I love you, Lucy-Claire."

"Lucy-Claire," she repeated. "I like that. A lot."

"No matter what we end up with, sweetie, there will always be a part of Lucy here, with us. And a part of Claire, too."

"Are you okay with that?"

"All I need is you."

They were the words that opened up the last lock on her heart and set her free.

EPILOGUE

ON THE DAY Chris and Emma Talbot announced that they were expecting their first child, Ramsey and Lucy-Claire Miller announced that they'd eloped. They told her family first. Rose and Frank, who'd eloped the week before, were at home. They called Cal and Morgan from their house. And stopped by to see Chris and Emma.

From there they got in their car, already packed with their suitcases, and set out for the long drive to their honeymoon in Florida.

They made a brief stop on the way. In Vienna, Kentucky, where Mr. and Mrs. Miller, Sr., welcomed them with tears and open arms. While they were there, Ramsey's mother pulled him aside—to warn him to be good to this girl who was too good for him, Ramsey was sure.

Instead, she apologized for blaming him for something he couldn't possibly have prevented. Diane could just as easily have taken those pills if Ramsey had been right there at the party with her. The choice she'd made was her own. Not Ramsey's.

And then she asked him, again, what town he lived in now.

She was fading. But she was at peace. And she loved her son.

Before they left, Ramsey promised his father, and himself, that he and Lucy-Claire would make frequent visits to

Vienna from that point forward. Life was too short, and too precious, to waste.

Lucy-Claire agreed with him completely.

* * * * *

#1830 WILD FOR THE SHERIFF
The Sisters of Bell River Ranch • by Kathleen O'Brien

Rowena Wright has finally come home to the Bell River Ranch. Most townspeople thought this wild child would never be back, but Sheriff Dallas Garwood always knew it. She *belongs* to this land. He's doing his best to steer clear of her. The last time they tangled, he almost didn't walk away. And now there's too much at stake for him to risk a second round with her.

#1831 IN FROM THE COLD
by Mary Sullivan

Callie MacKintosh is good at her job. That's why she's been sent to this Colorado town—to persuade her boss's brother Gabe Jordan to relinquish his share of the family land. But she soon learns there's more to this situation than she knows. And her skills are no match for a family feud that runs deep...or for her growing attraction to Gabe!

#1832 BENDING THE RULES
by Margaret Watson

Nathan Devereux has big dreams—and they don't include family. After years of raising his siblings, he's ready for some time to himself. But what is he supposed to do when faced with an orphaned thirteen-year-old daughter he didn't know about? He can't turn his back on her—or ignore her very appealing guardian, Emma Sloane. But when Emma announces that she wants to adopt the girl herself, all Nathan's personal rules about family suddenly seem to change.

#1833 THE CLOSER YOU GET
by Kristi Gold

As a country music superstar, Brett Taylor seems to have it all. But appearances are deceiving. He's learned the hard way that relationships and family don't mix with a life on the road. Then Cammie Carson joins his tour group, and the pull between them is intense. Suddenly he sees an entirely new perspective...with her by his side.

#1834 RESERVATIONS FOR TWO
by Jennifer Lohmann

Opening her own restaurant has been Tilly Milek's lifelong dream—and she's finally done it. And all it takes is one bad review to derail everything. Of course The Eater, the anonymous blogger all of Chicago reads, was there on the worst possible night! But when Tilly meets Dan Meier and discovers that he's the reviewer, she's determined to make him change his mind—no matter what it takes.

#1835 FINDING JUSTICE
by Rachel Brimble

For Sergeant Cat Forrester, there is only right and wrong. But when former lover Jay Garrett calls to say their friend has been murdered, those boundaries blur. Especially when he admits he's a suspect in the case. She needs to think like a detective and find the truth. But can she balance these instincts with her feelings for Jay?

YOU CAN FIND MORE INFORMATION ON UPCOMING HARLEQUIN® TITLES, FREE EXCERPTS AND MORE AT WWW.HARLEQUIN.COM.

HSRCNM0113ENHB

Wild for the Sheriff

by Kathleen O'Brien

On sale February 5

Dallas Garwood has always been the good guy, the one who does the right thing...except whenever he crosses paths with Rowena Wright. Now that she's back, things could get interesting for this small-town sheriff! Read on for an exciting excerpt from *Wild for the Sheriff* by Kathleen O'Brien.

Dallas Garwood had always known that sooner or later he'd open a door, turn a corner or look up from his desk and see Rowena Wright standing there.

It wasn't logical. It was simply an unshakable certainty that she wasn't gone for good, that one day she would return.

Not to see him, of course. He didn't kid himself that their brief interlude had been important to her. But she'd be back for Bell River—the ranch that was part of her.

Still, he hadn't thought today would be the day he'd face her across the threshold of her former home.

Or that she would look so gaunt. Her beauty was still there, but buried beneath some kind of haggard exhaustion. Her wild green eyes were circled with shadows, and her white shirt and jeans hung on her.

Something twisted in his chest, stealing his words. He'd never expected to feel pity for Rowena Wright.

She still knew how to look sardonic. She took him in, and he saw himself as she did, from the white-lightning scar dividing his right eyebrow to the shiny gold star pinned at his breast.

Three-tenths of a second. That was all it took to make him feel boring and overdressed, as if his uniform were as much a costume as his son Alec's cowboy hat.

"*Sheriff* Dallas Garwood." The crooked smile on her red lips was cryptic. "I should have known. Truly, I should have known."

"I didn't realize you'd come home," he said, wishing he didn't sound so stiff.

"Come *back*," she corrected him. "After all these years, it might be a bit of a stretch to call Bell River *home*."

"I see." He didn't really, but so what? He'd been her lover once, but never her friend.

The funny thing was, right now he'd give almost anything to change that and resurrect that long-ago connection.

Will Dallas and Rowena reconnect? Or will she skip town again with everything left unsaid? Find out in *Wild for the Sheriff* by Kathleen O'Brien, available February 2013 from Harlequin® Superromance®.

REQUEST YOUR FREE BOOKS!
2 FREE NOVELS PLUS 2 FREE GIFTS!

HARLEQUIN®

super romance®

Exciting, emotional, unexpected!

YES! Please send me 2 FREE Harlequin® Superromance® novels and my 2 FREE gifts (gifts are worth about $10). After receiving them, if I don't wish to receive any more books, I can return the shipping statement marked "cancel." If I don't cancel, I will receive 6 brand-new novels every month and be billed just $4.69 per book in the U.S. or $5.24 per book in Canada. That's a savings of at least 15% off the cover price! It's quite a bargain! Shipping and handling is just 50¢ per book in the U.S. and 75¢ per book in Canada.* I understand that accepting the 2 free books and gifts places me under no obligation to buy anything. I can always return a shipment and cancel at any time. Even if I never buy another book, the two free books and gifts are mine to keep forever.

135/336 HDN FVS7

Name _____ (PLEASE PRINT)

Address _____ Apt. #

City _____ State/Prov. _____ Zip/Postal Code

Signature (if under 18, a parent or guardian must sign)

Mail to the Harlequin® Reader Service:
IN U.S.A.: P.O. Box 1867, Buffalo, NY 14240-1867
IN CANADA: P.O. Box 609, Fort Erie, Ontario L2A 5X3

**Are you a current subscriber to Harlequin Superromance books
and want to receive the larger-print edition?
Call 1-800-873-8635 or visit www.ReaderService.com.**

* Terms and prices subject to change without notice. Prices do not include applicable taxes. Sales tax applicable in N.Y. Canadian residents will be charged applicable taxes. Offer not valid in Quebec. This offer is limited to one order per household. Not valid for current subscribers to Harlequin Superromance books. All orders subject to credit approval. Credit or debit balances in a customer's account(s) may be offset by any other outstanding balance owed by or to the customer. Please allow 4 to 6 weeks for delivery. Offer available while quantities last.

Your Privacy—The Harlequin® Reader Service is committed to protecting your privacy. Our Privacy Policy is available online at www.ReaderService.com or upon request from the Harlequin Reader Service.

We make a portion of our mailing list available to reputable third parties that offer products we believe may interest you. If you prefer that we not exchange your name with third parties, or if you wish to clarify or modify your communication preferences, please visit us at www.ReaderService.com/consumerchoice or write to us at Harlequin Reader Service Preference Service, P.O. Box 9062, Buffalo, NY 14269. Include your complete name and address.

HSR13